Happy Birthday,

Dear Beany

Lenora Mattingly Weber

THOMAS Y. CROWELL COMPANY

New York

jW 383 h

To Gayle Ellen Weber

Happy Birthday, Dear Beany

1

THE March wind was blowing a gale as Beany Malone drove up the wide driveway of the Malone home. She climbed out of the noisy little car that belonged to her brother Johnny, her plaid coat ballooning about her.

Wind or no, the usual welcome committee of two awaited her: their big Irish setter and Mike, the small young mongrel. As usual, the big dog greeted her with tail-wagging dignity. As usual, she had to fend off Mike's delighted greeting while the setter looked on with disgust that fairly said, "Will that fellow ever grow up?"

Beany's eyes rested on a print blouse on the clothesline. She had washed the blouse before leaving home this morning, and she must iron it to wear on her date tonight. She wished someone in the family had thought to bring it in, instead of leaving it to whip in the wind. This blouse with the pale green, bright green, and blackish green shamrocks was her best blouse, given her by her best friend Kay—

Kay. Beany felt her loss anew. For Kay was gone. Away from Denver, away from Harkness High, away from Beany. It had all happened so suddenly. Kay's grandmother, who lived in a small Utah town, had died. Kay's mother had told Beany when they were hurriedly packing to go to the funeral, "We'll just have to bring Grandpa home with us. He can't live on in that big house alone." . . . But the uprooting of Grandpa, so Kay wrote to Beany, was going to take time and tact. There had been no choice but for Kay and her mother to stay on with him, and for Kay to enroll in the high school there.

All during Beany's sophomore and this, her junior year, at Harkness, she and Kay had shared a locker, confidences, note paper, lunches. They had double-dated on weekends.

Life can change so quickly. A door can close so quickly. Beany knew that old saying: "For every door that is closed to you, another will be opened." But why did doors have to close? Why did best friends have to be separated?

It had happened to Beany before. When she was nine, her one and only friend, named Miggs Carmody, had moved away. Beany reached for the clothespins that held the flapping blouse and thought again, as she had thought so often in the years: I wonder why Miggs stopped writing to me? I wonder where she is now? I wonder if she thinks of me as often as I think of her?

The small dog was still leaping upon her. The book on dog training said that stepping on the offender's hind feet was the easy way to break the habit. But the trouble, Beany realized as she tried it, was that Mike's hind feet moved too fast for a human foot to land on.

The back door of the Malone house opened and two boys, munching doughnuts, came down the steps. She called out, "Hey, grab Mike, will you?"

The tall, dark-haired, dark-eyed boy was studying what seemed to be an old photograph and didn't even look up. The other, who was not so tall and had crew-cut blond hair, chirped to the dog, collared him and tucked him under his arm. He paused only to ask, "That a new rumba step you're doing, Beany?" and went right on talking about the picture. The two boys went across the yard toward the stately red brick house next door.

Beany didn't expect any more greeting than she received, inasmuch as the tall, absent-minded one was her brother Johnny, and the one with the crew-cut was Carlton Buell, the boy next door. She was thankful enough not to have Mike's paws dirtying up her plaid coat and matching plaid skirt.

She disengaged the whipping blouse and went into the kitchen. She was sprinkling it when her sister Mary Fred called out from the living room, "That you, Beany?"

"No, it's Orphan Annie."

"Don't waste time being funny. Put the potatoes in with the meat loaf and bring in the big wastebasket."

Beany carried in the red metal wastebasket. In the wide doorway between dining and living rooms she stopped in dismay at the scene before her. "My sainted aunt!" she murmured.

The top of the window seat under the five-windowed bay was propped open. The floor was a litter of old books, papers, a stray mitten or two, snapshots, playing cards, letters— Why, there was that history notebook Beany had hunted for last September.

Their tallest and brightest lamp had been pulled over

3

close. In its glow, Mary Fred sat in the midst of the debris, shuffling through negatives and holding each one up to examine it. "Kind of a mess, eh?" she murmured, without looking up.

For years that window seat had been a catch-all. For years either Mary Fred or Johnny or Beany had been saying, "We ought to take everything out of there and see what's at the bottom."

"How come you decided to clean it out now?" Beany reproved, thinking of the blouse she must iron. And she *should* put up her fluff of bangs on bobby pins.

"I'm not cleaning it out—I'm looking for a negative," Mary Fred answered, still sorting through the pile in her lap. "Of me and a filly—Miss Goldie. It was taken the night I rode her in her maiden hurdles—nope, this isn't it—remember, I won a ribbon?"

Mary Fred Malone was always winning ribbons at horse shows. She was a sophomore at the university, where Johnny Malone was a freshman. She was three years older than Beany, who would be seventeen on St. Patrick's Day, only two weeks off. Mary Fred was still in the jodhpur pants and bright red jacket she had worn earlier in the day at Hilltop Stables, where she taught children's classes to ride—"How to jounce properly," she always said.

Her brown hair was several shades darker than Beany's braids, which were pinned across her head. Like Beany, she had blue-gray eyes put in, as the Irish say, with a dirty finger, for they were shaded by dark, thick lashes and brows. That same dirty finger, much to Beany's regret, had shaken itself over her own nose and cheeks and left a sprinkle of freckles that defied all the freckle remover Beany paid out money for.

Mary Fred said, "Help me find it, lamb," and Beany

dropped down beside her, shoving aside some of the litter and a rumpled part of an old Halloween costume.

Mary Fred made jerky explanation as she held up dark rectangles to the lamp's light: "If I find it right away, I can take it next door to Carlton Buell and he'll blow it up for me—he's developing some of his and Johnny's in his darkroom. I'm standing at Miss Goldie's head—oh, she's the honey of them all—registered as Golden Miss, only McDevitt, who owns her, got to calling her Miss Goldie. Gee, now that she's in foal, we ought to call her *Mrs.* Goldie. See, Beany, here's the snapshot. Only Carlton says he can enlarge better from the negative. I want an enlargement for old Tom McDevitt because he's so broken up about everything—"

"Why don't you just give him this picture? And what is he broken up about?"

"This little snapshot? Why, he couldn't see where Miss Goldie stopped and I started. His eyes are bad—cataracts. He's been putting off an eye operation because he still has a few horses left in his stables. Poor old Tom, I'm afraid it's the end of the trail for him. Miss Goldie was always the pet of all his horses." Mary Fred paused a minute to sigh with longing. "What I wouldn't give to have Miss Goldie's colt. Not because it's sired by Sir Amber and has show-horse blood, but because Miss Goldie's so gentle—so loving."

Beany grabbed out a great pile of letters, cards, snapshots, films. "Honestly! Some of this stuff has been here in the bottom of the window seat since Mother died."

Mary Fred nodded. "I know. That housekeeper we got when Mother took sick—I can't even remember the woman's name—was a great one for chucking things out of sight."

"Here's one of you on a horse," Beany said.

Mary Fred reached for the film, held it up to the light. "That's a *horse*. I'm looking for me on a *filly*."

"Don't be so technical. A horse is a horse."

"Horse is the over-all term for the whole equine race. Miss Goldie was a filly when I rode her; now that she's in foal, she's a mare. And such a cutey. She doesn't like carrots, and sometimes I take her one just to tease her. She scolds me by nibbling on my shoulder. Then I give her an apple and all is forgiven."

Mary Fred delved into the window seat again. She brought up a small album from which snapshots spilled.

"Look, Beany, here's that album Mother was going to fill with pictures of you and little Miggs Carmody. See, she even lettered on the cover, 'Hand in Hand' because you two always were. Remember how you used to brag, 'I've got a twin, but she's not my sister'?"

Beany caught some of the spilling pictures. She and Mary Fred bent over them.

"This must have been the last birthday you spent together," Mary Fred said.

The picture was of a nine-year-old Beany, standing with a girl a notch taller than she. They both wore green skirts, Beany remembered, though the green didn't show in the picture, and white blouses on which green carnations were pinned. Beany turned it over, read, "Our twin Micks, nine years old."

"Yes, that's the last time Miggs and I were together," Beany said. "The Carmodys moved to Oklahoma right after that."

Mary Fred laughed. "I remember. You were so worried about writing her because you didn't know how to spell Oklahoma."

6

Beany mused, "Funny, how Miggs just dropped out of my life later—"

Yes, and funny how one minute you were completely absorbed in the present, and then the sight of yourself and your old childhood friend could pull you back to the past. Beany studied another picture. She and Miggs must have been about six in that one. She came to another—

"Oh, here's the very first one—the day they brought us home from the hospital."

The story all came back to Beany. It seemed an exciting legend to her because she was one of the central figures in it. Her mother and Miggs's mother had given birth to girl babies at the same hospital on St. Patrick's morning almost seventeen years ago. The two women had occupied the same room. They had planned to leave the hospital with their two baby girls the same day. Beany knew that part of the legend too—

"Katie had to come home with Mother because it was snowing so hard that her husband phoned and said he couldn't get the car through the lane from their farm to the highway." They had never called Miggs's mother "Mrs. Carmody"; it had always been "Katie."

"And it kept snowing night and day," Mary Fred filled in, "and so Katie stayed on here. And lucky she did, or you'd probably have kicked the bucket, what with Mother coming down with something the day after they got home. I suppose it was a virus, because she ran a high temperature, and her milk dried up, and you yelled like a banshee— I remember that—"

"Oh, you don't any such thing. You were only three."

"When events make an indelible impression on you, you can remember even earlier than that," Mary Fred said firmly in the voice of a psychology major.

7

"And so Katie nursed me, along with her own baby," Beany said.

"And saved your life," Mary Fred reminded her. "Because you couldn't take any of the formulas the doctor tried on you, and you began shriveling up. You were even too weak to yell." Mary Fred broke off with a triumphant whoop. "Here it is—the negative of Miss Goldie. I've got to rush it over to Carlton's darkroom."

Beany sat on alone with the tumbled array of pictures in her lap, looking at them and reliving those younger days with a reminiscent smile on her lips. Always their weekend visits with each other.

And always Katie in the background—working in her garden, tending the baby chicks in a brooder. Little memories leaped up and lodged in Beany's heart. Katie's hearty, infectious laugh. Katie's dark thick hair and the way she swooped it back from her face with side combs. She was always losing one—"Can you little scalawags find my comb for me?"

Beany stood up, making a sack of her plaid skirt, and peered into the depths of the window seat. She pushed aside a bedraggled mosquito-netting Christmas stocking and took out a bundle of letters and pictures. She felt a nostalgic longing to see or hear from Miggs again, to pick up where they had left off years ago.

She sorted through the scrabble of old newspaper clippings, Christmas cards, letters. Her fingers halted. Here was a letter addressed to herself. Why, it had never been opened. It was from Miggs—she remembered that childish scrawl so well.

In puzzled wonder and without getting up, Beany hunched closer to the lamp's light and tore it open. She read the letter written with pencil in a fourth-grade hand. She read it twice.

Dear Beany,

Can I come back and stay with you so I wont have to go to new York with mother and a sort of relative. They are going to buy a lot of dresses and things and I dont want to go becaus I am awful tired of going places where I dont know anybody becaus we move so much. Mother says I will be a botther to youre mother but if you and youre mother writes that I wont be a botther she will let me come. So please answer real soon becaus I have got my sutecase all packed up to come and see you. We have a real long vacation for Thanksgiven.

Youre loving friend, MIGGS

A jolted and bewildered Beany studied the postmark on the letter. Stillwater, Oklahoma, and the date was November 14, over six years ago. But how had she missed seeing the letter? How had it been thrust unopened into the window seat?

A hand of guilt clamped on Beany's heart at thought of Miggs's waiting for an answer to it. "But I never saw it," Beany kept murmuring aloud. "I never saw it until now." Miggs, with her "sutecase all packed up," waiting for Beany Malone and her mother to write and say, "Come." . . . November 14? Beany's mother had died November 20, six years ago . . .

She didn't even look up as Johnny and Mary Fred came through the front door on a windy bang. She had no eyes for the newly developed, limp pictures each one held, nor ears for Johnny's saying, "Look, Beany, at the reproduction Carlton made from an old photo taken eighty years ago. It's an early-day St. Patrick's celebration in a firehouse. We're going to copy the costumes and setting and put on a skit on the campus for St. Patrick's day."

And no ears for Mary Fred's, "Here's our Miss Goldie.

9

Now do you wonder why old Tom McDevitt made such a pet of her?"

Instead, Beany burst out, "Do you remember the date Mother took sick and the doctor hustled her to the hospital?"

Mary Fred was the first to answer after a sober silence. "I don't remember the date exactly—Dad would, of course. I know she got up with a sore throat, and by the time Dr. Hunter came in the late afternoon, he said it was pneumonia—"

"I remember getting home from school just as the ambulance was leaving—Dad was going with her," Johnny contributed.

"She was there about ten days," Mary Fred said. "And then, just when we thought she was better, she had a heart attack."

They stood, each one gripped in his own memories of that chaotic and tragic time.

"Why do you ask, Beany?" Johnny said.

"You remember Miggs Carmody and her mother?"

Johnny's dark eyes lighted. "Miggs and Katie? Sure. Remember how Katie had what she called Stomach-ache Day? It was when her strawberries were ripe and we'd go out and she'd let us pick as many as we could eat."

"All his memories are stomach memories," Mary Fred commented. "What about Miggs?"

Beany told them of finding Miggs's letter in the bottom of the window seat. "It wasn't even opened," Beany grieved. "I can't imagine anyone putting it in the window seat—"

Mary Fred broke in, "I can imagine our ultra-tidy housekeeper just gathering up everything in sight and chucking it in there."

10

"Well, you know how it was about then," Johnny, the charitable, excused her. "There were so many people dropping in to see if they could do anything for us, and she was a great one for having things 'tidied up,' as she called it."

"I keep thinking of how hurt Miggs must have been when I didn't answer her letter," Beany sighed. "They must not have come back to Stillwater after their trip to New York. Because I wrote to her after Mother died, and the letter came back, marked Unclaimed. But they did a lot of moving from one town to another. Oh golly, I'll bet that's why Miggs never wrote again—I always wondered why she didn't—I'll bet she thought I didn't want her to come."

"There ought to be some way of tracing the Carmodys," Johnny said with concern.

There *must* be some way, Beany thought, her heart heavy with remorse—some way to right things with Miggs.

"Our birthdays are only two weeks off. Just think, for nine years Miggs and I celebrated them together. We always had the same birthday cake."

"You were practically twins," Mary Fred agreed. "You were both christened Catherine, and then she turned into Miggs and you turned into Beany."

Beany's thoughts were brought back from the past by the hall clock's striking six—and her date would be calling for her at six-thirty. Hurriedly, she gathered up the clutter off the floor and crammed it into the wastebasket.

2

LAST October the father of the Malones had brought a new wife to the big rambling house on Barberry Street. Somehow the young Malones had anticipated that their stepmother would be a big-bosomed, housewifely type who would sew on missing buttons and always have a cake nestling inside the cake container. It had been something of a shock when the new Mrs. Malone turned out to be a smallish, youngish person, called Adair, who wore a size twelve, and was far more adept with a paintbrush than with a needle or mixing spoon.

For Adair was a portrait painter.

But because she was warm-hearted and impulsive, they forgave her pitiful attempts at baking spongecake or ironing blouses. She had become one of them, and the smell of oil paints, which had once irritated Beany, now seemed a reassuring part of their home.

Mary Fred had hurried to the kitchen to add water to her meat loaf, which had baked dry. As she wriggled out of her red jacket and into a flowered plastic apron, she asked, "Does anybody mind tomato and lettuce salad for the fourth night in a row?"

"A lot of good it would do us if we did," Johnny muttered.

"Just be thankful that tonight ends my stint of feeding the hungry Malones—and a thankless job it is," Mary Fred said.

Mary Fred and Beany took week-long turns at marketing and cooking. Breakfasts were easy enough, with the toaster sitting on the table, with the first one down putting on the percolator; when Johnny was the first one down, they had enough coffee for a threshing crew. School lunches were no great problem, though it was hard to keep one jump ahead of Johnny when it came to having cookies or cupcakes on hand.

The planning and preparing the evening meal was the hardest chore for a schoolgirl. But their father gave the cook-for-the-week an allowance which was generous enough to buy groceries and have some left over for the worker. Beany had found that if she planned and shopped carefully, if she made desserts instead of picking up pastry at a bakery, she could come out with perhaps six or seven dollars for herself; but that if she bought with last-minute hastiness, she was lucky to come out even.

Johnny grumbled on to Mary Fred, "So it's meat loaf again. I rue the day you ever read that recipe."

"Well, if you think I'm going to fill that hollow pipeline of yours with breast of squab and lemon chiffon pie, you're crazy," Mary Fred retorted.

Beany paid them no heed. She was used to this squabbling over Mary Fred's monotonous menus. She was still haunted by that unanswered letter from Miggs as she crowded broken boxes, that rumpled Halloween costume, and scattered comics into the wastebasket. She heard the front door open and her father and Adair come in just as she went out the back door with it.

She emptied the trash into the ashpit and lit a match to it. The wind swooped a few burning papers out of the top and skimmed them toward the garage. Beany stamped them out. She found a stick and, standing on her toes, poked the blazing, smoking debris far down into the black depths of the ashpit. She got a smudge on her chin and a scratch on her arm.

She turned as a car came racing into the driveway. Beany stared at it in startled admiration and no recognition. What a gorgeous car—a Lincoln, and that new shade called amethyst. Not many new amethyst Lincolns were listed among the friends of either the young Malones or their parents.

The driver got out and came toward her, the wind whipping his tie and ruffling his red hair that was exactly the same shade as their Irish setter's. He walked with a nervous, jerky strut.

Norbett Rhodes. Time was when Beany's heart would have lifted high in her throat at sight of him. Time was when she would have been all aflutter at his catching her at this menial task of trash-burning, with one braid loose from its moorings and a smoky smudge on her chin. Her eyes were watering from the smoke. She wished she had a paper handkerchief with which to wipe her nose.

Norbett Rhodes had been Beany's first love. He had been her very first date when she was a fifteen-year-old sophomore at Harkness High. What a high pedestal that

14

young Beany had set Norbett on. How hard she had strived to please him. The gray days, the sunny days in Beany's life had been set by him. When the world treated Norbett right, Beany exulted with him. When the world did Norbett wrong, Beany suffered with him. The heart-breaking quarrels they'd had . . .

And then Norbett had dropped out of her life by going to Ohio and staying for four months. When he had returned in January, it seemed to Beany that she would never be free of her fifteen-year-old idolatry of him. . . . But at last the day came when she found that she could go her busy way without being lifted to the clouds or crushed to the depths by the unpredictable redheaded boy. It was even hard for Beany to believe. ("Oh well," Mary Fred had said, "I suppose you just built up an immunity to him —the way you do to penicillin.")

It was even harder for Norbett to believe—or accept.

Yes, it was nice, this being able to say, "Hi there, Norbett," without her heart thudding like a trip hammer against her ribs. "How come the Easter-egg Lincoln? Did you answer the right question on TV?"

"It's not mine," he said, coming closer to Beany and the ashpit, from which flame still flickered and smoke still puffed. "You ought've known better than to light trash with the wind blowing such a gale."

He didn't offer to help her shove back a burning wisp of the Halloween costume. He was too dressed up in gray slacks and gray-checked coat. His hair had been freshly cut. He was flapping gray gloves.

Beany beat out the flame with her stick and wiped her watery eyes with her knuckles and wished again she had a handkerchief.

"There's only one other Lincoln in Denver like this,"

Norbett bragged. "This one belongs to Helena Stearns. I guess you know who she is." He said it as though he were saying, "I guess you know who Queen Elizabeth is."

At the blank look on Beany's face, he went on, "She's recently moved to Park Gate. Even though she's got a lot of money, she's very lonely. That's why she gave up her house and moved there. She's a friend of my folks and she eats dinner with us every night in the dining room."

Norbett, an orphan, lived with his aunt and uncle at the big Park Gate apartment-hotel.

"Is that why you're driving her Lincoln—because she's so lonely?" a puzzled Beany asked.

Norbett gave her a dark look. "No. But it's brand new and so powerful that she doesn't feel sure of herself, driving it. A lot of folks, who don't happen to know wealthy people, always think of them as snobbish and uppity. Helena Stearns isn't at all. She's always thinking of somebody else. She's worked like a dog to have the penthouse redecorated—"

The blankness in Beany's face lifted. "Oh, the moneyed woman in the penthouse at the Park Gate. Kay always called her Mrs. Penthouse."

Kay, too, had lived at the luxurious Park Gate before she and her mother left so suddenly for Utah. Beany had heard about Helena Stearns from her. And even more from Sidney Peale, an English boy in Beany's class at school, who also lived at the Park Gate—but in the basement apartment. For Sidney's father was custodian of the building.

Both Kay and Sidney had told Beany about the immense living room in the penthouse with windows on three sides, which Helena Stearns was calling the Sunset Room. The walls and hangings and furniture were all in

16

blues and lavenders and crimsons to blend with sunset colors.

"And the draperies, if you please," Kay had added, "are of sheer black material, shot through with a silver thread. That's to tie in with the sky at night."

Beany had asked, "Has your Mrs. Penthouse got a family?"

Sidney Peale, occupant of the basement apartment at the Park Gate, answered in his clipped British accent, "No. She's a childless widow. But I understand—" (his "no" was "nao," his "understand" was "understahnd") "—that she's preparing it for some beastly rich relatives from Texas to move in with her. A man and his wife and their child."

"Imagine the poor things," Kay had said on a giggle, "having to huddle there together with only four bedrooms and adjoining baths, and that Sunset Room, no bigger than a poolroom. And a dining room that only seats twenty-four."

Norbett was saying now, "Helena asked me to drive her out to the airport. She's catching the seven-thirty plane for Dallas. I want you to meet her, Beany. With all her money she's so humble—so sort of helpless. And she has a motherly instinct to do nice things for everyone. She told me to bring a date along and have dinner with her at the airport. So how about coming along?"

"Norbett, I can't. I'm sorry, but I've got a date tonight."

"You can break it, can't you? The dining room is on the second floor and all glass so you can watch the planes come in. There's dancing after eight. Helena says their lobster is superb."

How elated and cocky Norbett was at being "in" with

Helena Stearns and her penthouse-Lincoln crowd. . . .
Beany thought fleetingly, another time I'd have eeled out
of any date to go with him.

She said, "No, I just couldn't break my date."

"Must be specially special," he flared. "What is it?"

All right, he had asked for it. "It's a birthday supper-
party for Sidney Peale. Oh golly, and I have to iron my
blouse yet."

"Who're you going with?"

"Andy Kern."

"The policeman's son," he said belittlingly.

"Pardon me, Norbett, but your snobbery is showing.
Yes, I'm going with Captain Kern's son. And Andy's sister
Rosellen. She and Sidney Peale have an uncrushable crush
on each other, and she's baked his birthday cake. She's
still on crutches from polio, but you never saw such
cakes—"

"Who's Sidney Peale? Sounds like a third-rate actor."

"Don't you know Sidney—you, a resident at the Park
Gate? Sidney's father is custodian there."

"Isn't that kind of a fancy name for janitor?"

"O.K., then Sidney's father is the janitor. And Sidney
helps him. You've seen him around."

"Holy Toledo, you mean that guy with the Harvard
accent who runs the elevator and sets mousetraps for the
old ladies? You do hobnob with wonderful people,
Beany."

Beany said coolly, "Not a Harvard accent—British.
The Peales were bombed out in England and they came
here after the war. And Sidney's father had to take whatever job he could get. Sidney will be valedictorian of our
class at Harkness. Most likely he'll get a scholarship to
Harvard. Incidentally, he's the most courteous person

18

I've ever known. Are you just talking like a first-rate snob, or have you turned into one since you're chauffeuring for the clinging vine in the penthouse?"

Norbett's lean face flushed a brick red. "It's no crime to admire achievement, is it? It's no crime to be ambitious, is it? I even thought you'd be pleased to hear that I'm to do some special features for the *Tribune,* along with helping my uncle in his printing shop."

"You are! Back on the *Tribune.*" The *Tribune* was the rival paper of the *Call* on which Beany's father wrote a column. "I'm glad. Dad says you're a born newspaperman."

"Coming from Martie Malone, that means something," Norbett said mollified. "Beany, break your date and come with me."

"I can't. There're just the four of us and—"

"A cozy little foursome, huh? A thousand pardons, for thinking you'd prefer having dinner above ground at the airport instead of in the janitor's apartment at the Park Gate."

Beany laughed. "Not dinner. Either supper or high tea. Probably beefsteak and kidney pie and scones. Did you know you pronounce 'scone' to rime with 'done,' not 'stone'?" . . . Times had indeed changed. The old Beany wouldn't have been able to laugh at Norbett's sarcasm.

Norbett said airily, "Thanks for the brush-off. I'll ramble on and find someone else to have dinner with Helena Stearns and me at the airport."

"It shouldn't be hard."

Beany glanced into the dark recesses of the ashpit. The fire was out now. Only one silver wisp of burned paper lifted and floated, like a gray moth, up and down in the wind. In the March dusk Norbett's face had blurred; the iridescent amethyst of the big car was no color at all. Beany shivered as the wind edged through her yellow slip-over.

Still Norbett lingered. He said, and she realized he *wanted* to make her mad, *wanted* her to lash out at him, "You sure it isn't too difficult for you to wear that charm bracelet a first-rate snob gave you a year or so ago?"

It could still surprise Beany that she didn't get hurt and furious and bounce the bracelet on his chest as she had once done. She thought wonderingly: Strange, that when you care for someone, you want to hurt him. Strange, that when you stop caring so desperately, you pick out words that won't wound.

She said placatingly, "I like wearing the charm brace-let, Norbett. But if you want it back, all you have to do is say the word."

"I don't want it back," he shouted. "It's yours. All those fool dangles on it, I bought for you. But now you're wear-ing Andy Kern's wrist watch. So toss the bracelet in the ashpit with the rest of the trash."

"Oh, Norbett, you don't have to be so hateful. We can still be friends."

"Oh sure! You can be like a sister to me—phooey! I came back here from Ohio—I decided to stay on with my uncle at the Park Gate because I thought things would be the same with us. But no—" His voice took on a high mimicking tone which she realized was supposed to be hers. " 'Oh no, Norbett, I don't want to go steady with you—not now.' " His voice dropped to his own angry one. "Why don't you?"

She didn't want to add to his anger by telling him the truth: Because I stopped being fifteen at last. Because I stopped thinking you were wonderful. She said instead, "I don't want to go steady with anyone."

"Beany plays the field," he flung at her.

He started toward the car but stopped with a mocking smile to demand, "What's this wonderful Andy Kern got that I haven't?"

Beany had an instant picture of Andy Kern with his broad shoulders and dark hair and amused gray eyes. She was tempted to say, "It isn't what Andy's got but what he hasn't got. He hasn't got your moods, or temper, or flares of jealousy. He doesn't give me a bad time. I can always count on Andy."

But she only said on a weak laugh, "Norbett, I'm frozen —and I've got to iron a blouse—"

He didn't even say good-by. He went on angry strutting steps to the car, backed it swiftly out of the driveway.

Beany picked up her wastebasket and scurried for the warm kitchen. She found Johnny stirring the meat-loaf gravy. Mary Fred was in the butler's pantry, ironing Beany's shamrock blouse.

"Thanks for taking over," Beany said. "I'm way behind schedule."

"I got the biggest wrinkles out," her sister said. "I left the collar and cuffs for your expert hand. . . . I trust the delay at the ashpit doesn't signify the patching up of an old love affair."

"No, no patching up," Beany said, taking the iron from her. "Norbett left in a huff because I wouldn't break a date and dine and dance at the airport with him."

"Old all-or-nothing Norbett," Mary Fred commented.

Beany ran a swift iron over the white collar and flared cuffs. She pulled out the iron cord and folded the blouse over her arm.

Her father and Adair were in the back hall. Adair was still in the green choir-boy smock she always wore when she was painting. The smell of turpentine vied with the smell of coffee. Beany's father was rubbing spots of paint off Adair.

He turned to Beany to ask, "Can you figure out how any woman can get daubs of purple paint on her ear?"

Beany only smiled at them both. She asked, "Dad, you remember Miggs Carmody and her mother?"

"Miggs and Katie?" His face, even as Johnny's, lighted in a smile. "Of course, I remember them. They're the kind you never forget."

Martie Malone was a columnist on the morning paper, the *Call*. Like his son Johnny, he was tall with dark eyes, dark, wavy hair; though his was touched with gray at the temples. Like Johnny, he had a warm beguiling smile.

Beany could remember, as a child, noting the laugh wrinkles around his eyes and thinking that you could almost play ticktacktoe in the lines. Special assignments on the paper took him away from home so often that Johnny referred to him as "our off-again, on-again, gone-again father."

He explained to Adair about Miggs Carmody, who was practically Beany's twin, as they moved into the steamy and savory kitchen. He added, "That blessed Katie saved Beany's life by nursing her when her mother got sick. That's why we named Beany 'Catherine' after her."

"How could I find Miggs now?" Beany asked. "Wait till I show you the letter I found today that came over six years ago. We think the housekeeper must have dropped it in the window seat on one of her cleaning sprees."

Martie Malone read the letter, handed it back to Beany and said on a sober headshake, "Too bad."

"If only she had written again," Beany lamented. "I

kept thinking she would. Because my letter to her came back."

Her father's thoughtful eyes seemed to be looking back through the years. "Those were such black days, such confused ones, after your mother died," he said. "You remember that I bundled up all you children and we drove to Santa Fe when I was sent there on assignment. We stayed over Christmas, because we couldn't bear the thought of Christmas here in this house with her gone. I know that a lot of our mail went astray, what with the Christmas rush and our having it forwarded there. The child might even have sent you a Christmas card, Beany, that never caught up with us."

Oh dear! Fate and circumstances (as well as a too-tidy housekeeper) *had* seemed to take a hand in Miggs Carmody and Beany Malone losing touch with each other.

"Can you think of any way I could find where she is?" Beany appealed.

"What was Mr. Carmody's first name? And what did he do? Maybe you could trace him through his company," Adair suggested.

"We didn't know him very well," Beany said. "He was away from home a lot." She had only a hazy memory of a short, farmerish man with his hair beginning to thin on top.

"He sold machinery of some kind, as I remember," Martie Malone said. "I'm not even sure what kind, and I don't know what company he was with. I suppose most of his customers were in Oklahoma. That must have been why they left their little acreage out here at the edge of town and moved there. Oklahoma? He must have been selling equipment for oil wells, and that's why they kept moving from one town to another. I can't even remember the man's first name. Beany, you saw more of them than the rest of us did—can you remember what Katie called him?"

Beany shook her head. "She used to call him the Traveler. I remember her saying once, 'Look at the new blouse my Traveler brought me. He must have been ashamed of this battered blue one I've been wearing so long.'"

"Katie never gave a thought to clothes," Mary Fred put in. "She was on the plump side and she used to say, 'I'm like June—bustin' out all over.'"

"But what a fryin' arm she had," Johnny said. "I remember one birthday when we were out there a cloudburst came up. That lane that led from their house to the road was just a river. So we kids were marooned there. Katie made us potato pancakes, with some sort of honey and butter spread—"

"Stomach memories again," Mary Fred sighed. "I'll bet a psychoanalyst could do something startling with that."

"What was Miggs like, Beany?" Adair asked.

"We didn't look like twins. I was a freckled towhead, and her hair kept getting darker and darker. She was always shy with strangers, but she wasn't afraid of horses or a great big bull they had." Beany continued to reminisce. "She was always nursing hurt or sick animals. I remember a rabbit with a splint on its leg. I remember how we used to giggle ourselves to sleep—"

"Her black eyes could laugh out loud, or cry, or cuss you out," Johnny added.

What would Miggs be like now, Beany wondered. Was she still unhappily trailing along from one little Oklahoma town to another—"I am awful tired of going places where I dont know anybody." Again Beany was haunted

24

by the picture of Miggs waiting for Beany's answer to her, "Can I come—?"

This time it was the pealing of the doorbell that brought Beany back to the here and now. That would be Andy Kern to take her to the birthday supper for Sidney Peale. And here was Beany holding her best blouse, instead of being buttoned inside it.

3

SHE opened the door for Andy Kern, apologizing, "Oh, Andy, I'm sorry I'm not ready. But we were all talking and I didn't realize it was so late."

"I'm probably early," he said with his crinkly grin. "Rosellen was in a hurry to get out of the house with the birthday cake before the juvenile delinquents bounced a ball on it, or slupped off some of the icing."

It was his two young brothers, aged ten and twelve, Andy referred to.

"I'll be dressed in a jiffy," Beany promised.

"Take your time, doll," Andy said easily. "Rosellen wanted to wait in the car."

That was the nice thing about being Andy's girl, Beany thought, as she squirmed into her blouse, which was still damp at the seams; life was so comfortable, so free of tension. Norbett would never have said, "Take your time, doll." He'd have said, "Snap it up, can't you?" and stood at the foot of the stairs, tapping his foot. Instead, Andy was in the back hall, visiting with the family.

And that was the nice thing about Beany's family; they never minded delaying a meal, even if it meant reheating and thinning the gravy. Even if the coffee percolated overtime.

Andy met her at the foot of the stairs, sniffed her perfume in mock ecstasy, breathed out, with a rolling of eyes, "Heavensent!"

"No, it's my new Surrender."

" 'You Surrender' or 'I Surrender'? . . . Don't forget Sidney's present."

She had forgotten it. It was a dance record from the latest musical comedy, that she and Andy had bought two days ago. She took a flurried few minutes to look for tissue paper and ribbon to gift-wrap it. Funny, how you could always come across tissue paper and lovely lengths of ribbon when you didn't need them, but when you had a present to wrap—

"Never mind the fancy trimmings," Andy said. "Just bundle it up so it'll get there in one piece."

Beany reached for a copy of the *Call*, pulled out two sheets of it. As she did, her eye rested momentarily on her father's name, her mind momentarily registered an announcement which was boxed off in the paper, "Watch for Martie Malone's Columns on Uranium Companies and Penny Stocks." But she gave it no thought at all as she tucked the edges of the paper around the record and handed it to Andy.

He said, "I'm trying to talk Johnny into coming along with us. But even Rosellen's fresh coconut cake doesn't lure him."

"You children run along," Johnny said. "I'd just be a fifth wheel."

That was another upsetting thing about the departure of Beany's best friend, Kay—Johnny had lost a girl friend as well. Before Kay left, every Saturday night meant a foursome of Johnny and Kay, Andy and Beany. Occasionally it had been a sixsome with Rosellen and Sidney Peale joining them.

"Besides," Johnny added, "Carlton Buell and I are going to see what we can brew up for a St. Patrick's skit. We're going to work from an old photograph and reproduce the characters. I hope there'll be no turning over in graves when I put a lot of corny jokes in their mouths. Have fun, youse."

But as Andy helped Beany down the front steps, Johnny hurried after them. "Hey, I've got an idea. How about all of you taking in my show on the campus by way of celebrating Beany's birthday? I'll even have the harmonica player play Happy Birthday, dear Beany."

Johnny didn't notice and neither did Beany—not then, though she was to think of it afterward—that Andy didn't say, "Swell deal. We'll do just that." For they reached the car and Rosellen opened the door; there were greetings and Johnny's asking, "Rosellen, what does a guy have to do to rate a birthday cake?" and Rosellen's answering, "Just cue me a day ahead of time, Johnny."

With the cake on her lap and the crutches beside her, Rosellen edged to the middle of the front seat to make room for Beany. They drove off in the windy night.

Only Rosellen's body was slowed and hampered by crutches. Her interest in life, her spirit knew no bounds. She was always bubbling over with talk. They had driven several blocks before Beany realized that Rosellen was most untalkative. And so was Andy.

Beany started a conversation. "The Park Gate doesn't seem the same since Kay left." She laughed ruefully. "Johnny says it'd be easy for me to get in a rut, and I guess he's right."

"What's the matter with ruts, when they're nice happy ruts?" Rosellen said feelingly. "I like days to have a sameness."

Did Beany imagine it or did Andy nudge his sister? He said, "Life would be pretty static if it was all sameness."

"What's the matter with sameness, if it's a nice happy sameness?" Beany argued.

"Hey, you two crepe-hangers," Andy scolded. "We're going to a party, not a wake—remember?"

They *were* pretty doleful, Beany realized. She laughed and asked, "Can I talk about my long-lost twin?"

Her telling it filled the time until they reached the Park Gate. Rosellen cheered her by saying, "You'll find Miggs. It just came over me—the feeling that you would."

"No charge for the gal reading your future," Andy said.

He pulled up at the back entrance of the big apartment hotel, so that Rosellen would have a shorter distance to manage on her crutches. The wind flailed at them. Beany carried the cake and the wrapped record, leaving Andy to help Rosellen.

"Is Sidney to be surprised?" Beany asked. She had to yell it over the wind.

"I'd be surprised if he is," Andy yelled back. And Rosellen rested on her crutches to add, "The juvenile delinquents told him I was baking him a cake."

Steps led down to the basement. Rosellen said, "It's not so hard to go *up* steps on crutches, but going down you always feel as though you were about to fall on your face."

Andy solved the problem by handing the crutches to

the already burdened Beany, and carrying Rosellen down the flight and through the door, which Beany backed against to open and hold open. She thought with only fleeting amusement of Norbett's belittling remark about her preferring a basement to the sky room at the airport.

The door of the Peales' basement apartment was open in welcome. At sound of the crutches, Sidney came hurrying to meet them. Sidney was always flustered and unsure of himself—always, except when he was with Rosellen. If ever, Beany thought, the "You're so wonderful" technique worked wonders, it was on the painfully shy Sidney.

"Mother and Father just left," Sidney explained as he ushered them in and took the packages from Beany. "But Mother left everything ready for us, except making the tea. They went to an English movie."

"I'll bet they get homesick to hear Britishers talk," Rosellen said.

Sidney took her coat, seated her at the head of the table, which was set up in the living room, as though he were seating a queen. They each beamed admiration and affection at the other.

Beany realized, as she had only vaguely realized before, how much good those two did each other. Rosellen gave Sidney a sureness of self, whereas Sidney's attention gave Rosellen that most priceless thing to a handicapped girl —the feeling that she was desirable.

Beany looked at Andy and his small wink of understanding warmed through her.

"Father wouldn't have felt free to go," Sidney told them all, "if our exacting tenant in the penthouse hadn't left."

She was flying to Dallas, Beany remembered.

"What does she exact?" Andy asked.

"Service," Sidney said. "She's forever ringing Father to complain that her flat—I mean penthouse—is too hot, or the water isn't hot enough, or the lift—elevator," he corrected himself, "takes too long to come when she wants it."

Yet Norbett had said Mrs. Stearns in the penthouse was all motherly instinct, that she thought only of doing nice things for everyone. Perhaps much depended on the point of view.

"You ought to tell her to go soak," Andy Kern said.

Sidney made the tea and Beany carried in the teapot, swaddled in its padded tea cozy, and put it on the table, which was already laid with cold cuts and relishes. And scones, even as Beany had predicted.

"Food," exulted Andy. "And women. Who could ask for anything more!"

Andy ate with his usual hearty relish. "Don't throw away any lettuce or radishes," he warned Sidney. "The Kerns will take it home. The juvenile delinquents have a couple of pet rabbits. Tell them about the rabbits that are about to wreck our Home, Sweet Home, Rosellen."

Rosellen only shook her head.

What had happened to make her so sober and quiet? Yet she went through the ceremony of putting seventeen candles on Sidney's cake, of turning out the lights, of saying, "Now if you blow out all the candles, your wish will come true."

As though Beany couldn't guess Sidney's wish. It would be that Rosellen could graduate from crutches to walking with a cane. Sidney gave a great huff and every candle flickered out. But before Rosellen could cut the cake, the telephone rang.

Sidney said only, "Yes, ma'am," into the receiver again and again. He replaced the telephone and said with a shrug, "It's *she* again. She's ringing up from the airport to say she can't remember whether or not she left a window open in the Sunset Room, and would I go up and check."

Rosellen looked up with quickened interest. "And are you going up to the penthouse to see?"

"I'll have to, but I won't be but a few minutes."

"Oh, Sidney, I'm just bustin' to see that penthouse. I've never seen one. Couldn't I go with you?"

Sidney hesitated, and Beany said, "I'd like to go too. I've heard so much about it from you and Kay. Couldn't we all go?"

"Not me," Andy said. "I don't want any old pelican walking in on us snooping through her place."

"She's not an old pelican, according to Norbett. And she won't be walking in on us," Beany assured him. "She's taking the seven-thirty plane to Dallas."

"Go on—go on," Andy said. "I'm not grieving my heart out because I've never seen a penthouse. I'll stay here and play records and drink tea."

So it was that Beany and Rosellen, clumping along on her crutches, accompanied Sidney with his clanking ring of house keys. They took the elevator and Sidney told the operator, "Thirteenth floor."

The boy looked at the keys Sidney carried and grinned in understanding. "Some little chore madame thought up, no doubt."

"I'm to check to see if she left a window open," Sidney said.

"Service with a smile," the boy said, "or she complains to the management."

32

On the top floor, one of Sidney's keys opened an ornate door into what Beany supposed was called a foyer. Sidney, with something of proprietary pride, pressed on lights and said, "I'll show you the bedrooms first. All four of them with private baths."

Beany and Rosellen ran out of adjectives on the bedrooms. Rosellen, who read a lot, would murmur, "This must be that new bayberry green," or "Imagine putting chartreuse with tortoise brown."

"Even the telephones are in harmonizing shades," Sidney pointed out.

"Even wall-to-wall carpeting in the bathrooms," Rosellen breathed.

"This bedroom is called the April Room," Sidney said. "It's for the girl relation when she comes."

The room was like a bower with its white ruffled curtains—a bower with many mirrors and the palest of pink satin on the bed and two chairs which Rosellen said were "slipper chairs." Beany's eyes rested on the flowered wallpaper. "Apple blossoms," she said on an admiring whisper.

"No, nothing so common as apple blossoms," Rosellen corrected. "Camellias or maybe magnolias. Look, Beany, even hand-painted wall plates where you turn on the lights."

Sidney said, "I'll turn the lights on in the Sunset Room."

Beany and Rosellen drew a long, "Oh-h-h—" as they entered it. It was everything Kay had said: "Big as a poolroom. . . . Like a stage setting." Again Sidney, with proprietary pride, pointed out the dining room, which was two steps up from the living room proper, and which could be shut off by pulling panels that were of thin wood but gave the effect of gathered draperies. Sidney even demonstrated how easily they could be pulled out and pushed back.

"Like a scene in Technicolor," Beany paid tribute, her eyes roving over the sectional chairs and couches in shades of blue, lavender, gray, and crimson. Low tables of different shapes, but all of heavy glass on metal legs, were placed throughout.

"The carpet's so thick, you couldn't find a dime if you dropped one," Rosellen said.

Windows on three sides. Beany walked to one, looked down on the twinking, varicolored lights of the city. In the distance the outline of mountains loomed vaguely against the gray sky. The wind rattled at the windows.

Rosellen dropped down on a low and wide divan. Beany sat on a crimson one opposite her. "This is a conversational grouping," Rosellen informed them.

On the table between them were cocktail glasses and a decanter covered with silver lacework. On a lower shelf of the table sat a telephone. This one was of soft green. Beany picked it up and, with the affected air of a haughty woman, said, "Give me the mayor, please," and then, "Oh, Mr. Mayor, that neon sign on the boulevard offends me. It's an off-note in my color scheme. It upsets my psyche. Please see that it is changed immediately."

Sidney's usually serious eyes twinkled. Rosellen laughed gleefully. It struck Beany that this was the first time Rosellen had laughed all evening.

Perhaps it was that, perhaps Beany was carried away by "audience appreciation," for she went on with her act. She reached for one of the glasses and extended it to an invisible butler. Her voice was even more arrogant, her chin even higher, as she said, "Jeeves! You couldn't do this to me. Not an ice-colored ice cube in my drink. I must have mauve."

Again Rosellen laughed so heartily that she let go one of her crutches and it clattered against the wrought-iron legs of the table. If it hadn't been for that, they might have heard the elevator stop outside; they might have heard the outer door open. But Beany had one more line to add to the invisible butler, "Oh, and, Jeeves, peel me a grape."

It was the horror in Sidney's eyes, as they lifted to the doorway, that arrested Beany. Rosellen's laughter broke off with a gasp. Beany, who was sitting with her back to the door, turned her head.

A small woman with gray hair was standing inside the doorway. She was dressed in black—black fur jacket, black dress, a small black hat. Her collar-shaped necklace of silver sparkled frostily in the bright lights Sidney had turned on.

Beany knew instantly that this was Helena Stearns. . . . Well, Norbett had said he wanted Beany to meet the motherly Helena, who was humble and helpless. But had Norbett ever met the chill stare of those eyes?

Beany stumbled to her feet, upsetting the green telephone. She set down the glass she still held in her hand.

Rosellen for once was speechless, and Sidney stood in flustered chagrin, swallowing hard. Beany fumbled out, "Sidney came up to close your window—and we came with him— We'd never seen a penthouse apartment—I mean, we'd heard so much about your Sunset Room—and so we thought—"

Helena Stearns ignored both Beany's faltering smile and her words. She said, without raising her voice, "Would you mind replacing the phone you knocked over?" Her eyes lingered on Beany, who had a feeling that they were making note of every shamrock in her best blouse, and the braids pinned across her head.

It was a relief when the woman turned to Sidney and said in the voice one might use to a servant, "Will you turn out all the lights you've left on in the bedrooms and baths?"

Sidney hastened to do her bidding. The three in the Sunset Room waited in dead silence. Not even a click, because the light switches were the noiseless kind. Not even Sidney's footsteps, because of the thick carpeting. Only the muted swish of silk and fur as Helena took off her jacket.

Sidney returned. Helena said, "Now I'll ask you to close the window in the dining room which I phoned you about."

Sidney, taking his awed guests on a tour of the penthouse, had quite forgotten the reason for his coming.

There was the clatter of Rosellen's crutches as she gathered them to her. Even though Beany had never seen her use them so fast, it still seemed a mile across that expanse of gray carpeting with all the glass-topped tables to sidestep.

They were in the apartment hall outside and at the elevator before Sidney, looking guilty and chastened, joined them. No one spoke.

The elevator seemed to take forever to rise to the thirteenth floor. When it did, and its doors slid open, Norbett Rhodes stepped out. He was carrying two pieces of gray luggage. Beany realized dazedly that he must have been delayed in putting the amethyst car in the basement garage.

His surprise was equal to Beany's. He stopped and

surveyed the speechless trio. "Well," he finally managed on a nervous laugh, "fancy meeting you here."

Beany burst out accusingly, "Norbett, you told me she was taking a plane to Dallas. We never thought she'd be back."

"Don't blame me," he said. "Blame the wind. Her plane was grounded because of it. They announced it right after Helena called the janitor about the window she left open. What are you folks doing up here?"

"Come on," Sidney said nervously, guiding Rosellen into the elevator.

Beany wondered, as its doors shut out Norbett's surprised and curious face, just what Helena Stearns would say to him about the intruders in her domain. How much had she heard of that would-be bright little act about mauve ice cubes and "peel me a grape"?

4

BEANY, Rosellen, and Sidney rode in constrained silence to the basement floor. In slow pace with Rosellen, they walked the short distance to the Peale apartment.

Rosellen laughed almost too brightly. "Her ladyship returns and finds the peasants on her premises."

Beany said almost too glibly, "Thank heaven, I don't move in the same social circle as her ladyship. I'm glad I'll never have to face her frosty stare again."

Sidney tried to laugh. They were all skirting the same uneasiness, all remembering that her ladyship in the penthouse could make it most unpleasant for the Peales if she complained to the management.

Sidney managed to say, "Now that you've seen the palace in the sky, our digs will look like a hole in the wall."

"A nice warm hole in the wall, after the icy treatment up there," Beany said.

38

"Well, you wanted ice in your drink," Rosellen reminded her on a forced giggle.

They found Andy playing the record player loudly. He raised his voice over it. "Sight-seeing tour over? Let's carve the cake."

The basement apartment did seem smaller and shabbier after that brief and unhappy glimpse of elegance. Yet Beany looked around it with new interest. The crossed fencing swords on the wall, the trophies on the mantel which Sidney had evidently won for athletic events in his English school. The Persian print covering the couch, the wood carving of a dancer on the bookshelves. Everything in the room had a personal meaning, its own warm significance.

Sidney opened Cokes while Rosellen cut the cake. Andy put on a record with a catchy rhythm, said, "Let's do a rumba, Beany."

Dancing with Andy was so pleasantly effortless that Beany, without ever missing a step, told him about their embarrassing visit to the penthouse. "You know something, Andy? I wouldn't want to live in a place that looks like a furniture-store display."

"Shucks, and here I was going to rent you a penthouse."

Beany gave that only the smile it deserved, and went on, "That Sunset Room. At first, it takes your breath away—like when a curtain goes up on the stage—"

"And then the villainess came on," Andy grinned.

As Andy whirled her, Beany caught a glimpse of Rosellen and Sidney sitting at the table. How sober they both looked. She could understand Sidney's uneasiness—if only she and Rosellen hadn't insisted on accompanying him to the penthouse! But what was the matter with Rosellen?

She was about to ask Andy when Andy began to clown. He reached for one of the fencing foils on the wall, and went into the exaggerated heel-clickings and poses of a Spanish sword dancer. He dropped the sword to the floor, and edged around it with mincing steps. He struck a final bullfighter pose as the music stopped. And then he staggered over to the table like a man far gone in drink. He reached out and grabbed a bottle of Coke with jerkily shaking hands, and rasped out, "Drink never hurt me none."

Beany knew him so well. He was trying to lift the tone of poor Sidney's little birthday gathering. He was trying desperately to rouse Rosellen out of her unaccustomed low spirits. And he had succeeded only briefly. For, as they sat on eating Rosellen's fluffy cake and drinking Cokes, that gray pall seemed to settle again.

Beany groped in her mind for some cheerful, lifting-up something to say. "Johnny's going to put on a St. Patrick's one-act play out at the U. Old-time stuff. You know, a lot of whiskered gents in plaid vests, telling Irish jokes, I suppose. He thought it'd be fun if we could all go out to it, the four of us."

No answer from anyone. Beany looked at Rosellen, who was keeping her eyes on the crumbled cake on her plate. "Don't you think it'd be fun for all of us to go, Rosellen?" Beany prodded.

Rosellen lifted unhappy eyes—and suddenly burst into tears.

Andy reached over and mussed her dark curly hair. "For heaven's sake, snivelpuss—" But the grin he turned on Beany and Sidney wobbled at the edges. "I was saving the news till the party was over. I've already enlisted in the Marines."

"Oh no!" Beany breathed. "Oh no!" And then, "But,

Andy, you said you weren't going to—not until school was out?"

"I *was* going to wait," he said. "But I had a chance to get in at a bargain rate—three years marked down to two. Every so often the Marine Recruiting Office does that to fill their quota. So I figured I'd buy it. That way, I'll be home sooner."

"He's leaving—Monday," Rosellen gulped. "Sidney, have you got any paper handkerchiefs?"

Andy said scoldingly, "Look, Rosy-posy, there isn't even a war on. And just think, I'll learn to make my own bed."

The party was over. There was no use pretending any longer. Rosellen cried as they cleared the table of the clutter. Her tears fell as she wrapped a sizable wedge of her cake for Johnny. They got into wraps, said good-bys to Sidney, and left. (Andy had to run back to get the lettuce for the rabbits.)

He stopped at the Kern house first and helped Rosellen into the house. Silently, he and Beany drove to Barberry Street, turned into the Malone driveway. The Malone house was dark except for a light in Johnny's room and the hall light which had been left on for Beany—and maybe for Mary Fred, who was out, dancing.

For a long minute the two in the car sat in silence. Even though so many things were waiting to be said, wanting to be said. Beany tried to say to herself, There's no war on. Two years isn't so long . . . But she could think only of the empty days at Harkness without Andy Kern eating lunch with her and saying, "All donations thankfully received." Without Andy walking to French with her afterward and going through the act of an usher with a flashlight, showing her to her seat and saying, "Watch out for the step, Madam."

Andy's job was ushering at the Pantages Movie House. . . . No, and there'd be no more going to movies— "Courtesy of Andy Kern, head usher." No Andy, plopping a bag of popcorn in her lap—no plopping of himself down beside her during the show while he kept a wary eye out for any customers who needed seating.

She didn't know she was crying until she felt tears wet and chill on her cheeks. Andy shook her scoldingly. "I'm only going to San Diego. And I'll be home again on leave right after I finish boot training. What's there to cry about?"

Beany's laugh was choky. "Oh, Andy, I can't stand all the doors closing. First Kay, and now you. And don't you dare say anything about other doors opening for the ones that close. That's a lot of malarkey—and I'm sick of hearing it."

He chuckled at her flare of anger. "But it's life, knucks. You wouldn't want it to stay a same sameness, would you?"

She didn't answer that, but said, "I'll be so lonesome without you, Andy. I never realized how I depended on your always being there."

"It was nice for me to know you were always there, too. It's nice to know you'll miss me. Send me cookies, so I can brag about my girl to the other leathernecks?"

"I will," she promised. "What kind?"

"Filled ones, because they're extra fillin'."

The scratching at the car door, the whimpering came from Mike. He always slept in the yellow convertible that belonged to Adair, but he still had to take part in any of the happenings on the Malone premises.

"Don't let him in," Beany warned, "or he'll be all over us. . . . Will I see you tomorrow, Andy?"

"No, tomorrow our house will be overrun with all of

42

the Kern clan to give me a send-off. So this is good-by, pie-face." He reached over and kissed her—not a hurried or teasing peck, but a gentle kiss on her lips.

"Andy, maybe I'm in love with you. I like the sample kiss."

"But maybe someone will come along with a sample you like better. Better to be sure than sorry, knucks. I'll inquire into such matters when I come back from boot."

He opened the car door, scooped Mike up under his arm, and walked with her to the door. She said catchily, "I'll think of you whenever I wind your watch."

"Not my watch, *our* watch." Yes, she knew him so well. She knew by now that when Andy was most serious, he pretended to be joking. "When you wind it, you might even say a prayer for me. Who knows—it might keep me out of the brig."

5

THE telephone in the back hall was ringing the next morning when the Malones returned from Mass.

Beany answered it. It was Rosellen Kern, and she burst out, "Beany, you and Norbett are still on speaking terms, aren't you?"

"Well—yes, as far as I know. He was speaking to me last night when he wanted to know what we were doing in the penthouse."

"Then will you call him up and kind of feel him out?"

"What about, Rosellen?"

"About last night. Didn't you notice how worried Sidney was about Mrs. Penthouse walking in on us? I talked to him this morning, and he's still worried—"

Beany smiled to herself. It was so like Rosellen to forget her own grief over Andy's leaving by taking on Sidney's worry. "But where does Norbett come in?" Beany asked.

She could hear a loud commotion in the background in the Kern household. Rosellen said, "Wait a minute." She turned from the phone to call loudly, "Donnie, and all you kids, you'd better get those rabbits out of the living room before Dad sees them."

She turned back to explain to Beany, "The house is running over with relatives because it's Andy's last day, and the kids all want to play with the rabbits. But if Donnie knows what's good for him *and* the white rabbits, he'll keep them out of Dad's sight. . . . Where was I? Oh yes, about Sidney. He's even afraid his father might lose his job. Not that they'd fire him for that penthouse deal, but Sidney says that if they jumped on him—'reproved him,' was the way Sidney put it—his father had taken so much from Mrs. Penthouse that one thing more might make him lose his temper. Anyway, Sidney is sure in a dither about last night—"

"It wasn't his fault. We were the ones who insisted on going."

"That's what I want you to tell Norbett, Beany. And find out if she was awful wrathy about it—that is, wrathy enough to complain to the management."

"It's my fault if she was or is," Beany admitted. "I was the one that did the corny impersonation of her."

"It wasn't bad," Rosellen said on a giggle. "If it weren't for Sidney and his dad's job, I'd wish she heard every word of it. But anyway, call Norbett and ask him—"

"I'll smooth it over if I can," Beany promised.

She hated to call him. She even walked out into the kitchen and asked Johnny, who was beating egg whites for waffles, if she could help. Johnny's waffle breakfast after church was practically a Sunday ritual.

"No help needed," Johnny said. "I don't even want you

out here, telling me I can make waffles with two eggs instead of four. You do something to my culinary soul."

Her help would be needed, Beany thought with a shade of bitterness, when it came to cleaning up the mess Johnny always left in the kitchen. She drifted back to the telephone. Grasp the nettle tightly—meaning, do a job you dread as quickly as you can.

She dialed Norbett's number, which she still knew by heart.

The minute Norbett's voice said hello, she said, without pausing for breath, "It's Beany, Norbett. There's something I want to tell you about. About last night. You see, Andy Kern's going into the Marines tomorrow—only I didn't know until the party broke up—though I kept wondering why Rosellen was so down in the dumps—"

Norbett broke in exultantly. "He is! Beany, you were swell to call and tell me. I'll sure be glad to see that wrist watch off your wrist. It never belonged there, and you know it."

"But I still have his wrist watch. I'm going to keep on wearing it. But about last night, and Rosellen and my going to the penthouse with Sidney. Sidney's so worried about it. He's afraid maybe your Helena Stearns—I mean Mrs. Stearns—will go to the manager about it and make trouble for Sidney's father."

She waited for Norbett to say something. There was only silence at his end, so Beany went on earnestly, "It wasn't Mr. Peale's fault. He didn't know a thing about it. He wasn't even home. The four of us were there in the Peales' apartment, just ready to cut the cake—"

"All so chummy and cozy," Norbett put in.

Beany let that pass. She couldn't afford to antagonize him now.

"—and so when Sidney said he had to go up to close

46

a window in the penthouse, we were the ones that insisted on going. And when we were up there—well, as I say, Rosellen was lower than a snake's hind leg, and I was just putting on a silly act to make her laugh. What did Mrs. Stearns say about it—I mean, was she burned up?"

"Did you call me just because you were concerned about this worthy junior janitor and his family in the basement?"

"Yes, because Rosellen and I both feel to blame about it."

The unpredictable Norbett. He said airily, "No, Helena has more important things on her mind than the elevator boy bringing his girl friends up to snoop around. You know, you had me worried for a minute, Beany. I thought you were calling up to tell me there was nothing to stop *us* from going steady now, with friend Kern joining the Marines—"

"Oh," was all Beany could say.

"—because Helena has a cousin who is coming up from Texas with his family to live in the penthouse with her. And there's a daughter that she wants me to show around. Helena showed me her picture last evening. Pretty hot-diggety, hot-ziggety."

"How old is she?"

"I didn't ask for any birth certificate. Helena has already enrolled her at Huxley Hall. And there are all sorts of parties planned for her already. So it looks like I'll be kept pretty busy."

Beany replaced the telephone with mixed emotions. Would she ever understand Norbett Rhodes?

She telephoned Rosellen to assure her, so she could, in turn, assure Sidney that Helena Stearns's mind was occupied with more important things than the trespassers in her apartment.

"I'm still glad," Beany repeated fervently to Rosellen, "I'll never have to cross her path again."

Andy was gone.

Beany's fourth-hour sewing class on Monday was just a sewing class, instead of the class before her lunch period with Andy. Beany tried to concentrate on the rose-colored pedal pushers she was making and the two hems on the two legs that somehow wouldn't lie flat.

Across the table from Beany sat Dulcie Lungaarde. She was ripping out a seam in a tweed jacket in its early stages, and she muttered resentfully as she ripped. She had stitched up the underarm seam without basting it, and Mrs. Hilb, the teacher, had reprimanded her sharply, "When you're working with wool, the rule is baste, stitch, press."

Dulcie was a pert and bouncy girl with hair the color of burnt sugar, which she wore in a pony tail that hung —or flipped—behind her like a long curled plume. The jacket she was making was for Beany. Beany's stepmother, Adair, had given Dulcie a generous length of green tweed, enough for two jackets—one for Beany and one for Dulcie, herself.

Beany could see the smiles of satisfaction that passed around the class at Dulcie's discomfiture. For Dulcie was not popular at Harkness. She was still thought of as that "brassy new girl," for she had entered Harkness at midterm in January.

Her unpopularity was not because she was a carhop at the Ragged Robin, for there was little snobbery at Harkness. Nor because she was, and knew she was, the best sewer in the class. Nor even because she blackened her brows and lashes and reddened her lips too heavily.

It was because she was too flamboyant, too cocky, and

entirely too flirtatious. She had bragged too often about her late dates with the "college men" she met at the Ragged Robin. She was also known as a "snuggle-upper" which, in Harkness parlance, meant that she was amorous on dates.

Beany had tried hard to smooth Dulcie's path at Harkness. So far, Beany was her only friend. Yet even Beany could never think of Dulcie as *best* friend—not as Kay had been. Kay was gentle and understanding. If Beany told Kay that Andy was joining the Marines, Kay would never have said, "So what? You can do better than that wise guy," as Dulcie had.

Dulcie's father was a carpenter by trade, but, until recently, he had been a roving prospector in search of uranium. Dulcie liked to tell that she had lived in seventeen different places by the time she was seventeen years old.

Beany leaned across the table to ask her, "In all your moving about, did you ever know anyone named Carmody? A girl, Miggs Carmody?"

Dulcie lifted irate eyes from the stitched seam she was ripping. "No. No Carmodys." She didn't even ask why, but muttered, "If Hilb makes me baste every half-inch of this, you won't have your jacket by the Fourth of July."

"Hilb always turns pretty tense this time of year," Beany sighed, "because of her fashion show coming up. Gee, I'm glad I haven't made anything worth showing in it. I was in it last year and I just hated mincing across the stage in time to the music."

"This year it's worse," Dulcie muttered. "We all have to pose like mannequins in a store window, first. Hilb doesn't even want us to blink or breathe—"

"I know," Beany nodded.

She knew all about Mrs. Hilb's Easter Parade, because Beany was on the staff of the school paper, *Hark Ye,* and

49

their coming issue would be largely devoted to the style-show program, and pictures of its participants.

This year Mrs. Hilb was having the stage setting to resemble a department-store window—without glass, of course. Each parting of the curtain would disclose a group of girls, posing rigid and unmoving as store mannequins; and holding the pose while the narrator, in glib saleswoman fashion, described each costume. Then the mannequins would come to life and move across the stage in time to the music.

Beany was not actress enough for even that small role in the spotlight. Her part in it last year had been one of heart-thudding misery.

"But you'll be featured as the final number, Dulcie. You'll be a big hit in your mouth-watering formal," Beany told her.

"Hit with who—*whom?*" Dulcie grumbled, looking around the room at the unfriendly girls.

Beany felt a stab of pity for the blundering girl. Dulcie *wanted* to be liked! But she had got off on the wrong foot at Harkness. If only that very first morning, when Beany brought her to the sewing class, Dulcie hadn't looked around disdainfully at the cotton skirts and blouses the other girls were laboring on, and blatantly announced, "I'm going to copy an original. See, this one with the black lace bodice and white tulle skirt."

If only she hadn't bragged that she was making her formal to wear to the coming Harkness prom. That had made no hit with the girls who hadn't a date for it—and wished they had.

"Don't worry about it," Beany was saying, just as the bell rang for the first-hour lunch period.

Beany and Dulcie, carrying their sacks of lunch, walked to the lunchroom together. Beany's thought had gone back to Miggs Carmody. She told Dulcie about their birth at the same time on St. Patrick's morning, told of their shared birthdays for nine years—told of her finding the unopened letter from Miggs in the window seat—

Dulcie pulled out chairs for them at the end of a long table. She said as she dropped down, "I thought you were going to say the babies got mixed up. Now that would be interesting. But you look too much like all the other Malones. You all have grins like a crack in a five-cent watermelon."

"No, we didn't get shuffled up."

"Then what's the point of the whole story?" Dulcie reached for mustard to spread on the lunch meat in her sandwich.

"The point of the whole story," Beany said impatiently, "is that I want to find her."

"Why? You forgot her all these years—why this sudden passion to find her now?"

"I didn't forget her. I thought of her a lot. I wrote her to tell her that Mother died, but the letter came back. I kept thinking I'd hear from her. Dad thinks she might have written me the next Christmas and that it got lost because we were away from home. And then all at once— you know how life is—we'd lost track of each other."

Beany, too, dabbed mustard on the tasteless slice of Mary Fred's meat loaf between her bread, and bit into her sandwich. The mustard was little improvement.

"Yesterday, I wrote to Kay," she went on. "Her father's a mining engineer and travels a lot, and I asked her to ask him if he had ever met anyone named Carmody. Miggs's father travels a lot, too, selling machinery. I asked Kay to answer airmail, special delivery. I keep hoping—it's sort of a dream—that we could get together for our birth-day."

51

"O.K., so suppose you trace down your little hand-holding pal. She'd probably be so changed, you wouldn't even like each other. I'd forget it. What you need now, with friend Andy off the scene, is a new beau—not any dear little girl chum of long ago that shared your crib."

"Oh hush, Dulcie. You're just soured because Hilb made you rip out your jacket."

"Not *my* jacket—*yours,*" Dulcie reminded her. "And that's not what I'm sour about." She tossed down the crusts of her sandwich, lifted, then lowered, her unhappy eyes, and asked in a driven whisper, "Beany, does Carlton ever—well, mention me to you—at all?"

Oh dear! Beany wished she hadn't asked it. She wished Dulcie could forget the blond, crew-cut Carlton Buell who lived next door to the Malones. A romance had barely started between the two when it had been blighted by Dulcie's own flirtatiousness. For Carlton had seen her "cuddling" in the front seat of a car with a college boy Dulcie had met at the Ragged Robin—

Beany answered Dulcie with a shake of the head, "No, he's never said a word. But then, Carl isn't the kind to—I mean, he has a sort of old-world gallantry about talking about girls."

"Oh sure, sure. He has to put a girl on a pedestal and then if she falls off—then the great idealist turns his back and goes on his way." She bit into her apple with an angry crunch. "Darn me, anyway, for being so scurvy when— when it was Carl I was so crazy about. I just wish I knew if he still hates me."

Beany sighed. It was even hard for her to understand how anyone could pine romantically for the quiet, somewhat stocky, crew-cut Carlton. She said, "Carl's not the kind I could come right out and ask."

This same Monday afternoon when Beany returned

52

home from school, she saw Carlton in front of his house. Carlton, a student at the U, taught swimming and basketball three nights a week in a community center down under the viaduct. This afternoon he was loading into his car not only athletic equipment, but his mother's silver coffee urn, and a huge platter, swaddled in a sweat shirt. The pocket of his coat sagged with what appeared to be salad forks.

"Looks like you made a good haul," Beany said.

He turned his quiet grin upon her. "The girls' club at the center is putting on a spaghetti supper tomorrow night. They're asking their boy friends, and they'd like it to be pretty swanky. I'm taking down a few things the club is short of."

"Do you need anything else?"

He took a crumpled list from his pocket. "Do you have any candlesticks, or wooden bowls for salad?"

The Malones did. It ended with Beany pressing on him candlesticks, complete with red candles, the salad bowls, and bright-colored fringed napkins.

As they packed them in a carton, Beany asked, "Carl, you remember Miggs Carmody, don't you?"

Carlton remembered, because he had eaten a good many pieces of birthday cake on past St. Patrick's Days. He, too, had gone to the Carmody acreage out beyond the university on Stomach-ache Day—"One of them was a Bee-sting, Dog-bite Day for me into the bargain," he added.

"Maybe your father would know how I could go about finding the Carmodys and Miggs," Beany said. Carlton's father was Judge Buell. Surely a judge would be endowed with wisdom about such things.

"I'll ask him tonight," Carlton promised, as Beany held the door open for him.

This was Beany's week of dinner-getting.

The first thing she did was to look in a far corner of the icebox behind the milk bottles. Ah, the remainder of the baked ham from yesterday's Sunday dinner had remained hidden from Johnny. His hungry habit of piecing between meals was certainly a handicap to a cook who frugally counted on using leftovers.

Yes, enough ham to grind up and make into timbales. She could bake potatoes and apples at the same time.

Mary Fred came hurrying into the kitchen and picked out the two largest and reddest apples. "For Miss Goldie," she said. "Two, because she's eating for two."

"I'm glad she isn't eating for three, or there wouldn't be one apiece for the Malones," Beany said.

Mary Fred made no reply to that. She paused in the open doorway to say, "Poor old McDevitt worries about Miss Goldie. I think that's why he keeps putting off his eye operation. I told him not to worry—that I'd take care of her till he came back."

"How could you take care of her?" the practical Beany asked.

"I'd figure it out—somehow," Mary Fred said, squaring her chin, as she went on her way.

Adair was entertaining visitors in the big living room. Probably something to do with her forthcoming exhibit in the Art Gallery, for Beany could see that a number of her portraits were propped up on the window seat.

She was just closing the oven door on the potatoes and apples when the doorbell rang.

As she went through the hall, she could see through the glass in the outer door the silhouette of a young man— just the silhouette, because it was near dusk. Beany's heart gave a sudden joyous leap. Broad shoulders, head of short,

54

wavy hair. Andy Kern. Maybe he hadn't passed his physical—maybe he was coming to tell her that he wasn't leaving after all—

She threw the door open wide, said on a glad shriek, "Andy! I'm so glad to see you—so glad—"

She stopped short. It wasn't Andy Kern at all. It was all the more startling because the young man who stood there resembled Andy as to build and dark hair—even to his crinkling eyes and teasing grin. At least, at first glance he did. And then a flustered Beany saw that he was older and that behind his smile there was something wise and thoughtful—yes, and cynical.

Yet when he spoke it was in a slow, easy drawl. "Sorry, but I'm not your Andy. I'm just plain old Hank—Hank Willison."

"Oh," Beany said, conscious that she was staring at him. He wore heavy boots and a leather coat that wasn't buttoned, though the March evening was sharp. His boots were muddy. So was the front of his shirt.

"Your dad's Martie Malone, isn't he?" And, at Beany's nod, "Is he home yet?"

"No, not yet. Won't you come in? I'm Beany Malone."

He stepped inside. "If you don't mind, I reckon I'd better phone him down at the *Call.*"

A Southerner? He had that slurring of *r*'s. His "I reckon," had been an "Ah reckon." He followed Beany through the hall to the telephone. He looked at the three-legged stool, on which the Malones often teetered unsteadily during long conversations, and said, "That sure looks familiar. I've straddled many a three-legged milking stool in my young days."

. . . No, it was more of a hillbilly drawl that made Beany think of TV comedians . . .

Working in the kitchen, Beany could hear snatches of his conversation with her father. Something about a trip to Utah and the report he had brought back.

He came to the kitchen door and said, "Your dad wants me to bring our findings down to him and the financial editor at the *Call* office." At Beany's mystified look, he explained. "You might have heard about their investigating some of these get-rich-quick uranium companies." Again that slow, lazy smile. "Yep, your dad's out like a bloodhound to show them up, so people won't invest their hard-earned shekels in ones that are no good. He's got a point. We checked over holdings in Utah and Arizona that were just plain old cow pastures."

"Are you a geologist?"

"Almost. I'm a senior at the School of Mines. I drove this trip with Professor Naismith, who's the best in the state. His brains, my leg work. I've driven all the way from the wilds of Utah today." He gave a tired heave. "I sure didn't figure on sitting in on a conference at the *Call*. I had a rasslin' match with a flat tire out here a ways, and got my shirt all muddied up. And I live clear to gosh and gone on the other side of town. It'll take me over an hour to go home and slick up."

"I can sponge the mud off your shirt and press it dry," Beany offered. "It wouldn't take very long."

"Here I come in, a stranger, and you'd wash my muddy shirt?"

"I won't wash it all. Just the mud off the front."

"Bless your little old fat heart. Turn your back, then, while I peel. I'll sit in my leather coat."

Beany asked, "Are you hungry?"

"Since you ask—yes. I could eat a pork chop made out of pig iron."

Beany laughed. "Would you settle for a ham sandwich made out of ham? Would you like milk or instant coffee?"

Coffee, he said. He needed something to "hotten up" his innards. He made a great show of taking out a little black book. "I'm crossing out all the Bettys and Nancys and putting Beany Malone at the top," he said. "I never saw anyone so handy with a slicing knife. You hear about friends that'd give you their shirt. Now I can brag that I know someone so big-hearted she'd wash your dirty shirt."

Hot water and soap took out the muddy stain. Beany washed it at the sink. While Hank Willison ate his sandwich and drank his coffee, she ironed it in the butler's pantry.

He was still thanking her when Beany walked to the front door with him. She asked him if he came from the South, and he said, "I'm an Okie. But I've been around here, pulling myself up by what are known as bootstraps, for six years. I'm twenty-two. That's a doddering old man to you, no doubt."

"I'll be seventeen on St. Patrick's Day. Just a babe in arms to you, no doubt."

"In *my* arms?" he asked and laughed at Beany's blush that drowned out the freckles across her nose.

And that was how Hank Willison, with that puzzling something behind his lazy smile and slow drawl, entered Beany's life. Beany was to think afterward of how she had asked everyone else, "Did you ever happen to know a girl named Miggs Carmody?"

She was to think of it with a certain irony, for Hank Willison, whom she didn't ask, was the one person who could have answered it.

6

IT was late the next evening, and Beany, in her short plaid housecoat, was putting what Johnny called her top-knot up on bobby pins when Carlton Buell returned the things Beany had loaned him for the supper at the community center. The girls' club, in appreciation, had sent her a serving of spaghetti.

"I'll save your having a large nightmare by eating half of it," Johnny said—and did.

"Gosh, Beany, you look like George Washington with your hair flattened down like that," Carlton commented. "Say, I have a clue for you on your Carmodys."

"You have, Carl! What?"

"I talked to Dad about them, and he remembers that Mr. Carmody had him fix up the papers to put the little acreage in Mrs. Carmody's name just before they moved away. Dad was practicing law then. Seems that Carmody sold equipment for oil wells and sometimes gambled on them himself. Maybe he wanted to protect them—that is, know they had a home to come to, in case he lost his shirt. It might be they still own the little farm. It might be the tenants on it could tell you where the Carmodys are now."

"Why, sure they could," Johnny said.

"Carl, you're smarter than all the rest of us put together," Beany praised. She added dubiously, "But I don't know whether I could find the place on my own or not. I was only eight the last time I was there—and all that land beyond the university is so built up now—"

"I could find it, easy as pie," Johnny said. "It was a two-story green house with an apple tree all but leaning against it. We'll drive out there tomorrow afternoon, Beany, if you get home from school in time."

But she didn't get home from school the next afternoon in time to go in search of a green house with a nearby apple tree.

Beany was feature editor on the school paper, *Hark Ye*, and an important staff meeting was called after school.

It was not only to plan the forthcoming issue of the paper, but also their forthcoming dance. The dance was called the Bunny Ball because its date was always close to Easter. It was an annual event which the staff gave to make up—or partially to make up—*Hark Ye*'s deficit.

"So don't any of you babes get ideas of grandeur," the finance editor warned.

The Bunny Ball was to be held, as it had been for years, the Saturday night before spring vacation and would follow the Easter Parade. There were reasons for this. Many who came to the fashion show in the auditorium would stay on for the Bunny Ball in the gym. The patrons of the style show would buy hundreds of copies of *Hark Ye*, because its pages carried the program and were well splashed with pictures of the participants.

"Some of the proud parents buy a dozen extra *Hark Ye*'s to send to grandmas and Cousin Minnies," the finance editor said.

Their staff photographer had already taken pictures of some of the models in their "creations." Beany, sitting at the long scarred table in the journalism room, leafed through them. Umm, good of Dulcie Lungaarde in her bouffant formal. Though Beany could have wished Dulcie hadn't struck such a cocky pose.

The arguing over details became more heated. The deficit. Those mindful of it were all for keeping expenses down. "We're not aiming to splurge—we're only aiming to make dough," they said.

They talked down the ones who wanted an orchestra for the dance. "No orchestra. We'll have George."

George was the Negro piano player who would play for Mrs. Hilb's Easter Parade. He was a football player, and his long strong hands were equally adept at catching a pass or thumping piano keys.

Jennifer Reed, editor-in-chief of *Hark Ye*, said, "George can get his brother to play the accordion for our dance. And we think we can get a drum—"

"All this for free," reminded the finance editor.

"Piano, accordion, and drum," belittled the pretty and popular club editor of *Hark Ye*. "Sounds like the Salvation Army meeting on any corner."

Jennifer Reed turned her thoughtful brown eyes to Beany. "What do *you* think?" she asked.

Beany started. . . . She had been thinking bleakly through all this wrangling about the Bunny Ball that she wouldn't have an escort. Not with Andy Kern already in

60

Marine uniform in San Diego. Not with Norbett Rhodes tied up with Helena Stearns and some hot-diggety young relative of hers. If she went, she'd be a "cog." A fine thing for a member of the staff.

She hedged in her answer to Jennifer. "George can sure whale the piano keys, and he knows all the latest hits—"

The staff was still arguing when the janitor flicked the lights in warning that the building was about to be darkened.

But the next afternoon Johnny and Beany set out in search of the Carmody farm. Mary Fred went with them, too. "I know just how to get there," she said. "We take that main drag out past the U until we come to a gas station, and then turn right."

"I thought we turned at a grocery store," Beany said.

They drove past the university buildings and grounds. And then all landmarks failed. Where they thought to find a gas station or store, the new six-lane Valley Highway slanted widely across. Once they got onto it, they had to keep going until they came to a clover leaf where they could turn off. They found a less traveled road, and wound their way back.

"This new school—Huxley Hall—wasn't here when we used to come out," Beany murmured, glancing at its light brick buildings, tennis court, swimming pool, and riding stables. . . . So the young relative of Mrs. Penthouse would be coming here. And Norbett Rhodes would be very busy, showing her around. . . .

"Nice riding ring," Mary Fred commented. "I've met Huxley Hall girls at the horse shows. The daughters of wealth. One of the girls said they call themselves the hussies from Huxley."

"Keep your eyes peeled for a green house, complete with apple tree," Johnny said.

"How can we tell it's an apple tree, when it's not apple season?" Mary Fred asked.

Johnny drove slowly while they looked in every direction. Beany thought he had driven too far south, and Mary Fred thought he hadn't gone far enough.

"If it wasn't for that high-toned Huxley Hall sprawled all over the landscape, it wouldn't be so hard to get our bearings," Mary Fred muttered.

Up this road, down that one, they drove, craning necks for sight of a two-story green house with a widespread tree touching it. "And a big front porch," Johnny reminded them. He remembered standing on it that day when a cloudburst had detained them; the day Katie had made potato pancakes.

They passed by new little flat houses; dilapidated, tall, old brick ones. They saw one two-story frame house, but it was a bald-looking, unblinking one of mustard yellow, quite unporched, and quite untouched by a tree of any kind.

And finally it was dusk and Johnny gave a sigh of defeat. "Tell you what you do, Beany. Get Carlton to bring you out. He's like a beagle hound when it comes to directions and remembering landmarks."

They reached home, discouraged and dispirited. Later that night Beany's spirits lifted when Johnny returned from the Buells', and relayed to her the news that Carlton would go with her the next afternoon.

"He has to be down at the center about six-thirty. But he'll swing by Harkness and pick you up soon as his last class is over at the U."

The next afternoon, Friday, Beany was just pushing

through the wide doors of Harkness when Dulcie joined her. They were halfway down the steps when Dulcie suddenly clutched her arm. "Look, there's Carlton Buell's car. There, down near the corner."

"Yes, he's going to drive me out to see if he can find the old Carmody place."

Dulcie's face fell. "Oh gee," she breathed, "when I saw his car, I thought maybe—maybe—" She thought maybe Carlton Buell had Dulcie Lungaarde in mind when he parked near Harkness, she meant.

"We can drop you off at the Ragged Robin—it's your night to work there, isn't it?" Beany offered. "It's right on the way. Carlton wouldn't mind."

But Dulcie held back, shaking her head. "That's what I'm afraid of—of his being polite and not minding—because he doesn't care enough to mind. Beany, it doesn't seem right. Carlton doesn't mean a thing to you, and yet he takes you places. And he means so much to me—and he wouldn't take me any place. If I just knew for sure that it's hopeless, why then I'd *make* myself stop mooning over him. Do you suppose you could sort of—?"

"Find out what goes? I'll try," Beany promised.

She had no chance, on the drive out, even to mention Dulcie. For the talk was all about finding that elusive farmhouse with its porch and apple tree. "There was a willow tree by the strawberry patch," Carlton remembered. He was sure he could locate the place without going past the university and being thrown off by the Valley Highway.

But in another half-hour Carlton was saying, as he backed his car to make a turn and try another road, "It's the Huxley Hall grounds that keep throwing me off."

Again Beany turned her head in this direction and that,

hoping to catch sight of a two-story green house with a porch. Or any two-story house with a nearby apple tree. Again that bare-faced yellow house caught her passing glance. Why would anyone paint a house that ghastly shade?

They stopped and made inquiries. First of a man who was repairing a fence; but he had lived there only two years and had never heard of anyone named Carmody. Next they stopped at a chicken hatchery where the fluffy day-old chicks reminded Beany of Katie and her brooder full of them.

No, the woman in attendance didn't know anything about the Carmody place.

Again the March dusk descended, and with it a spitting snow. They drove farther until, as Carlton said, the visibility was nil, and then, quite discouraged, turned toward home.

"The Carmody house could have been torn down," Carlton said, "to make way for the highway, or maybe for Huxley Hall."

"It must have been," Beany agreed. "It's just disappeared."

She roused from her disappointment to say, "South Wyman is a through street. Let's drive down it till we hit College Boul." South Wyman was Dulcie's street, though it was more of a country road than a street. Passing Dulcie's home would provide a chance to talk of her.

The small Lungaarde house was in the process of being added onto and remodeled. Dulcie's carpenter father was doing the work himself. Beany said, "Look, Carl, at how much work they've got done already."

Carlton glanced ahead to it with only passing interest. "Yes, it's going to be nice."

Beany turned her next remark over in her mind. Carlton, of course, had no idea that she knew as much as she did about the shattering of his and Dulcie's romance. . . . Probably it was right about here, in front of the house, that Dulcie had been parked in a car the night Carlton drove by and glimpsed the loving scene in the front seat.

Beany said, "Poor old Dulcie. She never had a home the way you and I had, Carl. Before her father decided to settle down, she was always on the move. Maybe she felt she had to work fast to get acquainted so as to have dates. Maybe she didn't think it mattered so much—how she acted, I mean—when she'd be moving on and never seeing the same folks again. And then she always had to work to get pretty clothes. And she had to put up with all sorts of people, and no wonder she got a little hard-boiled."

"Yes, she had a rough go of it," Carlton agreed. "I used to feel sorry for her, rushing around to fill orders at the Robin, and the manager lacing her down every time he felt like it."

Beany felt a hopeful surge of peacemaking, of rece-menting the romance. "Carl, how'd it be if I fixed up a double-date some night with Dulcie?" She paused, thinking, but who would *I* get now that Andy's gone?

Carlton said readily, "That'd be fine with me. And I could take my car if Dulcie's date doesn't have one."

"Oh no! I meant for you to date Dulcie. Honest, Carlton, she's changed. You see, she wanted to be popular and have dates every night and—" Oh well, why beat around the bush? "—and she thought she had to love-it-up to have boys like her. But she isn't like that now—honest, she isn't."

No remark from Carlton, and Beany added, "She's really swell. Adair gave her enough tweed for two jackets to make in sewing, and she's making mine first—and just working like a gopher on it."

Carlton grinned at her, reached over and patted her hand. "That's fine, Beany. I was pretty gone on her a while but—" Carlton was careful not to explain the "but." He only added, "Once the fire's out, it's out—with me, anyway. Maybe other guys aren't like that. I notice that when a cigarette goes out, a lot of them pick it up and light it again. I don't. I don't like the stale taste."

Beany could only agree soberly, "I know. I don't smoke —only once in a while for kicks—but I know what you mean."

Carlton flashed her a look of understanding. "For the record, Beany, you seem more all of a piece since Norbett isn't around, giving you a bad time."

"I even feel more *me*," she answered. . . . But a sort of stranded me, she thought, with Kay gone and now Andy. Doors closing. And no opening of the door on an old friendship, no making amends to Miggs for her seeming neglect, no picking up where they had left off years ago. . . .

Carlton stopped in front of the Malone house on Barberry. "I'm sorry, Beany, I wasn't a better beagle hound. 'The little house that wasn't there.' "

"Thanks anyway, Carl," she said heavily.

"The pleasure's all mine," he answered.

She couldn't help but chuckle at that as she ran up the front steps. How many times had Carlton been stranded for a date for a dance on the campus and taken Beany? How many times, when Beany had been stranded for a date, he had come to her rescue? And always when she thanked him, he said gallantly, "The pleasure's all mine."

The Bunny Ball! As a last resort, she supposed she

could turn to Carlton. Still, a girl hated having to conscript her brother's best friend.

She stepped into the hall. On the newel post lay the day's mail. There was Kay's airmail, special-delivery answer to Beany. Of course, Utah and Oklahoma were far apart. But maybe Kay's father, who traveled a lot as a mining engineer, could have crossed paths with Miggs's father, who also traveled a lot, selling equipment for oil wells.

Beany's eager fingers tore open the letter.

7

BEANY read the letter.

Another of her slim hopes was shattered.

She heard the sound of Johnny's typewriter and climbed the stairs to his room. The rat-a-tat of the keys stopped as she opened his door. His dark eyes took in the disappointment in her face.

"So Carlton couldn't locate it, either?" he said, tipping far back in his swivel chair. The chair threatened to tip clear over, and he deftly hooked his feet on the desk just in time. He glanced at the letter in her hand. "What'd Kay say? Any luck there?"

Beany shook her head. She read to him:

> I asked Dad if he had ever met anyone named Car-mody. The only Carmody he ever met was a rich oil-man from Dallas at a banquet last year. Dad didn't know whether he had a daughter or not, but he said

his wife was very beautiful, and svelte, and looked like *The* Best-dressed Woman of the Year."

"The rich oilman from Dallas isn't our Carmody," Beany murmured, remembering vaguely the balding, farmerish Mr. Carmody.

"No, and *The* Best-dressed Woman of the Year isn't our Katie," Johnny said. "Not if she's svelte, which is a four-bit word for skinny. Not our Katie who was always bustin' out all over."

"And Katie's hair was always every whichway," Beany added. "I remember how she was always losing the heel off the one pair of high-heeled shoes she wore. She didn't even like to be dressed up. But she didn't need to be—she was so much fun, and she laughed so much."

Beany stood for a minute in unhappy reverie. Johnny, anxious to show his sympathy, said, "Come on, kid—I'll help you get supper."

That Friday night, perhaps because the thought of Miggs lay heavily on Beany's mind and heart, she dreamed of her. There was no coherence to the dream. It was only a mood, a voice. Beany wakened from a half-sleep and jerked upright in bed, with the feeling that someone had been standing beside her bed, speaking to her.

The person was Miggs Carmody. She didn't know why she knew, but she did. The words had come from Miggs. "Beany, oh, Beany, I'm so lost. I can't find her—I can't find her at all—"

Beany's lips were asking, "Do you mean your mother? You mean you can't find Katie?" Even as Beany wakened fully, she found herself saying, "I'll help you, Miggs— I'll help you—" But, of course, there was no answer. . . .

That feeling of Miggs's needing her was still strong upon Beany the next morning as she sat at the breakfast table and poured half-and-half on her cereal. She had to tell Mary Fred about it.

Mary Fred said, "That sounds more like thought communication than a dream."

"You mean telepathy?"

"Or extrasensory perception. There're innumerable cases almost like yours last night. Dr. Rhine at Duke University conducts experiments on it. Miggs must have been thinking about you—and wanting you. And the thought came through to you in your drowsy, receptive state."

Beany dressed for her Saturday job, still haunted by her dream—or thought communication. . . . "Oh, Beany, I'm so lost." . . . The longing to reach Miggs was now more urgent than ever. Wherever she was, she was thinking of Beany, and needing her.

In her abstraction, Beany climbed into Johnny's car before she remembered her shorthand notebook and pencil.

The morning paper for which Martie Malone wrote a column also ran a half-page of letters to and answers by a mythical Eve Baxter. These letters were an airing of love and marital and in-law problems. They were signed, "Once a fool," or "Brokenhearted," or "Unwanted." Thousands of subscribers read the letters, along with Eve Baxter's helpful or sympathetic answers, with their breakfast coffee.

The Malones all knew that Eve Baxter was, in reality, a seasoned newspaperwoman named Evelyn Bartlett. But because the paper wanted to keep her identity a secret, Beany was warned not to divulge it. Once when one of the *Hark Ye* staff said with wise cynicism, "That Eve Baxter! It's not a woman at all. It's an old broken-down sports reporter that grinds out all that stuff," Beany had to clamp her lips tight to keep from correcting him.

During the week, Eve Baxter dictated to a typist at the *Call* office. But, partly because she liked to stay home on Saturdays, partly because she was fond of Beany, she dictated to her on those days. Beany drove over to her home in Johnny's jalopy and took down Eve Baxter's answers in her school shorthand. Then at the *Call*, Beany typed both letters and replies and turned them in to the copy desk.

This Saturday morning, Beany drove through the park, passed the tall Park Gate with its penthouse and, a few blocks farther on, stopped in front of the trim two-story residence of Eve Baxter.

Beany always relished having the door opened for her by an elderly housekeeper, named Araminta, in a ruffled cap and apron. Of hearing, "Come in, Miss Beany. Let me take your wraps, dear. Miss Eve is expecting you." It was somehow like a page from an English novel. The faithful, devoted family servant.

But the illusion lasted only while Araminta led her up the stairs, opened the door to the big front room and announced, "Here's Miss Beany, Miss Eve. Now I'll go about my marketing." For then Miss Eve turned from her desk and snapped out, "That stubborn mule of a woman. Her, and her tea. Soon as the back door closes behind her, go down and brew up a pot of strong coffee."

This tea-versus-coffee was an unending feud between employer and employee. Araminta insisted that coffee ruined a woman's complexion and disposition. "I have to browbeat her into making it," Miss Eve often told Beany, "and then it tastes as though she dropped sachet powder in it."

This morning, as usual, Beany measured coffee into

the percolator with a lavish hand and set it on a high gas flame. It was while she was waiting for the burbling trickle in the glass knob to turn a deep brown that a hopeful idea came to her. A possible way of reaching Miggs Carmody.

She carried the coffee into the big sunny room upstairs and poured Eve Baxter a steaming cup. She even waited for her to take a few sips of it, knowing, from experience, that Eve Baxter's disposition was not ruined but improved by it.

"Eve, people in Oklahoma read the *Call*, don't they?"

"Yes, we have some circulation in Oklahoma. Why?"

"You know how people sometimes run a few lines in your column to someone they want to hear from. Like last week there was that one about would Eddie please contact his aunt because of an emergency?"

Eve Baxter lifted curious eyes. She was a slender woman with nervous decisive movements. Her red hair was sprinkled with white. It always reminded Beany of the cinnamon and sugar mixture they used on cinnamon toast.

In answer to the question in her eyes, Beany related again the story of the girl who was "practically" her twin. She ended, "It's sort of a dream I have—of spending our seventeenth birthday together. But I don't know—time's getting short. It's next Saturday, St. Patrick's Day."

Eve Baxter veered away from the subject a minute. "I see a notice in the art column this morning that your stepmother's showing of portraits opens that day."

"Yes, that was the time the gallery gave her. She feels kind of bad about it, because her opening is on my birthday and she's afraid I'll feel neglected." Beany chuckled. "And Johnny is worried because he'll be rushing around,

72

getting old-time costumes and props for the skit he's putting on at the university. He wants me to go to it. He's afraid I'll feel neglected if I don't have something special for my birthday."

"And what about Mary Fred? Is she worried about neglecting you?"

"Yes, because she'll be gone, too. You know the dude ranch she works on in summer? The manager called her to ask if she could come up and help out for a week, because they're having a plane-load of skiers fly out from New York. She'll have to miss a week of school, but her profs have given her assignments ahead, and she's working overtime to get them in. She needs the money."

Eve Baxter filled her cup again. "And what's all this got to do with your lost Miggs and our circulation in Oklahoma?"

"I wondered if you'd let me run one of those appeals, like Eddie please contact your aunt, in your column. Just on the chance that Miggs would see it and write to me."

"It's about as chancy as putting a message in a bottle and tossing it into the sea, but you can try it. Keep it short, and we can crowd it in. I'm running only two letters and answers this morning."

Eve Baxter picked up the letters, said on an exagerated sigh, "Ah, love, love! One of the letters is from a soldier who received a Dear John letter. The other from a girl who received a Dear Mary letter from her soldier. Both are disillusioned, brokenhearted, utterly shattered. Both are sure life is finished."

Beany waited till the woman took a long swallow of coffee, knowing she had more to say. "I'd like to bet that in six months—no, I'll make it three—each one will be thanking his lucky stars the romance was broken off."

73

"Why?"

"Because life seems to demand a certain amount of trial and error before young people find the right one. Because young people have to find *themselves* first."

Beany thought of Mary Fred's saying, "You turn into a different *you* as you go along." Of Andy's saying, "Better to be sure than sorry." She thought of her young infatuation for Norbett that was no more—

She asked, "Do you think that once a boy and girl have been crazy about each other, they can ever be—well, just friends?"

Eve Baxter's keen eyes raked over her face. "Who are you trying to be just a sister to? To that cantankerous redhead you used to be so dewy-eyed about?" Beany's blush seemed answer enough, for Eve Baxter went on, "So you've dropped the torch at last, eh? Well, I'm glad to hear it. That lad needs to find himself if ever anyone did."

Beany defended, "But Norbett had such an unhappy childhood. He's an orphan, and he had to live with his aunt and uncle—you know the Rhodeses at the Park Gate? And he was always made to feel unwanted. I still feel sorry for him."

Eve Baxter made a sound, halfway between a snort and a hiss. "Pity's the worst thing for a fellow like that. Beany," she said heatedly, "I'm fed up with people using their unhappy childhoods as an excuse for failure—even ornery dispositions. Who hasn't been whacked down by life in one way or another? If a ball is knocked in a gutter, it *has* to lie there—it's inanimate. But we're human beings—we're animate. We have free will—and guts. We can get to our feet, brush ourselves off and say, 'O.K., I'll just go on from here.'"

Beany was turning that over in her mind when Eve

74

Baxter said soberly, "You ask if you and the stormy petrel could be just friends. Yes, if he whittles down his ego. Some of the most beautiful friendships are between opposite sexes. To be sure, some men can think of women—or girls—only as someone to woo or impress. Some girls have no capacity for any relationship with a male other than as a possible mate. It's too bad, because each has something to give the other. Take it from an old maid who knows."

She pushed her empty cup from her. Beany picked up the percolater and cup and saucer. She carried them to the kitchen and washed them and put them away before Araminta returned. This was part of Eve Baxter's conspiracy with Beany.

Beany said as she returned, "I'm practically an old maid. Andy Kern's gone into the Marines, and I'm left high and dry."

Eve Baxter threw back her head and laughed. "I'll give you three months—oh no, even three weeks would be too long—before you have a young man at your beck and call. You'll never be an old maid with that Malone grin."

Later that morning at the *Call* office, Beany typed the letter from the girl who signed herself, "Heartbroken," and from the soldier who signed himself, "Through with Women," along with Eve Baxter's heartening answers.

Beany walked across the noisy editorial room to the desk with the name plate "Martie Malone" on it, and showed her father the copy with her message sandwiched in between the letters.

It read:

> Paging Miggs Carmody wherever you are. The only birthday present I want is to hear from you.
>
> BEANY MALONE

75

Her father reached out with his soft black pencil and made some hieroglyphics beside the message so that the typesetter would set it in blacker type than the rest of the column.

"Don't count too much on results," he said with a dubious headshake.

"I'm not," Beany said.

But she was counting on it. Surely it wasn't wishful thinking—that feeling that her birthday was to be more than a birthday.

She'd had the feeling all along, when Adair worried about her opening taking her away from the house on Beany's birthday; when Mary Fred said, "I hate to dash off to the ranch and leave you stranded, with no Kay, no Andy to make your birthday an occasion." When Johnny had said, "Cripes, Beany, I know you don't vibrate to old-time stuff, or to having a brother for an escort, but coming to the St. Patrick's skit would be a notch above watching TV on your birthday."

To them all Beany had said, "Don't worry about me."

She had even said to Mary Fred, "I have the dog-gonedest hunch that I'm going to hear from Miggs. Because if that *was* thought communication, she's got me on her mind, too."

8

MONDAY morning Dulcie Lungaarde didn't wait until she and Beany met in sewing. She was standing at the foot of the stairs so the two could climb them together.

"I'd have called you yesterday," Dulcie said, "only I was afraid Judge Buell's only son might be on the Malone premises."

Oh dear, Beany thought again, I wish I could tell her what she wants to hear. She said, "Carlton and I rode around for hours but we didn't find the Carmody—"

"I didn't think you would. Did you talk about anything else besides your precious Carmodys?"

"Yes, we talked about you. When we passed your place, I told him about your making my jacket, and then I suggested that maybe—"

"Oh, go ahead, Beany," Dulcie snapped, "and don't be so picky of your words. Just tell me whether I've got a chance or not."

They were outside the sewing room now. They stopped, letting some of the pupils push past them. "I don't think so, Dulcie," Beany said honestly. "He said the fire was out—and that going back to an old flame was like — Well, he said maybe other fellows—"

"What'd he say going back to an old flame was like?" Dulcie prodded sharply.

"He said it was like lighting a cigarette that had gone out."

"What a colorful little figure of speech," Dulcie mocked, but Beany saw her face go slack with disappointment.

"Did you read Eve Baxter's column this morning— her answers to the boy and the girl who were so broken-up and thought they would never smile again? Eve Baxter told them the only way to forget was to go out with others—"

Dulcie gave her burnt-sugar pony tail a toss. "I don't need Eve Baxter to tell me that. One of the football players at the U has been trying to date me, and I am not about to sit home and eat my heart out over any stuffed shirt."

They had reached their sewing table, and Dulcie opened her drawer and grabbed out the greenish tweed, which was beginning to bear some semblance to a jacket.

She looked at Beany with a twisted smile. "Carlton thought I was a model of maidenly virtue, and he was disappointed when he found out I was on the cheap side. This new bright-eyes is all primed to give me a rush because he thinks I'm a cheap little carhop. *He's* going to be disappointed, too, when he finds I'm a reformed character."

If only, Beany regretted, as she surveyed her own denim

pedal pushers, Dulcie had reformed a little sooner, Carlton would never have seen her and another boy in a clinch.

Dulcie added, "I saw your touching appeal to Miggs Carmody in Eve Baxter's column too. My eye, Beany, why can't you relax and let bygones be bygones? I'll bet this Miggs person has forgotten she ever knew you. I'll bet if you went rushing up to her and said, 'Remember me—I'm Beany?' she'd say, 'Beany? Beany who? Oh, Beany Maloney—or was it Beany Baloney?'"

"She hasn't forgotten me," Beany declared. "I know. Because Friday night when I was half asleep, it was as though she stood there in the room and spoke to me—"

"What'd she say?"

"She said she was lost. It wasn't what she said as much as the feeling I had that she needed me. Mary Fred said it wasn't a dream, but thought communication. That wherever Miggs was, she was thinking of me, and so the thought came—"

"Thought communication, my foot. Sounds like a nightmare. And don't you know dreams always go contrary? If you dreamed Miggs was down and out and needing help, it means that she's sitting on top of the world."

Mrs. Hilb interrupted. "Beany, will you ever finish those pedal pushers? You've been so long on them, they're practically out of style now."

"I've been practicing buttonholes," Beany said. She added low to Dulcie, "That Easter Parade is making the woman tenser by the day."

"She's not the only one," Dulcie muttered back. "I wish I wasn't going to be in it. I wish I'd never made that formal. I have nightmares in broad daylight about it—and they're not 'thought communications,' either. No one will clap for me."

"Dulcie! Beany!" Mrs. Hilb's voice was sharp. "This is a sewing class—not a tea party."

On Wednesday afternoon the *Hark Ye* staff met again in the journalism room for more discussion of their coming issue; for more heated argument over the coming Bunny Ball.

Those who longed to make it an occasion wanted dance programs. They always had programs at university dances, they said.

No programs, said those who longed to wipe out the deficit. What were programs anyway, but something for a girl to dangle on her wrist and later put in her scrap book or hang on a wall as a memento of a happy evening?

"You've got something there," sneered the club editor. "This promises to be an affair we'd best forget."

It was late when Beany reached home. The family were all gathered in the dining room.

"Here she is," Johnny announced. "We thought you'd never get here, little beaver. We have news for you."

And Mary Fred hurried in from the kitchen to say, "I told you it was thought communication. You're psychic. Oh, Beany, your wish came true. Just look." She was motioning with a wooden spoon to her father and the squarish white card he held in his hand.

Martie Malone handed it to Beany. "It can't surprise you any more than it did me," he said.

It was an engraved invitation. Beany read the words, "Mrs. Addison Jay Stearns" . . . "Honoring Mr. and Mrs. Perry Carmody . . . and daughter Catherine" . . .

Beany looked uncomprehendingly around at the family. Johnny reached over her shoulder and put a finger on the name, Mrs. Perry Carmody.

"Mrs. Perry Carmody is Katie. Daughter Catherine is your Miggs, stupe. Look at the where, look at the when."

Beany's dazed eyes dropped to the invitation again. "Park Gate Hotel" . . . "Five to Seven" . . . "The Seventeenth of March" . . .

Mrs. Addison Jay Stearns? Oh, Mrs. Penthouse—Norbett's marvelous Helena Stearns—who had walked in on the intruders in her Sunset Room and, without raising her voice, made them feel like three consecutive worms.

"Mr. Carmody's name that we couldn't remember is Perry," her father said.

"Fancy that," Mary Fred was saying. "Your Miggs and Katie being honored at a penthouse party. If I didn't have to be up at the ranch, untangling skis and skiers, I'd go along."

Johnny said the same thing, "And if I didn't have to be out at the Student Union, sticking handlebar mustaches on the cast, I'd go along."

"Did this come to me?" Beany asked, still staring confusedly at the card."

"It came to me at the *Call* office today," her father said. "To me and to you—Mr. Martie Malone and Miss Beany Malone."

"I wonder why it didn't say Mr. and Mrs. Malone," Beany murmured absently. She still couldn't associate the Miggs and Katie she had known with Helena Stearns and that luxurious penthouse apartment.

Adair said, "Whoever sent the invitation probably didn't know there was a Mrs. Malone now. Of course, I couldn't go anyway because of my opening, and the dinner afterward."

"You can represent the Malones, Beany, and give them my regrets," her father said. "Because I'll be going to the dinner they're giving, 'Honoring Mrs. Malone, the portrait painter.' "

Mary Fred prodded her with her wooden spoon. "Beany, come out of your trance. You and Miggs will be sharing a birthday just as you did in days of yore."

"Miggs and I— Why, of course."

It was just that the engraved and formal invitation had been so startling. But her wish had come true. She would see Miggs at last and explain about the unanswered letter. Tears threatened her, and she talked fast to keep them back. "Why, I'll bet Miggs saw what I put in Eve Baxter's column. And maybe that's why the Carmodys came to Denver and planned the party for our birthday—"

"Hardly that, Beany," Martie Malone said gently. "Mrs. Stearns is giving this party."

"I wonder where Miggs is. I wonder if I could phone her right away," Beany said.

"Maybe she's staying at the penthouse. If she isn't, this Mrs. Jay Addison—or Addison Jay—woman could tell you," Johnny said. "Call up and ask."

The thought of telephoning the penthouse was somewhat dashing to Beany. She had never mentioned her visit to it to the family; the very memory of it could still make her squirm—

"Go on," Johnny urged, "and see how you can get hold of Miggs—or Katie. I'd like to talk to them."

Well, it would be worth bearding the lioness in her Technicolor den to find Miggs, to hear her voice. Beany went resolutely to the telephone in the hall.

She dialed the familiar Park Gate number, asked for Mrs. Stearns's apartment on the thirteenth floor.

The girl at the switchboard said, "Mrs. Stearns is not to be disturbed this evening. I'll take a message if you care to leave it."

Beany hesitated, and then asked, "Do you know if anybody named Miggs—that is, Carmody—is visiting there?"

"No, I don't, ma'am," the impersonal voice said and volunteered again, "I'll take any message you care to leave for Mrs. Stearns."

"I—I don't know—" She couldn't think of how to word a message to go through Helena Stearns to Miggs. "Maybe —I'll call later."

The family were listening from the dining-room door. "Sidney Peale might know if the Carmodys are there," Beany thought aloud. "You see, he runs the elevator—"

"I'd wait, Beany, till you see her," her father advised. "You've waited this long—you can wait two and a half days more."

"Soup's on," Mary Fred reminded them.

Beany sat down shakily to Mary Fred's dinner. . . . You'd think Miggs would telephone her. But maybe Miggs was remembering that Beany hadn't written to her. . . .

She was barely conscious of Johnny's wail, "Meat loaf again. All you have to do is go through the store door, for the butcher to reach for the hamburger."

"It's cheap and filling," an unconcerned Mary Fred answered.

"What will you wear to the party, Beany?" Adair was asking.

"Oh—I hadn't thought. My best outfit, I guess. The shamrock blouse and the new green corduroy skirt."

"Oh no, this doesn't sound like a skirt and blouse affair, Beany."

"How about my cream-colored wool with what the clerk called a portrait neck?" Mary Fred offered. "It's just right for teas and frat firesides and such. It's got a mustard stain on the skirt—some joker dropped his hot dog in my lap the last time I wore it. But I'll take it up to the cleaners on my way to school tomorrow. I'll tell them you have to have it Saturday."

"Yes, a light-weight wool with a low neck would be better," Adair agreed. She burst out impulsively, "Beany, you should have one of those after-five dresses for an affair like this. I'd like to get you one for your birthday."

Again tears threatened the already shaky Beany at Adair's warm generosity. For Beany knew, as did all the Malones, that Adair was saving the money she made painting portraits to turn the room over the garage into a studio. It was not at all satisfactory for her to have "sittings" in the Malone living room with all the family hubbub going on in the house.

"That's swell of you, Adair, but I hardly ever need that sort of dress-up dress," Beany said earnestly. "I'm saving for a new formal. There's the Bunny Ball coming up—" But the Bunny Ball had suddenly faded in importance since she had heard from Miggs.

Both Beany and Mary Fred bought their own clothes out of the money they earned—Mary Fred with her riding classes, Beany with her typing for Eve Baxter—plus what they could save from the food allowance.

Martie Malone said, "Beany, maybe you shouldn't feed us so well. Maybe then you'd have more of a wardrobe."

Beany could only give him a tremulous smile. . . . Goodness, she did feel lumpy of throat since that invitation had come. . . .

"Mary Fred ought to have a closetful of finery," Johnny said. "What with her constantly poking meat loaf down our gullets."

No answer from his sister.

Adair reached for the invitation which Beany had

propped up before her. "Five to seven," she murmured. "That could be one of those predinner cocktail parties."

"Five to seven!" Johnny said. "That's eating time. How could they help serving supper?"

"Even if it is a predinner party," Beany said confidently, "I know Miggs and her mother. They'll want me to stay on. I can just hear Katie saying, 'You can't go till I've fed you. Let it never be said anyone ever left here hungry.'"

In all the planning excitement, the young Malones never noticed the sober, almost troubled looks that passed between Martie Malone and their stepmother.

Beany couldn't wait to show that invitation to the skeptical Dulcie. They were no sooner seated at the sewing table the next day than Beany handed it across to her.

"My hunch was right," she said. "Miggs and I will be sharing out seventeenth birthday."

"And in a penthouse!" Dulcie breathed. And then she, too, asked, "What're you going to wear?"

Dulcie was even dubious about Mary Fred's cream-colored wool being right. "This Carmody-Stearns combination sounds pretty 'café society' to me. I'll bet they'll all be wearing cocktail dresses. Not that I pal around with the Socially Prominent, but I see their pictures on the society page—'Mrs. Gotrocks was wearing an emerald green brocade frock with a torso waistline.'"

"What about a hat, Dulcie?"

"Definitely a hat."

"That's good. It'll cover my braids. I told you about Helena Stearns walking in on poor Sidney and Rosellen and me and giving us the frosty treatment. That's what worries me about this whole deal. That's why I'm glad I won't be wearing the shamrock blouse. I don't want her to recognize me—right off, that is. As soon as she knows I'm Miggs's best friend it won't matter. I'll apologize again for our intruding that night, and everything will be fine."

"We hope. . . . What coat are you going to wear?"

"What coat do you suppose? My winter one. I can take it off the minute I get there. Never again will I buy a plaid one. They're all right for football games—"

"But not for a penthouse party," Dulcie said. She held up the jacket of greenish tweed, which was far from finished, and announced, "You'll wear this jacket. Not that it's right for a five-to-seven gathering, but it's better than your tacky plaid. Yessir, it's full steam ahead on it—"

"But, Dulcie, you've barely got it stitched together. You've still got the lining and the pockets and—"

"I can take it home and work on it on our portable electric. Even if I have to sit up all night. I won't have your penthouse friends high-hatting you if I can help it."

Mrs. Hilb consented to Dulcie's plan when she was told of the emergency of the penthouse party on Saturday. "Yes, you can finish it at home, Dulcie. But you'll have to bring it back here and let me examine it before I pass on it."

Who could help liking Dulcie, Beany thought fondly. Blunt-spoken, brash, even ill-tempered as she was at times. Who but Dulcie, after scoffing at the possibility of Beany's renewing a childhood friendship, would work extra hours to finish a jacket for her to wear to the reunion?

9

THE seventeenth of March! St. Patrick's Day, and the birthday of Beany Malone and Miggs Carmody.

The day came in with dark skies and a chill bite in the air. Beany didn't mind that. This was the day she would rid herself of the nagging guilt over her unanswered letter to Miggs. The day of reunion. The day a door would open.

She would ask Miggs to come home with her from the party and stay all night. They had so much to catch up on. Beany surveyed her room, which was woefully small; she couldn't crowd an extra bed or cot into it. But Miggs wouldn't mind. She had shared that same bed with Beany so many times—so many years before.

The day was given an extra lift by the corsage which arrived just as Beany was leaving for Eve Baxter's. From Andy in San Diego. Bright green carnations in a nest of even greener ribbon. The card was in Andy's handwriting: *"Erin go bragh,* and stay as sweet as you are."

Beany tucked it into the vegetable compartment of the icebox, between a head of lettuce and a stalk of celery. A corsage *would* dress up Mary Fred's cream-colored wool.

She was so full of the party that she had to tell Eve Baxter about it and show her the invitation. The woman read it and her eyes narrowed in thought. "Helena Stearns. Now what ax do you suppose she has to grind?"

"Do you know Helena Stearns?"

"I'd hate to tell you how many years I've known her. We went to school and then college together. Helen Carmody, she was then."

"Carmody! Then she must be a relative of Miggs's father."

"Not a very close relative—no closer than a cousin, because she was an only child."

"I wondered why she was *honoring* them. I suppose they came to town for a visit and she decided to have a party for them. I tried to phone Miggs as soon as I got the invitation, but I'd have had to reach her through Helena Stearns and—"

She didn't finish. She hadn't told Eve Baxter about that ill-fated visit to the penthouse, either. She said instead, "Norbett says that with all her money, she's lonely—and that's why she gave up her big house and moved to the Park Gate."

"The lone, lorn widow!" Eve Baxter snorted. "She's one of the shrewdest businesswomen I know. She's the widow of the Stearns of the Stearns Blackwell Mercantile. He died some six—seven years ago, leaving her with plenty of capital to gamble with."

She set down her coffee cup with a vehement click. "I never liked her. Oh, I don't hold it against her because she wants to make money, but I don't like her using her social position to gain business ends. And I don't like anyone who acts a part he isn't. That clinging-vine act—just so she can find a sturdy oak or two to wrap around. . . . So she's having a big affair for Perry Carmody, wife, and daughter. I wonder what the woman's up to now."

"What makes you think she's up to something?" a puzzled Beany asked. "It's a party."

Eve Baxter gave her "whoosh" that was both a snort and a hiss. "Helena Stearns isn't spending a lot of money on drinks and caviar out of loving-kindness to her fellow humans. I must get hold of someone at the *Call* and ask what the score is. I've been so busy Eve Baxtering that I haven't kept up."

"But Miggs and her mother aren't the ax-grinding kind," Beany defended. "They always loved having company and feeding them."

Eve Baxter didn't answer. She thrummed thoughtfully on the desk for a minute before she said, "Let's get to our letters."

Beany was in the Eve Baxter cubbyhole, typing the column, when her father came over to her. "I'm free for lunch today, puss. How about a hamburger with me?"

"I'd like to, Dad, only you know, the party. Have to run downtown and exchange the stockings Johnny gave me for sheerer ones. Oh, and thank you and Adair for the new pumps. They're so nice and teetery. I'm wearing them to the party."

"You'll see some of the *Call* people there. Society editor, for one. Quite a few from the papers and radio and TV stations were invited." He paused as though he were debating whether to say something more. He said finally, "Beany, in case the party doesn't take up the whole evening, you know Adair and I would be glad to have you join the artists' crowd for dinner."

"I'd be way out of my depth with artists. What would I talk about?"

His eyes twinkled. "You could tell them about the ash tray you made in ceramics that looks like a bedpan."

Beany chuckled ruefully, and returned to the subject uppermost in her mind. "I'm planning on Miggs's coming home with me after the party."

Again Martie Malone hesitated. But he said only, "That *would* be like old times," and walked back to his desk.

Everything takes longer on a crowded Saturday afternoon. Beany exchanged her stockings for a pair of cobwebby sheer ones. She bought bone hairpins, thinking, as she often did, braids are old-fashioned. I ought to whack them off.

She drove toward home, and stopped on the boulevard to pick up Mary Fred's dress at the cleaners'. But even as she tried the locked door, the sign on it fairly leaped out at her:

CLOSED AT 1:30 P.M. ON SATURDAY

Oh no! Oh, why couldn't she *ever* remember which establishments on the Boul closed Saturday afternoons, and which kept open? She walked around and rapped on the back door, hoping to rouse someone. There was no response. She came back and stared through the front window. There was the cream-colored dress, hanging on the rack of clean garments—so immaculate, so enticing—

No use standing and coveting it, when a locked door

separated her from it. Helplessly, she got in the car and drove toward Barberry Street.

But her green corduroy skirt wasn't an ordinary skirt, she tried to console herself. It had come from Madame Simone's exclusive store and had cost twice as much as Beany had ever paid before. And the shamrock blouse was even more appropriate for St. Patrick's Day. . . . Oh, but Helena Stearns's cold eyes had seemed to fairly count those shamrocks. . . . But Beany Malone could keep her tweed jacket on—for a while, anyway.

Johnny was waiting for his car. Two stovepipe hats sat on his dark head and, as he came toward her, he clamped an auburn mustache to his upper lip for effect.

"Handlebar mustache for the bartender—no pun intended."

"Where did you get that, Johnny?"

"I fashioned it with my own little hands."

The shade was so familiar, and their Irish setter looked so reproachful, that Beany scolded, "Johnny Malone, you ought to be ashamed—whacking hair off poor Red."

"Why not? He's got more hair than he needs with spring coming on. I should pay six-bits to rent one? I'd have clipped a black one off Mike, if he'd stood still long enough." He climbed into the car, called back as he drove off, "When you see Katie, tell her I hope she hasn't lost her fryin' arm."

Beany was bathed and dressed by five. What had happened to Dulcie and the green tweed jacket she had promised? Beany had hoped she would arrive early enough to help her decide on a hat.

It was five-thirty before the chugging of a pick-up truck announced Dulcie's arrival. She came in the side door, panting out explanation of why she was late. The electrician had been working on the wiring in their remodeled rooms, and the current had to be turned off.

"I couldn't sew on the portable, I couldn't even heat the iron to press. But here it is. I didn't have time to put in the lining or the pockets, but I finished the slit openings on the outside so no one will know. Just don't forget and drop any fifty-dollar bills in them or they'll go through to the floor."

"It looks elegant," Beany complimented, and slid into it. "Now help me decide on a hat."

She had previously laid out on her bed her own navy-blue beret, her last spring's hat which was far too summery for this dour March evening. Mary Fred's small selection of hats was there too.

With Dulcie's head cocked critically to one side, Beany tried on all of them. Dulcie shook her head firmly as each hat went on.

"Adair's got a little feathery one—green and bronze. It does a lot for her," Beany said. She hurried in to the closet in the front bedroom, and reappeared with it. She tried it on. "Adair's head must be smaller than mine. When she wears it, this soft feather curls down toward her chin."

Dulcie reached under it to flatten Beany's braids; she shoved the hat down more firmly. "Wear it," she said without much enthusiasm. "At least it covers your braids."

"The jacket does look as if it belongs with the skirt, doesn't it?" Beany asked. "I'll keep it on until Mrs. Stearns finds out I'm an old friend of Miggs's."

"That old harpy. I hope none of her snobbery has rubbed off on your pals. Good grief, it's almost six. Come on, I'll take you over in the pick-up. I'll let you out on the corner so none of the upper crust will see you arriving in

92

a truck. Reunion with Miggs in a penthouse. Didn't I tell you that 'thought communication' about Miggs's needing you was a lot of malarkey?"

Beany had no answer for that.

On the corner near the Park Gate, Dulcie let off her passenger with the pinned-on carnation corsage, with Mary Fred's white gloves clutched in one hand.

Sidney Peale was running the elevator that took Beany up. "Why, Beany," he said, "I hadn't a clue you were you until you smiled. I've never seen you in a hat before."

"I'm hoping someone else won't have a clue I'm me," she said in a low tone, for the elevator was full of passengers who were evidently penthouse-bound, judging by the dark suits of the men and the fur wraps of the women.

Beany was the last one to step off the elevator at the thirteenth floor. As she dropped behind to push her hat down more firmly on her head, someone touched her arm and a voice said, "Blow me down—if it isn't the babe in arms, the washer of dirty shirts."

Beany lifted amazed eyes. It was Hank Willison, who was an "almost" geologist at the School of Mines, who called himself an Okie. Again Beany was struck by his certain resemblance to Andy Kern.

"Why, Hank Willison," she gasped. "What are you doing here?"

He grinned his lazy, crinkly grin. His hat was pushed back on his head; his topcoat was over his arm. "Do your eyes always have to bug out when you see me? What am I doing here? I came out with some of the folks from the *Call*. I wanted to say hello to the Carmodys—" There was a certain malicious amusement in his eyes, "Yeh, and watch a woman named Mrs. Addison-something Stearns grind her ax."

. . . Strange, that was what Eve Baxter had said. . . .

"Oh, do you know Miggs and her mother?"

He nodded. "I knew them in Oklahoma six years ago. I lived with them when I worked for Mr. Carmody. Your dad was telling me today you used to pal with Miggs when you were kids."

"Yes, we're practically twins. And this is our birthday. I can hardly wait to see her and Katie. Why are you leaving the party so soon?"

"I figured I'd better—before Helena Stearns separated the sheep and the goats. How about my giving you a lift home? I can wait downstairs for you."

"Oh no, don't wait, Hank. I don't know when I'll be leaving. I'm going to stay till the party is over, because I'm planning on Miggs's coming home to stay all night with me."

She didn't notice that the amused glee left his eyes, and that he looked at her with something of concern. She added happily, "Or else maybe Miggs and Katie will want me to stay here with them. Miggs and I'll have so much to catch up on."

The elevator had stopped, letting out three more party-goers. Sidney Peale announced, "Down. Down." Hank looked at the waiting elevator, looked at Beany—

She said, "I'd better hurry. I'm late already."

Hank even looked back at her soberly as she followed the guests through the open door to the penthouse apartment.

A maid was taking the wraps from the guests. She asked Beany, "May I take yours, Miss?"

"No—well, no—not yet."

A confused Beany found herself in the Sunset Room in a bedlam of chatter. Her first panicky thought was, This certainly isn't a skirt and blouse affair. Such lovely dresses, such a lot of jewelry.

94

The black silver-shot draperies were drawn back from the windows. But no one was looking at the murky sky or the shadowy outline of peaks. The people—and it seemed to Beany there were hundreds—were milling about with glasses in hand, laughing, greeting one another. She didn't see a familiar face. She didn't even see Helena Stearns, for whose benefit she was wearing this tight hat that kept working up on her head.

Flowers—what masses of flowers. And all in yellows, blues, and corals to blend with the furnishings. Beany's own corsage seemed suddenly glaringly green. But it's St. Patrick's Day, she told herself.

She backed against a wall between two great splashy pictures, her eyes still searching through the crowd. Where was Miggs? Where was her mother? Was that the receiving line over by the fireplace, where the people were knotted most thickly?

Waiters were weaving in and out with trays of canapés and drinks. One stopped in front of her. It was Amos from the dining room downstairs, and he recognized her because, on several occasions, she had dined there with Kay and her mother. He explained gently, "Miss Beany, these drinks are for the grown folks. There's punch for all the young folks in the dining room."

Beany turned her eyes toward the dining room on its higher level. The pliable partition, which Sidney had demonstrated to Rosellen and her, was pushed far back. Miggs must be in there. But there was so many girls and young men, all of them laughing and quite at ease as they drank from glass punch cups.

Her eyes studied the girls; she couldn't see the ones behind the table for the high floral centerpiece. She didn't see anyone who looked like Miggs. After-five dresses. They were all wearing them. If only the cleaners hadn't been closed. . . . She felt sudden stage fright. She just couldn't go bolting in there to ask, "Which one of you is Miggs?"

She'd find Katie first. But she didn't see anyone who looked like Katie, either. She did recognize Mr. Carmody, though her memory of him was her haziest. He was talking to three men and, except for his better grooming, his wider bald spot, he hadn't changed from the quiet, ruddy-faced man Beany remembered.

A woman, hurrying into the big room from the hall door, brushed against Beany. It was the young blond society editor of the *Call*, whose desk Beany passed every Saturday on her way to Eve Baxter's cubbyhole. It was such a relief to see a familiar face that Beany clutched her arm, said, "Hello, Dorothy. Did you just get here?" Even "Society" was wearing a black faille dress and sparkling earrings.

"Hello, hon. Oh no, I've been on the job. As always, I move about, stuffing my brain with who is wearing what until I'm glassy-eyed and then," she gave Beany a conspiratorial wink, "then I dash into the nearest john and grab out little book and pencil—"

"Oh. Aren't you supposed to jot down notes as you go along?"

"Sometimes you have to—you know, opening night of Symphony or Opera where they come in droves. But here I'm sort of a working guest." Her eyes sorted through the guests as she talked. "I wish the governor and his lady would appear—although I'll bet she'll be wearing her same brown brocade—because I have to tear off and buy groceries and baby food." She murmured in a tone of mental note-taking, "Mayor's wife—black dress—sequin hat."

Beany asked, "Which one is Katie—Mrs. Carmody? I can't see her."

"There, in the silver lamé sheath, standing by Mrs. Stearns. You can usually pick out the hostess and honor guests in a mob scene like this by the orchids on their shoulders."

Yes, there was Helena Stearns in lavender velvet and a white orchid, shaking hands and introducing guests with winning graciousness. As though her only concern was their happiness.

Then Beany's eyes rested on the slim woman close to Helena Stearns, in silver with a green orchid on her shoulder.

"Oh, that's not Katie. Not in that dress that looks as if it was sprayed on her. I used to know her—and she was plump and always busting out her seams. She was no Best-dressed Woman of the Year."

Dorothy Cobb, society editor, murmured, "Maybe it's a different Mrs. Carmody. These rich oilmen have a way of changing models."

The woman in question turned her head just then, and Beany saw the flash of her dark eyes. "Oh, my goodness!" Beany breathed. "It *is* Katie."

She leaned weakly against the wall. Katie did look like the Best-dressed Woman of the Year. . . . Then it must have been these Carmodys that Kay's father had met at a banquet. Then Mr. Carmody must be the rich oilman from Dallas. . . . Then the Carmodys were the rich relatives from Texas who were to live in the penthouse with Helena Stearns—the "beastly" rich ones, according to Sidney Peale.

A dazed Beany was still turning that over in her mind when Dorothy left her. . . . Norbett Rhodes had said there was a daughter who was already enrolled at Huxley Hall—a hot-ziggety girl, who was to have the pleasure of his company. Miggs. Then the crowd in the dining room around the long table, with its lace tablecloth almost touching the floor, was the Huxley Hall crowd—

Yes, she'd visit with Katie first.

She made her way through the crowded room. As she passed Mr. Carmody, he gave her the vague smile of a man who is thinking, now who is she? She looks a little familiar.

Beany stood in front of the slender and chic woman in the silver lamé and said shyly, "Mrs. Carmody, I'm Beany. Remember Beany Malone?"

The fixed smile on the guest of honor gave way to almost breathless surprise. "Beany Malone!" And Beany felt her hands clasped tightly in the cold ones of the honor guest. "Beany grown up. What a surprise! I never expected to see you—"

"You didn't? But I got an invitation."

"I mean that Helena made out the guest list." Katie began talking nervously fast. "Everything's been so rushed. We only arrived a few days ago and—you know —shopping and fittings. Perry only flew in this morning —we were afraid he wouldn't make it—"

Beany burst out impulsively, "Katie, you've changed so. I didn't know you."

"I worked at it," Katie said a little wearily. "Heavens, wasn't I a mess when you knew me?"

"Oh no, Katie—no, you weren't," Beany said earnestly. "You were wonderful. Johnny said to tell you he hoped you still had your fryin' arm."

She waited for Katie's laugh—that old explosive and

infectious laugh. It didn't come. The lavender velvet dress, with Helena Stearns in it, had edged closer, but Beany hurried on with what she had to say—

"Miggs wrote me a letter that I never got—not until two weeks ago. It came while Mother was in the hospital, and we think the woman who kept house for us—"

Mrs. Stearns had taken Katie's arm. "Catherine, here are the governor and his wife just coming in. I invited them so you and Perry could meet them—and so Cathy could meet their daughter—"

With firm insistence she guided Katie across the room, motioning to Mr. Carmody to follow.

Beany found herself standing alone and feeling a stranger among strangers. . . . Catherine and Cathy, eh? Not Katie and Miggs. . . .

Why, there was Norbett Rhodes coming into the room —the unpredictable Norbett, Beany's first love. She watched him, sure that his nervous eyes would see her, and wondering if he would play the role of friend or enemy. She need not have wondered. He didn't even look her way. His eyes flicked briefly over the roomful and on toward the dining room and the young folks. He went directly there, like one sure of his welcome.

A rebuffed Beany moved across the room through the thinning crowd to the one person she felt at home with— the society editor.

"I was right," Dorothy said. "The brown brocade on Mrs. Governor. I'm sure they're the last arrivals. So me for the supermarket."

But as she turned toward the door, Beany detained her to ask, "What is Miggs Carmody wearing? Only Mrs. Stearns calls her Cathy."

Dorothy said low over her shoulder, "Champagne lace —you know, dirty white. Sculptured wool lace—and wouldn't I like to have one!"

She went hurrying off.

Beany looked toward the steps leading to the dining room. She was engulfed in stage fright. This whole party was so different from the way she had imagined it. Somehow, she had pictured Miggs—even Katie—there to greet her the minute she stepped in the door.

She was hot and uncomfortable in the tweed jacket, and Adair's feather hat pressed her braids and bone hairpins into her scalp. She was awed by all those girls in their after-five dresses. One of them, in gray taffeta, wore long pink gloves to match her pink pumps and pink bag.

A champagne lace dress? That was Miggs, then, at the end of the table, ladling out a drink of punch for Norbett Rhodes. Norbett's standing close to her somehow added to Beany's discomfiture.

Supposing Miggs had changed as much as Katie? Supposing that unanswered letter lay between them? Supposing Miggs wasn't glad to see her?

On unsteady knees Beany started for the dining room.

10

BEANY went up the two steps to the dining room, her eyes on the girl in the champagne lace dress. The dark head of the girl was lowered and she was half smiling at something Norbett Rhodes was saying. The long table was between her and Beany.

Beany's trepidation increased. The girl in the off-white lace with her corsage of small purple orchids looked so *right*. And Beany felt so *wrong* with her shamrock blouse showing under the tweed jacket Dulcie had hastened to make wearable, in the green corduroy skirt which had cost her three Saturdays' work for Eve Baxter.

She could only stand beside the table, gripping her gloved hands.

Then the girl at the punch bowl lifted dark eyes. They rested for a blank moment on Beany before she faltered out, "Beany—why, Beany!" and started toward her. "I didn't know whether you'd come or not—I kept looking for someone with braids—and then I decided you hadn't come."

And at the same time, Beany was saying catchily, "I'd have been here sooner, only I had to wait for my jacket. And then I didn't know which one was you. Miggs, did you see the message I put in the *Call?* It was in, Monday. . . . Hello, Norbett."

"Well, hi, Beany. I didn't know you knew Cathy."

"A message in the *Call?*" Miggs answered. "No, I didn't see it. But then everything's been so jumbled up and so rushed."

"I thought surely you had," Beany hurried on. "Because I said wherever you were, I wanted to hear from you for our birthday, and then it was just two days afterward that we got the invitation—and today's our birthday and so I thought—"

"Yes, it's our birthday," Miggs repeated. She was holding a glass of green punch in her hand and she thrust it at Beany with a nervous laugh. "Here, you haven't had any punch yet, have you? We can drink a glass of it for our birthday."

Norbett Rhodes spoke up, "Oh but, Cathy, Beany prefers tea. Tea and scones. She's become very British, doncha knaow?"

Cathy—or Miggs—had no chance either to answer that or to drink a glass of punch with Beany, for several of her young guests pressed up to tell her good-by. Miggs went through a spatter of introductions of Beany to the girls and boys about the table; Norbett seemed already to know them all.

An ill-at-ease Beany tried to acknowledge the introductions with ease. . . . Odd, how when one person
102

meets a whole group of people who know one another, the stranger feels so outsidish, so one-against-the-pack. Did everyone feel it? Not Johnny Malone, because his friendliness reached out even to strangers. Not Mary Fred, because she had a happy confidence in herself. But Beany stood, tongue-tied and awkward, and a little envious of their laughter and banter. . . .

Beany was again shoving her hat down firmly on her head when one of them asked, "Where do you go to school?"

"Me?" Oh, she should have said *I*. "I go to Harkness High."

"Harkness High," the girl repeated. Did a sensitive Beany just imagine that she said it in the same tone she might have said, "School for the underprivileged"? The Huxleyite added only, "I used to know a girl who went there," and turned back to her friends.

Some of the departing Huxley Hall girls were telling Miggs they would see her the next day at a reception; they would brief her on which were "snap courses" at Huxley.

Beany sipped her punch, her eyes on Miggs. Her hair had darkened to almost black. It was cut short and close to her head. She was taller than Beany. She was so poised —even a little lackluster—as she smiled and answered.

Beany wished desperately they would all say good-by and go. And Norbett, too. So she, Beany, wouldn't feel such an intruder with her old friend.

She pushed her way over to Miggs, hurried to say, "I never got that letter you wrote—the one where you wanted to come up while your mother went to New York. I never saw it until two weeks ago when we were hunting through the window seat. Remember the one in the living room we used to sit on? Oh, Miggs, I've been haunted ever since by thinking of you, waiting down there with your suitcase packed. I was afraid you'd think we didn't want you."

"I didn't know what to think," Miggs said with a shaky smile. "And then I wrote to you at Christmas."

"Oh, golly, I was afraid maybe you had."

The girl with the long pink gloves interrupted. Something about her wanting to make a phone call before they went downstairs to dinner. Miggs went to show her where to find one of those colored telephones.

Amos, the waiter, was standing at the table, and he said, "Miss Beany, better try some of these little cream puffs with lobster filling. We're about to clear everything away."

She reached for one. Um—mm, delicious. She realized that the hollow and jittery feeling inside her was partly hunger. She had been so hurried and excited she had eaten no lunch.

Norbett was acting as self-appointed host. He said, "Try these hot rolled-up deals. Mushroom filling. You could take off your gloves, you know."

Old show-off Norbett, Beany thought, and said on a thin laugh, "Not *my* gloves; Mary Fred's."

She pulled them off and thrust them in her pocket. The rolled up canapés, full of chopped mushrooms, were delicious, too. She reached for an olive and nibbled on it, waiting until Miggs was free again.

The crowd was miraculously melting away. One of Beany's new birthday pumps pinched, and she thought of dropping down on the nearby chair while she waited, but the pink purse, belonging to the telephoner, lay on it.

Miggs came back to the table. Norbett filled a glass with punch and handed it to her as though it were up to him to look out for Miggs Carmody. "You look as if you could stand some," he said. Miggs did. She looked tired and strained.

Beany turned to her again. She still had so much to say. "As soon as I got the invitation I tried to phone you, but the girl at the switchboard said I'd have to leave a message for Mrs.—" Oh-oh, she'd better not mention to Miggs—not yet, anyway—that she was scared of her Cousin Helena. She burst out instead, "Miggs, come home and stay all night with me."

If only they could have an uninterrupted time of getting back on the old footing!

Miggs looked at her out of troubled eyes. "I don't see how I can, Beany. You see, Helena—well, she gave this big affair as a sort of get-acquainted party for—for all of us—" She seemed to be fumbling for words. She looked toward the Sunset Room and the small knots of people still lingering there.

"Oh, but I can wait till they're all gone," Beany said. "I won't mind."

"But you see, Beany—"

Oh no! Here was Helena Stearns to interrupt again, to lay a peremptory hand on Miggs's arm. "Cathy, I've been trying to catch your eye. The governor's daughter came with her parents. Come along child, and meet them."

Beany's eyes followed them as Helena piloted Miggs down the steps of the dining room and into the Sunset Room. Norbett refilled his punch cup, said, "Some party, eh! But then, Helena can handle a horde like this, and still make everyone feel perfectly at home."

"She can?" Beany couldn't help saying with thin sarcasm.

Norbett gave her a reproachful flick of hazel eyes. He

said, "You haven't any way to get home, have you? I can run you home in Helena's Lincoln. I know she'd want me to."

His very patronizing air angered her. "That's big of you, Norbett." She lied in self-defense. "I have a ride home, thanks."

"Who with?" he demanded.

"Oh, a man I happened to meet here. A man who called Helena Stearns an ax-grinder." She couldn't help adding that, either. Norbett stalked away from her and into the Sunset Room. She watched him paying attention to two girls from Huxley Hall who seemed in no hurry to leave.

Beany lingered on, waiting for Miggs to return.

Amos, the waiter, stepped up to her to ask, "Miss Beany, do you know which gentleman is Mr. Carmody?"

"Yes, he's the one by the mantel, talking to the gray-haired man. See, he's holding his pipe."

"Oh yes. The headwaiter sent up word to tell him and Mrs. Stearns that the table is all set for their dinner party in the Paris Room downstairs." He moved on toward Mr. Carmody.

The table all set in the Paris Room downstairs for a dinner party? Then this party, honoring the Carmodys, *was* the prelude to a dinner. The mayor and his party, no doubt; the governor and wife and daughter. Maybe a few of the Huxley Hall girls and their young men. And Norbett Rhodes, as partner for Miggs. That was why he was lingering on, so sure of himself.

But not Beany Malone—definitely not Beany Malone.

She clutched her purse to her, reached in her pocket for her gloves—Mary Fred's white gloves. Her hands went straight through. Dulcie had warned her *not* to put anything in the pockets.

She moved hastily around the table to see where the

gloves had dropped. She saw one and bent to pick it up. The other had somehow been kicked or shoved under the table. She had to drop down on her knees and duck clear under the overhanging lace tablecloth to reach it.

From that spot she could see a pair of pink pumps going toward the chair at the end of the table. The girl with the long pink gloves, returning for her purse. She was not alone. Helena Stearns was with her, for Beany caught a glimpse of a lavender velvet skirt. They didn't see her, and Beany, not wanting the embarrassment of backing out from under the table in front of Helena, paused, waiting for them to leave.

In her crouched position, Beany heard Helena's plaintive voice; it was not lowered, for she evidently thought she and the girl were alone by the table. "I can't imagine why Cathy would suggest that I ask that pushy little person in the feather hat to join us for dinner. Dear me, such a clutcher. I've done nothing but pry her loose from Mrs. Carmody and Cathy—"

The voice trailed off as the two went down the steps into the big room.

Beany backed out and stood up, clutching Mary Fred's gloves. Her breath was suddenly a hurting thing. She wanted nothing but to get out.

She ducked into the hall and down its length, without ever a glance at the remaining few who were getting into wraps. Outside the apartment a knot of people waited for the elevator. A stairway led down to the twelfth floor, and Beany bolted for it.

She didn't even wait there for the elevator. Some of the sacred dinner guests might be on it. Or if Sidney were running it, he would ask, "Have a good time at the party, Beany?"

From twelfth she took the stairs to eleventh, and on

down—and down . . . She, in her blundering ignorance, staying on and on. . . . The pushy one. The clutcher. . . . Her cheeks burned with shame.

At last she was taking the wide marble steps that led into the lobby, and crossing it swiftly, furtively—still fearful of running into some of the party on their way to the Paris Room. She pushed through the heavy revolving door into the dark chill of the March night, barely noticing the heavy wet-feather snow that was falling.

She was going blindly down the steps when someone took her arm, and an easy, drawling voice said, "Seems like we always get a snow on St. Patrick's Day. My car's right down here a ways."

Hank Willison again. Then she hadn't lied to Norbett after all. He guided her to the car, opened the door for her. He slid under the wheel on his side. "I just figured I'd better wait for you."

"You were smarter than I was. You said Helena would separate the sheep from the goats. I was one of the goats she had a hard time shoving out the door."

She meant to laugh as though it were very funny, but the laugh choked in her throat.

"That witch!" he ground out. "That syrupy old witch. I'm going to pull the rug out from under her—so help me!"

Beany couldn't answer. She pulled off the uncomfortable hat. She sat huddled in the car and wept. . . . The party she had looked forward to. Mr. Carmody hadn't even recognized her. Miggs's mother hadn't expected to see her. And Miggs? Had Miggs really wanted her to stay on to the dinner? Or had she known only panic when Beany said she would outwait the guests, so that she rushed to Helena and asked that Beany be included? Beany didn't know. . . .

Almost as though he were reading her thoughts, Hank Willison growled, "Helena is running the show, Beany. I don't think they know it, but she is."

He started the motor and the windshield wipers and deftly swung away from the curb. He stopped at the light on the corner, and Beany managed to gulp out, "If you turn into the park, it's—it's the shortest way to Barberry—Street."

"I'm not taking you home. I'm taking you someplace to eat. It's way after seven, and all those appetizers sure churned up my appetite. And besides, it's your birthday, babe-in-arms, so no back talk from you," he said bruskly. And took the opposite turn.

11

AN hour later they were sitting across from each other in a corner booth in a steamy little Chinese restaurant. They were full of chop suey and egg rolls, and were now drinking their second pot of tea. Hank had slid the first pot and two miniature bowls across to Beany and said on a bow, "Will Miss Malone pour?"

She had cradled her hands around her first cup, grateful for its warming of her chilled hands, grateful for the hot liquid that dissolved the lumps in her throat. They had eaten hungrily, with only snatches of surface conversation. And now they pushed back their empty dishes.

Hank lit a cigarette. Beany unpinned her green-carnation corsage and laid it on the table. It had been all bitey, exhilarating fragrance when she put it on. Now its perfume seemed wilted and bruised.

Hank asked, "Does your heart belong to this Andy person, the one you thought I was? Your face dropped a foot that evening you opened the door and saw me there."

Beany shook her head slowly. "No—but I miss him. He joined the Marines." She added, "You do remind me of Andy. I mean, the same description would fit you both: broad shoulders, dark, wavy hair, gray eyes, and a crinkly smile—"

"Yes, yes, go on. I can feel the 'but' in your voice."

Beany laughed. It was the first time she had laughed since leaving the penthouse. She knew by the pleased look in his eyes that he was trying to make her forget her unhappy exit.

"But what?" he prompted.

"Andy has a sort of—oh, tough and glib and wise-guy way on the outside. But on the inside he's sentimental and—soft. And you act and talk so lazy and easy-going, but on the inside you're not. You're kind of hard and—I guess cynical is the word."

"Beany, I didn't know you gazed into a crystal ball."

A waitress in a flowered mandarin dress removed the dishes and set before them a plate with two cookies, shaped something like snail shells.

"Fortune cookies," Hank said. "Here, let me open yours so you won't tear the slip of paper inside. Pick one."

She handed him the cooky closest to her. "You mean it tells your fortune."

"Absolutely." He pried open the thin crust and extracted a tiny slip of paper and pretended to read: "You are so glamorous that when the man you are with kisses you good night, he will never be the same again."

Beany giggled, and took the slip from him and read it rightly: "Old friendships, new friendships will weave like a garland of flowers through your life." . . . Like a garland of flowers with thorns, she thought. . . .

She reached for the other cooky, said, "I'll read yours to you."

She opened it, intending to ad-lib something foolish as he had done with hers. But she was too surprised to do anything but read the words aloud: "In your life the closing of a door will benefit you. For you will gain strength and knowledge to open others."

Beany added, "Always doors closing. I don't like them to close."

"Neither did I," Hank said.

"Oh, have you already had a door closed on you?"

"Yes ma'am—and with a bang. Seeing as how Helena Stearns kicked it shut. Figuratively, that is. By the way, what did the old witch say to you, or do to you, to give you that slapped look?"

Beany said slowly, for the words still hurt, "I was under the table getting one of Mary Fred's gloves, and I heard her call me a pushy little person in a feathered hat. And a clutcher."

She took a swift sip of lukewarm tea to keep her lips from crimping. "Only don't tell anyone. I won't tell Dulcie. She's the one who worked like crazy so I could wear this jacket. She said all along I was building fool hopes on Miggs and Katie being the same. Katie wasn't. And I didn't have a chance to find out whether Miggs was or not. Not with all the interruptions, not with *her* prying me loose—"

Again her lips wobbled. Hank reached across the table and squeezed her hand. "Say, let's you and me form a Hatin'-Helena partnership?"

"I'd be glad to. Hank, how did she slam a door shut on you?"

He told her. "When I was fifteen, I worked for Perry Carmody in Stillwater. I'd help him tote oil machinery and do anything that took brawn but no brains. But first, I'd better back up and brief you on the whole tribe of Willisons. None of them amounted to a hill of beans. None of them but me ever got through high school. All any of them ever wanted was a job that gave him enough to eat—and not even fancy vittles. One of my uncles was a school janitor, another worked at a filling station—when he felt like it. My dad always said he never wanted more than a hundred dollars, because it would be too hard to count. And here was Hank, cut from the same take-it-easy pattern."

"Where does Helena Stearns come in?"

"Keep your tired little eyes propped open a while longer. I'm setting the scene. When I was sixteen, I moved up from roustabout for Carmody to driving for him; I knew all that country like the palm of my hand. I thought I had it made. I figured I'd had enough schooling—"

"How far had you gone?"

"Second year, high. Now let me tell you about the Carmodys. Perry was shrewd, and he was in the know on oil deals because of selling machinery. He had a chance to take a flyer, and Cousin Helena stepped forward and lent him the money. He hit it big. It made him a rich man. Naturally, the Carmodys thought her a beautiful and generous fairy godmother. And Helena kept telling them how she was alone in the world, except for them—"

"The lone, lorn widow," Beany murmured, quoting Eve Baxter.

"The clinging vine in need of a sturdy oak." He went on, "She was there visiting them in Oklahoma that summer when I was driving for Carmody. She had a new car, and when it came time for her to return to Denver, she wanted someone to chauffeur her. She didn't feel sure of herself with a new car."

"She doesn't with her amethyst Lincoln, either," Beany remembered. "She's always having Norbett Rhodes drive it."

"So Carmody asked me to drive her back to Denver. And that was the end of Part One in Hank Willison's life." He shook his head with a thin smile.

"Did you have a fight with her?"

His smile twisted. "Nothing so down-to-earth as a fight. Just remember, though, to give the devil his—or her—due. I was a big dumb clunk who didn't know a certain amount of bowing and scraping went with a chaffeuring job. I didn't open the door for her and help her in and out. It was hotter'n the hubs on that drive from Oklahoma to Denver, and I didn't know enough to stop and get her cool drinks and bring them out to her—but the women of all the good-for-nothing Willisons waited on themselves. So-o, when I stopped in front of her big house, she asked me for the car keys and said, 'I won't be needing you again. I've heard of dumb Okies, and you're the epitome of them all.'"

"She did?" Beany gasped.

"She did. And then she walked into the house and shut the door—she didn't even slam it. Every inch a lady."

"Did you go back to Stillwater?"

"I couldn't. I didn't have bus fare. I worked and got it —but I didn't go back. There it was—'dumb Okie.' I had to admit, much as it hurt, that she was right. So I rustled such jobs as I could, and started to school. It wasn't easy —tending furnaces, shoveling snow, pearl-diving—"

"Pearl-diving?"

"Washing dishes to you, babe. Studying was murder,

114

because I had always slid through classes the easiest way in Stillwater."

"But you're a geologist—an almost one anyway. Did you always want to be one?"

He flashed her a rueful smile. "Didn't I tell you that in my early years I wanted to be nothin' in the easiest way? But one summer I was doing yard work for Professor Naismith, and sometimes I'd drive him out on expeditions—"

"You live with them, don't you?"

He nodded. "Yes, and they've prodded me on. That's why I'm grubbing like a gopher at the School of Mines. And if I can inject one note of braggadocio into this sordid tale, I *am* old Naismith's prize pupil. That's why he took me to Utah to do the leg work on the investigation of uranium companies. The whole trip, spiked by one Martie Malone and the financial editor on the *Call*. . . . You don't suppose they'll charge us rent for sitting here so long, do you?"

Beany glanced at her watch. Almost ten. "I'm glad we're so late. I'd rather not get home until after Dad and Adair do. I'd hate them to know I wasn't asked to the dinner."

"You're a loyal little cuss. Stubborn, too. The set of your jaw tells me that—no crystal ball needed. Let's have another pot of tea and some lichee nuts."

"Are you sure you can—I mean, when you're working your way through school?"

"Honey-chile, I love you for thinking about my pocketbook. I'm solvent these days—I got paid for the Utah trip —so we can live it up."

Beany laughed, and he added, "Did anyone ever tell you that your grin is like the sun breaking through on a drizzly day?"

"I've been told it was like a crack in a five-cent watermelon. . . . Katie Carmody," she mused. "Oh, Hank, she used to be so different—so different from the Mrs. Carmody in the silver lamé dress today."

"I liked the old Katie best, too. I was the hollowest, hungriest lug you ever saw, but Katie filled me up. And Miggs was a sweetie."

He chuckled in reminiscence. "I'll never forget one time when I was driving her downtown to get her a pair of ballet shoes for a dancing class. And I got reckless in my driving, and dented the fender of her dad's car. I can see Miggs yet, shoving her shoe money at me. 'Here, Hank, you get it fixed right now so Dad won't scold you. I don't need the ballets today. You pay me back when you get paid, and then I'll get them.' And that's what we did. But imagine, that eleven-year-old kid, wanting to save me from a lacing-down from her dad."

"I can just see her," Beany said.

Hank added soberly, "I was in on the transition of Katie. I saw her change."

"You mean money changed her?"

"Money—and Helena. There's no slavery like that to someone you look up to, or feel obligated to. I don't imagine Helena lets them forget that if it wasn't for her, Perry Carmody would still be peddling machinery."

They dawdled a little longer over the last pot of tea.

When they reached home, Adair's convertible was in the driveway, which meant that Beany's father and Adair were home and retired.

They walked through the slushy snow to the front door. Hank suddenly framed her face in his hands, and even while Beany was saying, "I don't kiss boys good night on

116

my first date," he kissed her first on one cheek, then on the other.

"One for your seventeenth birthday, one for being in a Hatin'-Helena partnership with me," he explained and went down the steps, whistling under his breath.

Well-well, was all Beany could think as she opened the front door softly, he is like Andy—he is different from Andy.

She had one thing to do before she went to bed. She tiptoed into the dining room and hunted for the envelope in which the square, engraved invitation had come. She found it in a sideboard drawer.

It had been addressed in a firm adult hand to Mr. Martie Malone, care of the *Call*. "Miss Beany Malone," had been added in a girl's handwriting and with a ballpoint pen.

Miggs must have added it, without even telling Helena Stearns. Beany couldn't understand it. If the party was honoring the Carmodys, why had only Martie Malone been invited? When Martie Malone was the one who had known Miggs and her mother the least?

12

No one had ever been able to figure out how Red, the Malones' Irish setter, always knew when it was seven o'clock in the morning. By the sun slanting in the east windows? But even on cloudy mornings he came just the same to nudge Beany to wakefulness. Could he count the strokes of the hall clock? But even when the clock was out of order, Red never failed.

Ordinarily on Sunday mornings, Beany would murmur, "It's Sunday, Red," and he would subside on the rug by her bed, while she burrowed into her pillow for an extra nap.

But this Sunday morning when Beany was seventeen years and one day old, she came to instant wakefulness at the touch of his cold nose. And stayed awake. It was the very vacancy inside her. For so many days she had been heady with anticipation of meeting Miggs.

. . . Well, she had met her. And Miggs was going to Huxley Hall and had a bevy of friends there already, including the governor's daughter—thanks to Helena Stearns. Miggs had a handy boy friend named Norbett Rhodes—also thanks to Helena. Miggs was even now sleeping in that pink and white bower in the penthouse —the April Room. . . .

Then it hadn't been a thought communication from Miggs. She didn't need her old friend Beany. No, it had been nothing but a silly dream, and Dulcie was right when she said that dreams always go contrary.

Beany threw back the covers and got up. She dressed quietly so as not to waken the sleeping house. She would go to eight o'clock Mass, instead of waiting and going with the family at nine-thirty. She wasn't ready to answer all their questions about the penthouse party—not yet.

At church Beany glanced toward the pew across the aisle and winked at Rosellen Kern. She was with her father, Captain Kern of the police force, and the two "juvenile delinquents." Beany's glance strayed back to them. Usually Rosellen had to give them reproving looks or a jerk now and then to keep them quiet. This morning they sat in gloomy dignity.

When Mass was over, Beany walked out with Rosellen, slowing her steps to Rosellen's crutches. Captain Kern helped her down the steps, said, "You girls visit here while I bring the car around."

Beany was just telling Rosellen of the birthday corsage that had come from Andy when one of the boys asked, "Hey, Beany, do you know anybody that'd like two *real nice* white rabbits?"

Beany shook her head. "Gosh, Donnie, I don't."

"I'm Pete," he corrected her.

Rosellen sighed. "Isn't it too bad rabbits and kittens have to grow up? At the stock show last January Donnie took a chance on two baby rabbits—and, doggone, if he didn't win them. They were cute as buttons at first. But now—why, they're almost as big as your Mike. Donnie kept them in his room until—well, the house didn't smell like Chanel Number 5. Then we put them in the basement, and that wasn't much better, and besides, they chewed up Mom's dahlia bulbs—"

"Only eight of them," Donnie defended.

"Can't you put them outside?" Beany asked.

"Not in the garage. There's barely room for Dad's car. We can't let them run in the yard without buying ninety-two dollars' worth of mesh fence to keep the dogs out. And the landlady tells us we can't put up a rabbit hutch on the premises. Dad's fit to be tied. He's threatened to sell them to the vegetable man—"

A wail burst from the smaller Pete. "And he'd eat 'em for Easter. He said he would."

Donnie said stoutly, "Not our rabbits. I won't let him."

Beany said sympathetically, "We couldn't take them on account of our dogs. Red wouldn't hurt them, but that Mike—"

"Somebody could make a lot of money on them," Donnie said. "They could grow hundreds and hundreds of white rabbits."

"That's what *we're* afraid of," Rosellen said under her breath, just as her father pulled up to the curbing in front of the church.

As Beany turned away from the Kern car, she saw her father and Adair and Johnny going up the church steps. No time for even one question about the penthouse party.

Beany walked slowly home, her mind reliving that disappointing reunion with Miggs. She even thought with sad irony of her hoping to do something for Katie in return for Katie's saving her life when she was a baby. As though there were anything she could do for Mrs. Perry Carmody now!

At her own gateway, Beany stopped short, her eyes widening in amazement. A car had driven into the driveway and pulled up onto the garage's cement apron. But that wasn't the surprise. Two men had evidently just unfastened a horse trailer and, even as Beany stood staring, they backed a glinting sorrel horse—no, according to Mary Fred, a mare—down the plank and onto the ground. Even Beany's inexperienced eyes saw that the beautiful, white-touched mare was going to have a colt or, again quoting Mary Fred, "was in foal."

An elderly man stood at the mare's head. His face looked all the more seamed and weathered under his white thatch of hair. He was wearing a dark suit and white shirt that didn't seem to belong with the wide Stetson pushed back on his white head, or the worn riding boots.

The other was a gangling farm boy in overalls and blue shirt. He fastened the end-gate of the trailer and backed it close to the side of the garage. From the trunk of the car he lifted out a sack of grain, which he carried into the garage. He then unloaded three bales of hay; and lastly, a carton of brushes and bottles. As though the horse—no, mare—was to be left here on the Malone premises.

Through Beany's mind flashed what Kay Maffley used to say, "Something's always happening at the Malones'."

As Beany approached, the old gentleman turned bright but poorly focused eyes on her. "There you are, Mary Fred. We've brought Miss Goldie in to you. I'm having to take you up on your offer to look after her while I'm gone."

Miss Goldie? Oh yes, "the honey of them all," Mary

Fred had talked so much about that afternoon when she hunted for the film in the window seat. The film Carlton had enlarged for her to give to old Tom McDevitt. Then this was Tom McDevitt patting Miss Goldie's neck so lovingly. What else had Mary Fred said about him? Something about his not seeing at all well because of cataracts. And something about his having to sell his stableful of horses.

Beany said, "I'm not Mary Fred. I'm Beany."

He didn't seem to hear. Perhaps because Mike, shut on the back porch, was yelping to get out and see what was going on.

The man laid a gnarled hand on her shoulder and said, "I remember that day you cried your eyes out because your black horse died. I thought then that you were the kind who ought to have a horse of your own and so—"

"You mean that's why you brought in Miss Goldie?" a startled Beany asked.

"I want you to have her foal. Ah, that colt will be a sweetheart, and you can have it for looking after Miss Goldie for me."

The mare took a notion to examine a nearby lilac bush, and her owner moved indulgently along with her.

The boy explained to a bewildered Beany, "He has to catch that ten-thirty train to Omaha. His nephew is an eye doctor back there, and he's been after him to come back to his hospital so's he could operate on those cataracts. And old Tom has been putting it off—putting it off. But last night this doctor-nephew telephoned and told him he dassn't put it off any longer. He wired the old gentleman a ticket to come back today. And he's going to meet his train at Omaha."

Tom McDevitt and Miss Goldie rejoined the two. The old man went on, "I didn't mind selling the others, girlie

—Red Roderick, even Starlight—but you know what a pet I've made of Miss Goldie. I couldn't turn her over to just anyone. You always loved her, that's why I know you'll take good care of her."

A sudden panic came over Beany. She couldn't have this pregnant mare left on their hands. She moved closer to say again, and loudly, that she wasn't Mary Fred, but Beany. And that Mary Fred wouldn't be home for a week.

Even as she opened her lips to say it, a velvet nose reached out and nuzzled at her neck. It was almost a plea, as though Miss Goldie begged, "Don't you see how shaky and confused and driven he is? Don't let him down. Let him think you're Mary Fred, so he'll go off with an easy mind."

Beany said nothing, but reached up to stroke that kitten-soft nose.

Old Tom McDevitt went on, "You'll have a colt to be proud of. Out of Golden Miss and sired by Sir Amber. Remember to sprinkle a little salt on her oats. No alfalfa now. Marvin, you brought in hay?"

"Three bales." The boy added, "Come on, Tom, we ought to be at the depot right now."

Tom McDevitt started toward the car, turned back for one more gentle ruffling of the mare's cream-colored forelock. "I don't know just how long I'll be gone, girlie, but when I come back—" He paused a troubled moment as though he were thinking—if I come back—

"Don't worry about Miss Goldie. We'll take care of her," Beany promised.

"She's a spoiled wench," he said on a shaky chuckle. "Nipping you, if you offer her a carrot."

He turned suddenly and went on groping, jerky steps to the car.

Beany, a lump in her throat, ran after him. She caught

his arm and said, "Write to us. Be sure, now, and let us know how you get along." And, as though she were Mary Fred and had known and loved him for years, she reached up and kissed his weathered cheek.

She watched the mud-splashed car leave their driveway. She turned and looked into the topaz eyes of the young mare. How beautiful she was. Her sorrel coat was like a brand-new penny. Her mane and long heavy tail were creamy white, as were her feet and the splash from her forehead to her nose.

Miss Goldie's soft intelligent eyes roved over the buildings, the wide yard, and she gave a heavy heave that was like a sigh of acceptance: This is the way life is. We can't be choosy about where we are taken, or whom we are left with.

Beany had never been the horse-lover that Mary Fred was. But now, left alone with Miss Goldie, her fingers seemed suddenly to know what spot of the forehead to scratch. Soothing, endearing words came to her—"There, there, my lovely, I'll take care of you. We'll all be good to you, you blessed—"

The mare reached out to a spot of snow, shaded from the day's bright sun. She must be thirsty. Beany hunted up a bucket in the basement, scoured it out, and filled it with water. She was carrying it out when the Malones returned from church.

It was typical of her family that they should admire and pet Miss Goldie even before they heard Beany's lengthy explanation. She ended, "She ought to be all right here until Mary Fred gets back. Johnny and I can get straw and keep her in one side of the garage. We can keep the gates shut and let her have the run of the yard."

The Malone grounds were wide and deep, for there

were only three houses in their block; Judge Buell's on one corner, a white-trimmed Colonial on the other, and the Malones' in the middle.

Johnny said, "Sure, let's keep her all summer. And then I won't have to mow the lawn."

Martie Malone shook his head. "No, we can't keep her here. An ordinance was passed a few years ago, forbidding the keeping of a horse inside the city limits. We'd only get ourselves in hot water."

"Oh," Beany breathed, aghast. She had never given a thought to city ordinances. Old Tom McDevitt must not have known about them, either. Her father was saying, "You telephone Mary Fred at Willow Springs Ranch and see what she says. She'll know what to do about Miss Goldie."

"She might even come whisking down when she hears she's to fall heir to her colt," Johnny said.

13

THE Malones lingered long over Johnny's waffle breakfast. There was so much to talk about. The opening of Adair's exhibit. They all read the complimentary write-ups in both papers. Johnny had much to tell about his St. Patrick's skit, and the auburn mustache—courtesy of Red —which did *not* hold together. Then Miss Goldie and old Tom McDevitt and the operation on his eyes occupied a good portion of the conversation.

But there was no escaping the barrage of questions about Beany's reunion with Miggs. She went into great detail of telling how Katie looked and how Miggs looked, and the food and drinks that were served.

"The Carmodys are rich now," Beany said. "They are the rich relatives from Texas that Mrs. Stearns had the penthouse redecorated for."

"Yes, I know," her father said.

"Why didn't Miggs come home with you?" Johnny wanted to know.

"The party lasted so long," Beany evaded. "And it was such a madhouse, we could hardly get in two words without someone interrupting. And then Hank Willison was there, and so I left with him—and we had supper at a Chinese restaurant."

Her father said, "Hank fools a lot of people with that easygoing drawl of his. He's sharp as they come, and a hard, conscientious worker."

"When will you and Miggs get together for a real visit?" Adair asked.

"She'll probably phone," Beany hedged again. She added, "I'd better put in a call for Mary Fred. Sometimes it takes a while to get through to Willow Springs."

It took many rings, and the operator saying in her sing-song voice, "The circuits are busy. I'll ring you just as soon as I can reach them." And finally, "I have a circuit for you now. Just a minute."

But when someone answered at the ranch, sixty-three miles away in the Rockies, that someone reported that Mary Fred Malone was gone for the day with the skiers. The operator requested that Mary Fred Malone call operator 37 as soon as she returned.

Beany was still sitting on the three-legged telephone stool when the doorbell rang. She hurried to answer it.

Four callers entered, in response to Beany's startled, "Oh—oh, come in!" Helena Stearns, Mr. and Mrs. Carmody, and daughter Miggs.

Helena Stearns was the one who said with an apologetic smile, "Are you sure we're not disrupting your Sunday by dropping in?" and Beany said, "Oh no. Oh no."

In the brief moment it took her to usher them into the

living room, her surprise gave way to wondering joy. Miggs and her mother had come to see her. Everything was going to be the same as before. Beany had expected too much at the penthouse party. How could they have given one guest any special attention when there were hundreds there?

Beany's father and Adair came in, and there was the small hubbub of greetings and introductions, of the visitors explaining that they were on their way to a reception at Huxley Hall. And Helena, filling in with small talk.

Slowly, Beany's joy began to wilt. It wasn't the same. Katie, in her black dressmaker suit and furs, hadn't her old-time easy warmth. Miggs, on the window seat beside Beany, sat in stiff constraint. Only Mr. Carmody seemed his usual quiet, thoughtful self.

It was Helena Stearns who was overly friendly. She was *so* happy to meet the Malones after hearing such wonderful things about them from the Carmodys. What a lovely —what a *homey* room! She even thought Mike was "cunning" when he rushed in like a cyclone and had to be collared and carried out.

For a brief moment, when Johnny bounded into the room and threw his arms around Katie, she seemed like the Katie of old. She scolded, "You skinny string bean, when are you going to put some meat on your bones?"

"I'm waiting for your potato pancakes, Katie. Looks like you could stand an extra pound or two yourself. Don't they feed you enough?"

Miggs, too, broke into a laugh when Johnny clutched both her hands, and groaned out, "Why didn't someone tell me you were going to grow up into a luscious babe?"

"You mean you wouldn't have kicked me on the shins when I tried to ride your bike?"

Helena Stearns said archly, "Oh, Cathy has been looking forward to meeting her childhood sweetheart."

Miggs's laugh froze. She seemed to draw back like a child who is being pushed into something.

Beany said, "Remember, Miggs, when we used to sit here on the window seat, and our legs wouldn't touch the floor?"

Miggs only nodded.

Helena Stearns was doing all the talking. She was saying to Martie and Adair, "I owe you both an apology. About the party for the Carmodys. There was such a stack of invitations to address, that I slipped up on putting 'Mr. and Mrs. Malone and family' on yours. It was purely an oversight."

Miggs put in—but with no show of warmth, "When I mailed them, I added Beany's name to Mr. Malone's."

"That's quite all right, Mrs. Stearns," Adair murmured. And Martie added, "Neither of us could have come anyway. Yesterday was opening day for Adair's showing. Then some artists gave a dinner for her afterward."

"Yes, indeed, I read the rave review in the morning papers," Helena praised. "And I've heard glowing reports of your portraits from friends of mine."

She turned almost a doting smile on Beany. "But we were so happy you came, Beany. We had a little informal dinner afterward, but you got away so fast we didn't have a chance to ask you to join us. That's the trouble when there's such a big crowd."

Beany's jaw dropped. She couldn't answer. She couldn't even smile back. She, Beany, got away so fast. Yet she couldn't contradict the gushing woman and say, "Like fun, I got away before you knew it. I was the clutcher. You were kept busy prying me loose—remember?"

Puzzled, she looked over at Miggs. But Miggs's uneasy half-smile told her nothing. Beany looked back at Helena Stearns and knew a sudden urge to puncture her false effusiveness. She said, "You met me before, Mrs. Stearns. I was in your penthouse that evening you came home unexpectedly from the airport. Sidney Peale, the janitor's son, is a good friend of mine, and so Rosellen—the one on crutches—and I went up to see what a penthouse looked like."

Even that didn't dim the woman's fond smile. "I'm glad you did. I hope you didn't think I was abrupt that evening, but I was terribly upset because the flight was canceled. I'm afraid I was hardly myself. I had planned to fly to Dallas and bring Cathy back with me."

She said to the roomful, "It didn't seem right for Catherine and young Cathy to be moving around so much, not having a place they could call home to bring their friends to. And then, of course," she added on an appealing laugh, "I was selfishly thinking of myself. I'm just not the kind who can be happy alone. I like my own folks around me. I was never lucky enough to have children of my own. Perry and his family are the only ones I can call family."

No wonder Helena Stearns had fooled Norbett Rhodes, Beany thought. If I hadn't seen her that first night in the penthouse, if I hadn't been under the table yesterday and heard what she said about me, I'd think she was generous and loving, too.

Katie got restlessly to her feet. Johnny said, "How about a cup of coffee? Anyone who wants one, put up his (her) hand. The watering-down process depends on how many hands. Come on, Katie."

Beany moved closer to Miggs on the window seat.

Maybe if she asked her up to her room and they were alone together, they could pick up where they left off. But before she could suggest it, Helena smiled at them and said, "I imagine you girls would like to get off by yourselves."

Again Beany sensed that tightening-up of Miggs. "We'll have to go on to the reception as soon as we drink our coffee," she said. Beany had the feeling that this visit had been forced on Miggs by Helena, and that Miggs was unhappy about it. But why?

Helena leaned forward to say to Beany's stepmother, "Yes, I've been hearing so much about your portraits. That's one reason we stopped by. I wanted to ask you to do a portrait of Catherine."

"You mean Katie?" Adair asked.

Helena nodded, smiling at Katie's husband, Perry, who was quietly puffing on a pipe, even as Martie Malone was, and at Miggs, who was looking at her hands in her lap. "I'd like them to have a recent picture of Catherine. I thought yesterday that she made a beautiful picture in her silver lamé, standing there at the windows with the black and silver drapery as background."

"It would be very—effective," Adair said.

Martie Malone interrupted with a question to Perry Carmody, "Then you folks are planning to make your home here?"

Before he could more than take the pipe from his mouth in leisurely fashion, Helena answered for him, "Oh yes, Cousin Perry is to head a new company we're organizing. It took a lot of persuasion on my part to get him here."

Beany's eyes were on her father's face. She saw his eyes narrow with quick interest.

Helena added, "Perry's oil business kept him traveling

all over Texas. You're a family man, Mr. Malone, so I know you'll feel, as I did, that it was a wise move for him to locate here in Denver where he and his family can be together."

Martie Malone didn't answer that, but turned to Perry Carmody to say, "You know who Stan Lowell is—the financial editor of the *Call?* We've started some investigating of new and old uranium companies. Some of them we feel aren't on too solid a footing. We feel they need publicizing, in order to protect investors, especially the workingman who thinks 'penny stocks' are a quick way of getting rich."

"That's right," Perry agreed. "There're too many of these fly-by-night companies unloading worthless stock."

Beany wondered what all this talk was about—wondered about that odd quality in her father's voice.

Johnny and Katie came in with the coffee. Helena said swiftly, as though she wanted no more talk about uranium companies and investors or investigations, "Catherine, Mrs. Malone has consented to paint your portrait. What would you think about mornings for your sittings?"

"Yes, mornings would be all right. I don't have a thing to do in the mornings." Katie added with a wondering smile, "I never thought I'd be saying, 'I don't have a thing to do in the mornings.' Used to be I couldn't get up early enough to get everything done."

Her husband smiled at her with quiet pride. "It's high time you don't have to get up at dawn and work till dark."

And so it was arranged that Adair should start the portrait the very next morning. The guests finished their coffee, and took off with smiles and handshakings all around.

In the doorway, Beany caught at Miggs's arm. "Couldn't we get together soon?"

A bleak look flicked across Miggs's face. "Oh yes, it will be—arranged."

They left behind a puzzled Beany. Nor was she the only one. Martie Malone stood leaning against the mantel, taking a long and thoughtful time to loosen the charred tobacco in his pipe, an even longer time to pound it out against the brick—

14

MARY FRED'S call from the Willow Springs Ranch didn't come through until nine o'clock that night.

Even at the hall telephone, Beany could hear the mare in the garage thumping at the door to get out. So the minute Beany heard her sister's hello, she burst out, "Mary Fred, for John's sake, why did you tell Tom Mc-Devitt you'd look after Miss Goldie for him? Because he went back to Omaha for his eye operation and he brought her in in a trailer and left her here. This morning."

"He did?" an amazed voice said. "But oh, Beany, isn't she a lamb?"

"Well, a very oversized one. The old man thought I was you and told me I could have her colt."

She held the phone away from her ear because of Mary Fred's wild whoop. "He did! I can't believe it. A colt sired by Sir Amber out of Golden Miss. I wonder if it'll be marked like the father or—"

"Start wondering about what to do with Miss Goldie. We can't keep her here. Dad says there's an ordinance against horses in the city. Can't you come down, Mary Fred?"

"Not a chance. We've got a full house up here, and so shorthanded that I'm making beds and sandwiches and rubbing liniment on stove-up skiers. Tell you what, Beany. Call up Mack out at Hilltop Stables. He'll keep Miss Goldie until I get home."

"When will you be home?"

"A week from tonight on the nine-thirty bus. McDevitt left the trailer, eh? Remember, Beany, there's a trailer hitch on Dad's Dodge. Drive slow and easy when you take her out to Hilltop."

"What about her board?"

"I'll take care of that with my pay for teaching the kids to ride out there. Tell Mack that."

The operator broke in to say that three minutes were up. Mary Fred's last words were, "Call Mack tonight."

Beany called, but there was no answer from Hilltop Stables.

She called again in the morning before leaving for school. Bob, the helper in the stables, answered and before Beany told her whole story, said, "Gosh, kid, we can't take any boarder now. Friday, we had a couple cases of distemper break out. We're working overtime to keep it from spreading, but it'll take two, maybe three weeks to get it under control."

"Do you know of another stable where they'd take her, Bob?"

"Try the Bridle Path. They board horses for folks in town."

Beany dialed the Bridle Path. No—oh no, they didn't

have an extra stall, what with spring coming on and their taking on riding classes from the Military Academy. He suggested she try Frazier's Barn.

She had only time to snatch up her books and hurry off to school.

She carried the unfinished jacket back to the sewing class and Dulcie. She must be chary of what she told about the whole penthouse and Miggs Carmody affair to keep Dulcie from saying, "I told you so."

Sure enough, Dulcie asked, "Well, did Miggs fall over in a joyous faint in the Sunset Room when she saw you?"

Beany laughed. "Not in a *dead* faint. Not in the Sunset Room."

"What did she say?"

"Oh, Dulcie, what can you say in a mob scene like that? We'd no sooner get together than someone would be saying hello or good-by."

"Did they go on to dinner after all the liquid refreshments and bite-sized hors d'oeuvres?"

"Yes—I guess so. But Hank Willison was there, and he asked me to have chop suey with him. And I did."

"You did, huh? Well, but did Miggs and her mother and old every-inch-a-lady *ask* you to their dinner for the elite?"

Beany sidestepped further. "I didn't wait around—oh, as I say, they had to pay attention to the mayor's party and the governor—"

"So the gov was there! Then Miggs didn't come home with you?"

"No, but they all came to see us yesterday." Beany had an instant's picture of Miggs sitting on the window seat with that constrained smile on her face. Beany shifted the conversation to old Tom McDevitt and his bringing in Miss Goldie.

136

But Dulcie was not to be put off. "Did Miggs ask you to come over and share her April bower with her?"

Mrs. Hilb's presence interrupted. "Dulcie, let's see how far you got along on the jacket at home."

Beany hurried home from school that afternoon with Miss Goldie on her mind. She telephoned Frazier's Barn. But Frazier's Barn did not have room for a mare in foal.

Beany went down the listings in the back of the phone book, and called the remaining five riding stables. The answers were all no, with either brief or lengthy explanations. Their stable room had to be given to horses they could rent for riding. They didn't have enough stalls as it was.

Beany said desperately to the rambling talker at the Belmont Ranch, "Do you know *any place* I could board her? We have to keep her shut up in the garage because of the city ordinance."

"You know, Miss, I think your best bet would be some little acreage at the edge of town. Most of these farmers have a barn of sorts. Most likely, they'd be glad to make some extra dough."

If only she knew someone on a nearby farm. If only she knew someone who knew someone.

The next few days at school, Beany made frequent inquiries among her classmates. "Do you know of anyone who'd keep this mare, Miss Goldie? She's so gentle—"

They teased her about it. She had only to enter her French or math class to have someone chant, "Anybody *care* to board a *mare?*" Or else, "Anybody want the bother of a dear expectant mother?"—pronouncing "mother" to rime with bother.

Very funny, Beany thought wryly, until you, yourself, were faced with the bother of a four-legged expectant mother.

She had asked Dulcie first, "Could you keep Miss Goldie on your place? You've got a barn."

"It's crammed full of sacks of cement and lumber and kegs of nails. Is it true a horse's board is more than a human's?"

"It's true," Beany admitted. "But Mary Fred could have taken care of it at Hilltop out of her riding money."

Miss Goldie posed a touchy problem for the Malones. Martie Malone was often referred to as the watchdog of the city, because in his column he called the public's attention to any law that was not being enforced. Even city officials were not immune to his scathing attacks if he felt they were lax in their duties.

There was no keeping secret that there was a sizable and lovable piece of horseflesh on the Malone premises. All the neighborhood children were constant visitors. Beany had to watch that too many apples weren't fed Miss Goldie.

Rosellen Kern had said of her father when she told about the worrying white rabbits, "Dad's fit to be tied." Martie Malone was not that. But he explained to Beany, "I've made enemies in this town because I've stuck my neck out for what I thought was right. And you know the rivalry between the evening *Tribune* and the *Call*. The *Tribune* could make a headline story out of our keeping a horse here when it's against the law."

On Thursday of that week, Beany walked down the school steps with Dulcie. "I've got Johnny's car," Beany said. "He heard of some people named Schneider who might take Miss Goldie. They live out beyond you on Wyman. Do you know them?"

Yes, Dulcie knew them. She offered to go with Beany.

The girls found the Schneiders friendly and sympa-
138

thetic. But they shook their heads when Beany mentioned an equine boarder. No, they were taking a trip back to Iowa and didn't know how long they might stay.

Dulcie and Beany drove on, stopping at every little farm which boasted a barn. They waded up muddy paths to many doors and listened to many excuses for not keeping a mare. One barn was used for chickens; another, to house a vicious dog. One farm wife said she was afraid of horses.

Finally Dulcie said, "Let's call it a day. Let's stop at Downey's Drug and have a hot chocolate."

They were in a booth sipping their chocolate when Beany, who was facing the door, breathed out, "There's Miggs—and Norbett."

The couple looked toward them and Beany said, "Hello, Miggs. Hello, Norbett."

Miggs was wearing a jumper dress with white blouse, low heels and expensive camel's hair coat. Dulcie muttered under her breath, "Simplicity is the keynote for the Huxley Hussies."

Miggs came over to the booth and Beany introduced the two girls. Dulcie invited, "Sit down and join us in a drink. The boy friend seems to be busy."

"He wrote a feature story for the *Tribune*," Miggs said as she sat down. "And he wants to see if it's in tonight."

"I'm certainly glad to meet you, Miggs," Dulcie said. "Good grief, that's all I've been hearing from Beany for weeks—Miggs this, Miggs that. She grieved her heart out when she found that letter from you that she hadn't answered. She turned into a regular sleuth—"

Beany broke in to ask, "Want chocolate, Miggs?"

"Coffee," she answered, and Beany got up to tell Mrs. Downey behind the fountain.

She came back to Dulcie's, "—every night after school she was out combing the countryside to find the place you used to live, because she thought whoever was on the old homestead could give her your address. And then she dreamed that you needed her and so she put a plea in Eve Baxter's column—"

"I never saw it," Miggs said. "I wish I had."

Beany broke in to ask, "How do you like Huxley Hall, Miggs?"

Dulcie gave Miggs time for only a murmured, "It's all right," before she went on, "Then when Beany got the invitation to the penthouse party—Holy Toledo! you'd have thought it was a summons for a tryout in Hollywood. So I put on full steam to finish her jacket I was making in sewing. She went minus pockets, but what was a pocket or two when she was going to see Miggs, who was practically her twin?"

An embarrassed Beany crumbled the wafer that came with her chocolate. What in heaven's name had got into Dulcie? She kicked her under the table.

But Dulcie paid no attention.

"Everybody tried to tell Beany that this was no birthday party with a birthday cake the birthday twins would cut. We tried to tell her it was a cocktail party, but she kept saying, 'Oh, but you don't know Miggs and her mother. They'll want me to stay for supper.' She all but tucked her pajamas under her arm, so if you couldn't come home with her, she could stay with you."

Now Beany understood. Dulcie knew, even though Beany tried to hide it, that she had known sick disappointment. And Dulcie was taking this way to rub it in to Miggs.

In loud desperation, Beany said, "My feet are soaked.

Dulcie and I have been out interviewing farmers to find a place for a mare that was left on my hands." She rushed on to tell about Miss Goldie and the colt-to-be. She ended on real despair, "I just don't know what to do about it."

Miggs said evenly, "We can take her out to our farm."

"You still have the farm?" Beany asked. "We couldn't find it."

"It's still there. There's a barn and a field behind it where the mare could graze."

Beany could only stare at her in limp relief. Even the talkative Dulcie's tongue was silenced. As Miggs drank her coffee, Beany told her about the trailer, and about her father's car, which had a trailer hitch.

Norbett appeared at their table. He had the evening *Tribune* opened wide at page seven, and he said, "Nice spread they gave me on my story and the pictures I rustled up."

Beany ran her eyes over the pages Norbett spread on the table. He had interviewed people in different walks of life who had invested in uranium penny stocks. Each one told a success story.

Dulcie bent over it. "Well, well, here's a waitress who made enough on her investment in penny stocks to realize her lifelong dream of a trip to Mexico. If I cultivate you, Norbett, will you invest my tips at the Ragged Robin so I can drive around in a purple car? Oh, and here's a humble gardener who bought shares in a new uranium company years ago, and now is able to raise his own rutabagas. Good*nuss!*"

Norbett gave her a dark look. He said, "I guess this will pull the fangs of the alarmist on our rival paper."

Was Norbett aiming to impress Miggs Carmody, or

antagonize his old girl friend, Beany Malone? The alarm-ist on the rival paper must be Martie Malone.

Miggs stood up. "Beany and I are taking a mare out to our farm."

"But you can't, Cathy," Norbett said. "We've got Helena's car. We promised to pick her up at the Park Gate and take her to tea at the consul's."

"You pick her up," Miggs said. "You can show her your spread in the *Tribune* and get a pat on the back. Tell her I had an errand with Beany Malone. We'll go in her car."

Both Beany and Dulcie opened purses to pay for their drinks.

"I'll take care of them," Norbett said largely.

"Had I but known, I'd have ordered a double banana split," Dulcie said.

A half-hour later, Beany was driving the Dodge with Miss Goldie in the trailer behind it, with Miggs telling her which turns to make. "It's easier to go past Huxley Hall, and then double back." And finally she was pointing ahead, and saying, "There's the house."

Beany gasped, "Why, we passed right by that house. You mean that bald-looking mustardy one?"

"Or stewed squash. Yes, that's it."

"But your house was green, with a porch clear across the front!"

"One of the renters decided the porch was an eyesore, and ripped it off and put that little eyebrow over the front door. Of course, the house had to have a new paint job. Maybe they liked yellow—maybe they got the paint at a bargain."

"And we kept looking for a big apple tree close to the house."

"The present tenants did away with the tree. The woman said it was a nuisance—that the apples rotted on the ground and drew bees. I'm glad they left the willow tree there at the end of what was Mom's strawberry patch." She added, "Don't mind all the complaining of Mrs. Tenant. They were glad enough to get the place a year ago, when the husband was out of work and they couldn't pay their apartment rent. They put up such a sad tale that Mother let them have it, rent-free, if the man would keep it in repair. But now he has a job—machinist or mechanic. And now nothing is good enough for the woman. She gripes about no phone, and this dirt road leading from the highway to the house."

Beany drove with slow care up the rutted lane to the farmhouse, because of the mother-to-be in the trailer. She stopped in the yard between house and barn, which had once been gay with Katie's flowers, and which was now littered with car parts.

"It doesn't seem like the same place," Beany said.

"It isn't," was the cryptic answer.

Miggs had not exaggerated about the woman tenant. No sooner had the car stopped and Beany and Miggs climbed out, than a thin waspish woman in a flowered dress, and with a man's khaki coat thrown over her shoulders, came out the door. And demanded, "You surely aren't going to leave that horse here, are you? Orville don't have time to take on any extra work. And I can't stand horses—just can't stand them."

Beany was daunted by this remark, but Miggs went right on pulling bolts out of the end-gate. "She won't be any extra work for you," she told the woman. "She can have the run of the barn and the field behind it. I'll drop by on my way to and from school and feed her."

Beany climbed up into the trailer and untied Miss

143

Goldie's halter. She backed her down the ramp and onto the ground.

"Oh, good heavens!" the woman exclaimed. "She looks like she's going to have a colt."

"But not right away," Beany said.

The woman and her complaining voice followed them as they led Miss Goldie toward the barn. She didn't know what Orville would say; Orville had all his car parts in the barn—he was planning on making them into a truck—

"Orville can go blow," Miggs muttered to Beany as she opened the creaking barn door.

In the dusk the interior of the barn seemed at first only gloomy clutter. The window that faced the pasture was boarded up. Miggs opened the door that led out to it. Beany lifted a couple of old tires out of the manger.

Again Miss Goldie's limpid eyes studied her quarters resignedly. There was little space for her in the hodge-podge of accumulated odds and ends of machinery. Beany rubbed her nose, murmured, "There, there now, you'll have a pasture anyway—and Mary Fred will soon be home." She said to Miggs, "I can get up earlier in the mornings and drive out before school and feed her."

"You don't need to. It's so close to Huxley, it won't be five minutes out of my way." She was brushing out the feed box, shaking oats into it. Beany filled the manger with hay.

They tried to make more room by piling up some of the least heavy car parts. They pushed aside an old whet-stone. Beany said, "Oh look, Miggs, your mother's old brooder. I remember it full of little chickens. It was more fun to come out on hatching day."

Miggs said harshly, "Yes, fun for us. And hard work for Mom. She used to get up in the night and come out to see if the little stove was warm without being too hot. I was too little to realize how hard she had it."

"So was I," Beany admitted.

"And that strawberry patch was a back-breaking job for her. Weeding it, and taking off the runners and planting them. And watering it. She had so little when we lived here. You remember that old pick-up she drove and how it was always breaking down. No wonder she laughed till she cried when Dad gave her a pale blue Cad for her very own when he hit it big."

"She seems so different now," Beany mused.

"Naturally. Why shouldn't she get a kick out of buying clothes that aren't bargain basement? Or stepping in a florist shop and ordering flowers she hasn't planted and hoed and debugged herself?"

Beany said nothing. How could she say, "But I wish she didn't have so much. I've always wanted to do something for her, because she did so much for me."

Miggs said, "Helena's been so good to us. I don't know what we'd have done without her."

Beany had no answer for that, either.

Miggs rubbed a wisp of hay off Miss Goldie's bulging side. "She's all taken care of now. I'll drop by tomorrow."

As they walked to the car, the unhappy tenant was taking some washing off the clothesline. She kept her back to them and snatched angrily at each clothespin. Beany noted that at each yank on the line, one of the posts rocked insecurely.

Miggs spoke to the woman's back, "You'd better have your husband fix the latch on the barn door. It doesn't hold tight."

The woman vouchsafed no answer.

Miggs was silent as they drove back. So was Beany. Yet

there were so many things she would have liked to ask her: Why did your Cousin Helena do such a right-about-face? She wasn't even civil to me at the party. And why have you changed? Even though you were so crowded at the party, you were still glad to see me. But now—now, even though you've done the great favor of taking Miss Goldie, you're standoffish.

It happened that just as Beany was letting Miggs out in front of the Park Gate, the amethyst Lincoln drew up and Helena Stearns got out. Norbett, as chauffeur-friend, drove on to put the car away in the basement garage.

Helena walked over to the girls with a beaming smile. "Norbett said you two had a project concerning a horse."

"A mare," Miggs corrected her. "We took her out to our farm. The barn's a mess, but if we can clean it out and put straw on the floor, it'll be better." And then, with an odd smile, she added, "I thought you'd be glad for me to do a favor for the Malones."

Her words were like a chill jolt to Beany. What did Miggs mean? For that matter, what did Helena mean when she said, "Beany, be sure and tell your father how happy we are to help out friends like the Malones. If you need straw, I'll order it sent out tomorrow—and anything else the horse needs"?

15

ON Sunday night Beany and her father drove to the bus station to meet Mary Fred's nine-thirty bus. It hadn't arrived at ten—ten-thirty. The only information they could obtain was that a blizzard on Berthoud Pass must be delaying it.

This was the first chance Beany had had to talk to her busy father. She told him of Miggs's telling Helena Stearns that she should be glad of her doing a favor for the Malones. And of the woman enjoining Beany to tell her father they were glad to do anything for such good friends.

Martie Malone gave a mirthless chuckle. "That, my dear, is known as Public Relations. I'm the 'Press' and Mrs. Stearns wants to keep on very friendly terms with me."

"Was that why she asked so many newspaper and TV people to her party?"

"Right. I'm afraid that's the only reason I was asked. I didn't like to tell you at the time—"

"But Miggs added my name," Beany defended.

"Yes, bless her heart. And there's no reason why all Helena's sudden playing up to the Malones, because of my column, should spoil or tarnish your and Miggs's friendship. Don't let it, Beany."

She wanted to say more, but there was a quickening in the bus depot, a moving toward the big outer doors that told that the delayed bus was pulling in.

It moved in, like a thickly iced cake on wheels. The driver came stiffly down its steps, fastened back the door with a weary whew-ew!

A tired, bedraggled crowd climbed out. Mary Fred was one of the last. She was with a young mother who carried a tiny baby in her arms. Mary Fred, herself, held a little boy, well wrapped in her red coat. She gave her father and Beany only a fleeting smile until she delivered her burden to the man, evidently husband and father, who was meeting his family.

Beany took the red coat and tucked it around Mary Fred, who was shivering in the stale cold air outside the waiting room. "The little tike was sick and feverish," she murmured. "He kept crying all the time. His mother had her hands full with the baby, so I held him."

Martie Malone led the way to their parked car, and helped them in. Mary Fred explained between chattering teeth, "We were stranded on Berthoud Pass, waiting for the snow plow. Then we had to crawl along behind it through the snow."

Her father gave her an uneasy look. Of course, he couldn't scold her for wrapping her coat around a sick child; he would have done the same thing himself.

Mary Fred asked, "Is Miss Goldie all right out at Hill-

148

top? If the bus had got in on time, I planned to run out and see her."

Beany explained about distemper at Hilltop Stables. "But we've got her out at the old Carmody place. Miggs showed me where it was. We're looking after her." She didn't want to stress the worried days of hunting a place for Miss Goldie, or even to mention her grudging reception from the Carmody tenants. She asked, "Mary Fred, when will she have the colt?"

"About May, I imagine. That's the time they usually plan for a mare to foal. Didn't you ask Tom McDevitt?"

"I didn't think of it. The boy kept hurrying him off to catch his train."

Martie Malone said, "Don't worry about it tonight, Mary Fred. You get into a hot tub, and then to bed."

At home, Beany made her sister some hot tea and a piece of toast. Mary Fred took only a sip of the tea and a nibble of the toast. "I'm achey all over—from sitting in that cold bus so long, I suppose. Tomorrow I'll run out to McDevitt's old stables. Surely someone can tell me when Miss Goldie's colt is due."

But the next day Mary Fred did not leave the house or her bed. She was sick. When Dr. Hunter came that evening and took her temperature, he shook his head. "It's this bug that's going around."

They told him of the sick child Mary Fred had held in her arms on the long bus ride. "She probably picked it up from him," he agreed.

He left two prescriptions which Johnny had filled at Downey's Drug.

It cast a pall over the Malone household to have Mary Fred—old bubble-and-bounce, Johnny always called her —lying in a hard-breathing stupor. For three days she roused only to take her medicine.

Beany had telephoned Miggs to explain why she hadn't been able to help care for Miss Goldie. Beany would have liked to chat on with her, but Miggs said only, "I told you I'd look after Miss Goldie. Adair told us that Mary Fred was down with a virus."

At Harkness High each day seemed to grow more tense. It was the week before spring vacation. Each day brought the fashion show, the fashion-show issue of the *Hark Ye*, *and* the Bunny Ball closer.

Already there was the sound of hammering and sawing on the auditorium stage as the "store window" was being set up. Already you could hear George rehearsing his piano numbers, and Mrs. Hilb's reproving, "Girls! Girls! Walk to the music. This is no foot-race."

. . . Glory be, Beany thought, I've escaped that this year. . . .

But had she? For Mrs. Hilb came to the table where Dulcie and Beany worked, and said, "How nearly finished is Beany's jacket, Dulcie?"

Beany's heart started an uneasy beat. Mrs. Hilb studied the coat and planned aloud, "This is Wednesday—you have only to put the lining in. You sew so fast, Dulcie, that I don't see why you couldn't have it finished. Beany, do you have a light-colored wool dress you could wear under it?"

"Mary Fred has a cream-colored wool, but—but you see—"

"I'd like to use you in the first number," Mrs. Hilb planned on. "That's the showing of school clothes. One rehearsal for you would be enough."

Oh no, oh no! As though Beany didn't have enough worries without a part in the Easter Parade.

Mrs. Hilb was saying, "There's a machine free now, Dulcie. Stitch your lining together as soon as it's basted."

Alone at the table, Beany whispered to Dulcie, "Don't let her throw me to the wolves. It gives me goose pimples, just to think of standing up there with the spotlight on me."

"Gives *you* goose pimples? Why, you'd get a big hand just because you're Beany Malone. What about me?"

"Oh, but, Dulcie, you're to be the *pièce de résistance* in your formal—that gorgeous, drooling formal."

"Yeh, but *I'll* be inside the formal. And nobody drools over *me*." She lifted haunted eyes from the green lining she was basting together. "No one will clap for me. Can you imagine any nightmare worse than walking across the stage—and nobody clapping for you?"

"Oh, Dulcie, they will."

Yet, even as she said it, Beany was not so sure. If only Dulcie hadn't rubbed the whole student body the wrong way. If only she had been less flip and cocky. If only they could see under that to the real Dulcie, who wanted to be liked, who only put on a bold front because she was unsure of herself. . . . But it was so hard to undo a first impression, Beany realized.

Dulcie said suddenly in a conspiratorial whisper, "Beany, I won't rush the jacket through—and then you won't have to be among the jittery participants—if you'll do something for me."

"Sure. What?"

"Don't have Carlton Buell bring you to the show and the Bunny Ball."

"But I almost have to. I don't have anyone else, now that Andy—"

"It won't kill you to come without a date just once. You'll be better off than I will, because the fellows on the *Hark Ye* staff will dance with you—"

"Don't you have a date, Dulcie? What about the college boy that was waiting to give you a rush? Can't you come with him?"

Dulcie's lips curled. "It was evidently my reputation that attracted him. His idea was to make cozy with me in a car. And he parted from me in a huff because I didn't have the same idea." She added with bleak irony, "Unlike friend Carlton, he *didn't* want a girl on a pedestal."

It's too bad that it's even harder to undo a bad reputation, Beany thought with an ache of sympathy.

"All right, Dulcie, I won't come with Carlton. I never thought about your feeling bad to see him with me."

"That's not it. That, I could take. But I don't want him to witness my being a flop. I don't want him to see that nobody gives the little girl a hand." Her voice thickened, and she choked out, "I wish I'd never made that fool formal."

What could Beany do to help her? She could bring Johnny. Nobody could clap louder than he. Maybe she could get Adair and her father to come—no, Martie Malone was taking the plane Friday evening for Washington.

She murmured aloud on a desperate thought, "Dulcie, do you suppose you could ask Norbett Rhodes?"

"He's pretty busy jumping through hoops for his penthouse chums. Norbett's all right," Dulcie added, "if someone could whittle him down to size."

Beany stopped on her way home from school to buy a chicken to make broth for Mary Fred. She found her, lying with two pillows under her head and looking like a wan ghost of her old red-cheeked self. And far more interested in Miss Goldie's diet than her own.

"How are the oats and wild hay holding out, Beany?"

"There's enough to last out the week. I showed Miggs the measure to use for the oats."

"Did you tell Miggs she likes apples?"

"I think I did. I can't remember."

"Oh, Beany, do you suppose you could run out and see for yourself how she's getting along? And pick out the apples in this basket of fruit someone sent me. I feel uneasy about her."

"O.K., I'll drive out right away. I'll put the hen in the pressure cooker, and tell Johnny to watch it."

It was not entirely a happy trip Beany made to the Carmody acreage. First, there was the surly reception by the woman tenant when Beany knocked at the back door and explained that she had brought out apples for Miss Goldie.

The woman only snapped, "We don't have any say about who comes or goes or brings what. Orville don't like this horse business any better'n I do," and turned back to the stove.

Somehow, it didn't seem right to see another woman there in Katie's kitchen, at Katie's stove, Beany thought, as she went on to the barn.

She had no sooner stepped inside than she saw that Helena Stearns had kept her word. There, crowded between Orville's car parts, were bales of straw, of wild hay, and a bulging gunny sack of oats. It made Beany uncomfortable to be—through Miss Goldie—a recipient of such generosity. She wished Helena had let the Malones buy Miss Goldie's groceries.

The happy part of the trip was that Miss Goldie was in high spirits. She nickered and tossed her head and bunted at Beany, coaxing for another apple from the sack Beany tucked down behind the straw.

"Not tonight," Beany told her. "That apple was as big as two—and you have to watch your diet these days, young lady."

She left a note for Miggs, telling her where the apples

were hidden. She petted the mare and then, mindful of the Malone dinner to get, hurried off.

At home, when she opened the kitchen door, she found Hank Willison standing at the stove, sticking a fork in the chicken in the pressure cooker. Again he was wearing his leather coat and heavy boots.

He turned his slow, warming grin upon her. "Done to a T. I'm pinch-hitting for Johnny while he rigs up a bed light for Mary Fred. I'm waiting for your pappy to come home. Got another report to turn in to him."

"Fine," Beany said. "We'll set an extra place, and I'll stir up an extra dumpling or two."

"You're right up there at the top of my list, Beany."

The top of his list? She wondered if he really meant it. The Bunny Ball just three days off, and Beany Malone with no date for it. But Hank was a college senior. No, she mustn't take his soft soap too seriously. . . .

One other surprising evidence of Helena Stearns's generosity came that evening. It was after dinner, after Martie Malone and Hank had been closeted in the study and were having an extra cup of coffee in the kitchen. It wasn't surprising that the boys who dated Mary Fred, as well as her riding pupils, should send her flowers when they heard she was sick. The surprise was a huge florist's box, containing roses, gladiolas, and some blue flowers no one knew the name of.

"From Helena Stearns," Beany said, reading the enclosed card.

She had to reach down three of their biggest vases from a cupboard shelf to accommodate them. As she filled the vases at the sink, her father looked up from his coffee and said with unwonted irritation, "Beany, put those flowers where I don't have to look at them, or smell them."

"He means," Hank said, "that they smell like an ax grinding."

Beany grinned. "I thought it was Public Relations."

"Same thing," her father grunted.

Adair, too, looked at the profusion of flowers with a dubious frown. Adair had been keeping her morning appointments at the penthouse to paint Mrs. Perry Carmody's portrait. She wore a constant harried pucker between her eyes over it. And that was most unusual. Usually she was all eager enthusiasm over any portrait she was working on.

She righted one of the blue flowers in its vase, and burst out to Beany, "I'm certainly making a botch of Katie's portrait."

"You are? Why?"

"I don't know. I just can't get the feel of it. The pose is dramatic. Katie—Catherine to Helena Stearns—is standing at the window with those black and silver draperies behind her. But nothing—that is, the real person doesn't come through to me. The picture's got about as much life as an ad for vanishing cream." She laughed ruefully, "Today, I fiddled all morning, doing the sapphire bracelet she's wearing."

The next afternoon the final meeting of the *Hark Ye* staff was held for "putting the paper to bed," which meant having every write-up and picture placed on the dummy for the printer.

The staff was tired and edgy. The girls who had wanted an orchestra and programs were grumpy over their defeat by those in favor of keeping down expenses.

"Should we ask our dates to bring tin cups for the punch?" one of them sneered. "Or will there be any punch served at this penny-pinching affair?"

"I'd like to serve a punch or two," the business manager snapped. "Can't you get it through your noggins? This dance is to get us out of the red."

Claude Metz, proofreader, was to sell *Hark Ye* issues to the Easter Parade audience at the door of the auditorium. He said, "Beany, I might need a helping hand during the rush Saturday night. Your date wouldn't mind shifting for himself briefly, would he?"

"I'll help," Beany answered.

. . . Her date, indeed! She was in the same boat with Dulcie, who had said today, "I'll grit my teeth and do my strut across the stage, sans applause, and then I'll fade." Well, Beany Malone would help Claude take in money and then she'd fade, before the dance started.

Jennifer Reed, senior, was editor of *Hark Ye*. She was a poised and competent dark-eyed girl. She murmured to Beany and her helpers, "It's hard to pick which photographs to put on page one—and which to put inside."

Beany shuffled through the pictures. Here was Dulcie Lungaarde. Her formal was by far the most outstanding garment. Their staff photographer had managed a picture so clear that the rose design in the black lace bodice showed. And that billowy skirt of white tulle with the uneven facing of black tulle, edged with cut-out black roses. Beany remembered a weary Dulcie, whipping each one of those roses on by hand.

She said impulsively, "Let's put Dulcie on page one."

"Glory, no!" one of the girls said. "That gal's too big for her toreador pants already. She'd strut all over the place, if we gave her a place of honor on the front page."

"She isn't cocky," Beany defended. "Not really. She just puts on that sort of—façade—because she isn't sure of herself."

"Beany, you must have read a book," another girl said. "Not cocky? Why, if just once I saw that girl acting as though she didn't own the world, I could take her to my bosom."

Beany turned hopeful eyes on Jennifer for her decision. Jennifer was fair. . . . But Jennifer said after a thoughtful moment, "I think we'd better put Dulcie on page two."

This was Beany's turn to lose her temper.

"Why put her in at all, Jennifer? Now that you've all made her so miserable, why not give her one big kick and get it over with?"

Jennifer didn't answer. She went on numbering the photographs to correspond to the squares marked off on the dummy.

She waited until the other three girls left. Beany was reaching for her coat, when Jennifer said with an angry flash of eyes, "Wait a minute, Beany. For a nice person, I never saw anyone so quick to jump to the worst conclusion. I shouldn't tell you why I'm not putting Dulcie's picture on page one, but I will. Dulcie's still a new girl here, and she's made herself unpopular—"

She waved back Beany's defense of Dulcie and went on, "I'd put her on the front page in a minute, if I thought it would help her. I like her. But it would only make the other girls resent her and dislike her even more. Now do you understand?"

Beany said sheepishly, "Yes. Yes, I guess you're right. I didn't think of that."

Jennifer only gave her a weary smile. "Try counting to ten the next time, before you leap—to conclusions."

16

FRIDAY, the last day of school before spring vacation.

Beany walked out of Harkness, her arms loaded with books, the square of gingerbread she had made in cooking, and her cooking apron in need of laundering.

An automobile horn sounded. It was Miggs Carmody in her Cousin Helena's amethyst car. She swung open the door for Beany, said, "I wondered if you had time to ride out to the farm with me to see Miss Goldie."

Beany's heart gave a joyous leap at this overture of friendship. She climbed into the car, deposited her load, and broke the gingerbread in half. "I was just wishing I had someone to divide this with. Yes, I've got lots of time. Just so I'm home in time to tell Dad good-by. He's catching a plane around six for Washington. Mary Fred's temp is down. But she's limp and wobbly, and the doctor says she can't go out for a week. Johnny said he'd get supper."

They sat, eating the gingerbread, and Beany bubbled on, "Dulcie and I pulled a snide trick on our sewing teacher—but it's such a relief not to have that clammy feeling inside me about being in the fashion show."

She told about the tweed jacket she would have had to model if Dulcie had finished the lining. "I don't know what she did to it, but it wasn't right. And I was saved by the bell. But the fashion show is always too long, anyway. The more time it takes up, the less time we—they—have to dance at the Bunny Ball."

Miggs started the car. Beany pressed a button and the window on her side rolled down. She said, "Oh, this is fun—riding in such elegance."

Miggs said, "Helena told me to take her car. She thought you'd like riding in it."

The smile was jolted off Beany's face. Out of her hurt, she burst out, "Miggs, why do you act as though you *have* to be friendly with me? Why does Helena have to prod you into it?"

Miggs took her eyes off the road and glanced at Beany's flushed face. She answered with the same vehemence, "Don't you know why? Because Helena says it's better to have the good will than the ill will of a sheep-killing dog. Meaning Martie Malone."

"Meaning Martie Malone?" Beany repeated stupidly. "Dad? A sheep-killing dog?"

"Well, let's not carry that figure of speech too far. Helena says that his column carries such power and is so far-reaching. And that right now he's out after uranium companies. She says that one blast in his column could knock the props out of the Mid-Century which is being founded. And which Dad plans to take over."

"Oh-h-" Beany breathed.

Now she understood. Helena Stearns was afraid of Martie Malone. She had seen that boxed-in announcement in the *Call*, "Watch for Martie Malone's Columns on Uranium Companies and Penny Stocks."

Maybe, after the penthouse party, Miggs had mentioned Beany Malone, and Helena had found out she was Martie Malone's daughter. Helena had probably said to Miggs, "Oh, my dear, you must renew your friendship with the Malones." No wonder Miggs had acted so unnatural, so pushed.

Beany said earnestly, "If you knew my father, you wouldn't believe any of that. He wouldn't write a word that he couldn't prove was true."

"And if you knew my father, you'd know that he wouldn't go into anything that wasn't perfectly on the level," Miggs answered.

Beany asked, "Does he believe what Helena says—that Dad is the sheep-killing dog you have to keep on the good side of?"

"She didn't say anything to him about it. She said he had enough on his mind right now. She just told me what she was afraid of."

"She's all wrong," Beany repeated. "Why would Dad want to hurt you folks? He isn't that kind."

Miggs gave a rueful laugh. "My gosh, Beany, we're like a couple of kids fighting and saying, 'My dad's honester than yours.'"

Beany laughed too. "The whole thing's so cockeyed."

Yet somehow their very frankness had cleared the air. Miggs went on as they stopped for the light at College Boul, "You were saying how much Mom has changed. Can't you see why? Because she never had anything before. As a kid, she lived on a dry-land farm with never an

160

extra pair of shoes to her name. Then about six years ago, Dad hit it big in oil. He wouldn't have, if Helena hadn't come forward with the money to invest. But Helena's like that."

She paused—maybe waiting for Beany to praise Helena. Beany didn't.

They were on the stretch of road that carried them past the Huxley Hall grounds. They both stared ahead, trying to decide just what the moving object was in the road ahead.

Beany murmured, "Reminds me of an ant carrying something bigger than he is."

Even as they watched, the small human ant let down his burden as though it were too much for him. Why, it was a small boy and his load was a large and seemingly heavy carton. It was Donnie Kern.

Miggs slowed to a stop, and Beany called to him, "Hi, Donnie, what are you doing so far from home? What've you got in the box?"

He looked quite spent and woebegone, standing there in the raw March wind. Tears had reddened his blue eyes and streaked his face. He said in a thin voice, "My white rabbits. The box keeps sort of tipping over because I got a dish of barley in one end."

Miggs offered, "Why don't you get in with us, Donnie? We're going out to feed a mare, and then we'll take you home."

His lips worked before he could answer, "I'm not going home. The vegetable man comes on Saturday—that's tomorrow—and if he comes—they'll give him the rabbits—"

So he was running away from home with his precious rabbits.

In a low voice Beany told Miggs about the two baby rabbits Donnie had acquired; how they had grown to full stature and to an insoluble problem. And the ultimatum Donnie's father, Captain Kern, had been driven to make: that unless the rabbits were disposed of, the vegetable man was to have rabbit for his Easter dinner.

Miggs was out of the car the minute Beany finished. She said warmly to the boy, "I like white rabbits. I know a place we can take them. See that yellow house over there? See that barn? There's a lean-to at the end, and when I was a kid your age I kept rabbits in it. We might even find part of the old cage."

The runaway lifted his tear-smudged face, in which hope and doubt struggled. "You don't mean you'd eat 'em?"

"Heavens, no, I wouldn't ever eat a rabbit," Miggs assured him. "We'll fix them up in a box, and then you can come out and help build a runway outside. I used to pull clover for mine."

"I could come out and pull clover," he said. "Pete and I could pull a lot."

"Pete's his brother," Beany explained.

"Sure, you could bring Pete. Here, let's load the carton in the back seat. You can sit by it to see if they're right side up."

With their added cargo Miggs drove on. Her eyes smiled into Beany's in happy conspiracy. Ah, this was the Miggs that Beany had dreamed of finding. She said impulsively, "Miggs, please don't believe Helena. About Dad's lying in wait to do you dirt."

"All right, Beany. I hated to think it."

They turned into the rutted lane leading to the yellow house. Beany said, for Miggs's ears only and not for the

162

owner of the rabbits, "I hope your complaining tenant won't blow a gasket when she sees more livestock coming in."

Miggs swung into the yard. Even as she stopped the car, she nodded toward the house. "Looks as though she already has."

A great assortment of suitcases, folded coats, bedding, and cartons sat outside the back door. It opened, and the woman, wearing the same flowered print, but with her hat and coat on, flounced angrily toward them.

"I'm glad you've come, so I could tell you we were leaving—and why. I've been trying to get hold of your mother, but she wasn't home. Just as soon as Orville comes in his truck, we're leaving and going to my sister-in-law's. There's a limit to what a person can put up with."

The limit, the girls gathered from her sputtery indignation, was Miss Goldie. She kept pushing open the barn door and coming to the house and making a nuisance of herself—

"If Orville had fixed the latch on the barn door, she couldn't have bothered you," Miggs reminded her. "Mother let you have the place without paying rent, because Orville agreed to keep up repairs."

That fell on deaf ears. The woman stormed on, "And today, just when I had the lines full of washing—if she didn't come up and scratch herself on one of the clothes posts till she pushed it over. And my whole washing went in the dirt."

"Oh, that's too bad," Beany said. "But the clothes post *was* loose."

The woman's answer to that was to go into the house and slam the door.

"O.K., Bud," Miggs said to Donnie. "Carry your rabbits out to the barn."

"Golly, Miggs, I'm sorry that bringing Miss Goldie here has made trouble with the tenants," Beany said.

"It's a blessing. It'll be a relief not to have to listen to that woman. And I hope Orville loads up his junk so we can clean out the barn."

"But what will you do, Miggs? You'll need someone here to look after things."

"I know someone who'll do a better job than these folks ever did."

Miss Goldie was in fine spirits—as though she relished having knocked down the clothes post. Beany led her in from the pasture. She nuzzled playfully at Beany, all the while she gave her oats and hay and fresh water.

Miggs and Donnie did indeed find a remnant of the old rabbit cage in the lean-to off the barn. "This isn't too good, Donnie, but we'll fix better quarters later on," she promised. "When you come out next time, bring a hammer and any nails you can find."

Yes, this was a different Miggs. She laughed as she said, "Remember, Beany, how Mom used to say she didn't know whether to call this place Aching Acres or Stork's Stopover. Our cat was always having kittens, our cow even had twin calves. Stork's Stopover is about right for now. I suspect we have," she nodded toward the rabbits, "another expectant mother."

They drove home, going to the Kern house first to let out Donnie. Beany said, "There's Rosellen. I'll bet she's worried about you, Donnie."

"I told Pete not to tell *anybody* I was running away," he muttered.

Rosellen, on her crutches, was standing at the curb with the smaller Pete beside her. When the car stopped, and Donnie climbed out, she burst into relieved tears. She gave Pete an admonishing shove. "Go find Sidney—go tell him Donnie's back."

Beany and Miggs got out to explain. Their words and Rosellen's were all tumbled together. For Pete had confessed that Donnie had run away, and Rosellen had been beside herself—

"Mom is out helping Aunt Beth with her new baby—and I didn't want to call Dad—because when he found Donnie, he'd have blistered him. So I called up Sidney—and he's been running his legs off. Here he comes now."

Donnie shamefacedly ducked into the house and Pete followed.

Rosellen turned wet but shiny eyes to Miggs. "No wonder Beany thinks you're wonderful. I do, too, for being so good to Donnie and his rabbits."

Sidney joined them, short of breath from his search. Rosellen, the hospitable, invited them in, but Beany said her father was leaving and she must get home.

Then Rosellen detained them further.

"Miggs, Sidney and I have been talking about that story Norbett Rhodes had in the *Tribune* about all those people that got rich, buying uranium stock for almost nothing. Sidney said that one day in the elevator, he asked Helena about this new Mid-Century."

Sidney said shyly, "I get paid by the hour when I'm on the elevator. And I'm saving it for college. But I was thinking I'd like to invest it and have it double or treble, the way it did for the ones Norbett wrote about."

"Double or treble!" Rosellen broke in. "Gosh, one man bought stock for seventeen cents and it went up to ten dollars!"

Rosellen, the emotional, could shed tears one moment and then be dancing with joy the next.

She laughed now as she said, "I've got the swellest idea, Miggs. You know, my brother Andy went into the Marines. He had some pay coming to him from the Pant movie house when he left, and the manager gave him fifty bucks as a parting gift. Andy told me to put it in the savings bank. But wouldn't it be fun if I put it in Mid-Century uranium stock? And Andy would be rich when he got out of the Marines. Your Cousin Helena told Sidney it was bound to soar."

Miggs's eyes left Rosellen's eager face and rested on the shabby half of a double house the Kerns rented. Beany couldn't translate the odd look that flicked across Miggs's face, as she said swiftly, "I don't know anything about it." And to Beany, "We'd better go, so you can see your father before his plane leaves."

She didn't speak on the brief ride to the Malone home on Barberry. Adair's yellow convertible was parked in front. Johnny was carrying out his father's luggage.

He hailed Miggs with a warm smile. "Park that Easter-egg car and come on in. I'm the chef at Chez Malone tonight. I've got our biggest casserole full of Eggs Italienne. I've already persuaded Hank Willison to stay. He's been in a huddle with Dad in the study. We haven't seen enough of you around here. How about it? I woo women with my cooking."

Miggs said unexpectedly, "Yes, I could stay. I'd love to."

"You don't suppose we could get hold of Katie, do you, and have her come over, too?" Johnny asked.

Miggs shook her head. "No, she and Helena are all tied up with that International Style Show. They're going to a committee dinner."

Beany walked in the gate ahead of them. Adair and

Martie Malone came out the door. Beany held her father's briefcase while he squirmed into his topcoat.

"I left a job for you, Beany," he said. "Clean up my column and retype it for me, like a good girl. It has to be down to Stan Lowell at the *Call* tonight, so it'll be set up for Sunday's paper. Stan is always there till nine on Friday nights. Hank said he'd stay and take it down."

He kissed her good-by and added on a sigh, "Maybe after tonight you'll wish you had a carpenter or a haberdasher for a father."

He looked up to see Johnny and Miggs. He folded Miggs's two hands between his, said with his gentle smile, "It seems like old times, having you with us. I'm sorry I'm taking off right away." He hesitated a minute, as though there were something he wanted to say, and perhaps didn't have time or quite know how to say it.

Adair reminded, "Martie, it's almost plane time."

Martie only stopped and kissed Miggs on the cheek, even as he had Beany, and said, "Good-by, child. It's good to see you and Beany together."

17

BEANY, herself, had made this same recipe of Italian Eggs. She had boiled the eggs, removed the yolks to mash with parsley, cream, and chopped mushrooms, already sautéed in butter. She had poured a cream sauce over the stuffed eggs and baked it all in a slow oven.

But she had to admit this evening, as she pulled the bubbling casserole from the oven and caught its savory aroma, that Johnny's dish, with its dash of this and that, always had a more exciting flavor.

The kitchen had a noisy, party gaiety as Johnny issued orders. Miggs and Hank spread the slices of crusty bread with garlic butter. Johnny wore a paper sack on his head, chef-style, and a tea-towel around his waist. He was making tossed salad.

Beany had to admit that Johnny's salad surpassed hers, too.

"Just the old creative instinct," Johnny bragged as he shoved the buttered bread into the oven, "that gives food that indefinable, ineffable something. . . . Beany, if you dish that egg concoction up on cold plates, I'll clobber you."

Adair had telephoned from the airport to say that Martie's plane would be late taking off; she would have a sandwich with him there, and then go on to the gallery and her showing.

Johnny carried a tray up to Mary Fred. He came leaping down the stairs to say, "Hey, let's put our suppers on trays. The patient is beyond the point where anybody will catch anything. She's looking sort of wistful. She wants to ask Miggs all about Miss—or Mrs. Goldie, also."

Each one carried a full tray and climbed the stairs to Mary Fred's room. It was the living room of a two-room suite with the glassed-in sleeping porch adjoining. Ordinarily, Mary Fred slept on the unheated porch. "Since I'm puny, I have to sleep indoors," she complained. "Imagine me, the hardy garden variety, turning into a hothouse flower."

She looked a little like a hothouse flower after her five days' illness. Even her bright red robe could not coax any color into her cheeks.

She listened, eager and anxious, while Beany and Miggs answered her questions about Miss Goldie. Yes, the mare seemed happy and content in her quarters.

"That's because she has a pasture to run in," Mary Fred said. "She's like me—just a Girl Scout at heart." They even told her about Miss Goldie's rubbing down the clothes post, and feeling no shame because the washing fell in the dirt, but was friskier than ever because of it.

"I wish we knew when to expect the colt," Mary Fred

169

worried. "The very first day Dr. Hunter will let me, I'll drive out to McDevitt's stables. Even though he's sold out, I might find someone around there who knows. If no one does, I'll have a vet check her over. Miggs, has your mother seen her? She was always smart about such things."

"No. Mom hasn't been out to the farm since we came back. I guess she remembers the place as Aching Acres. Besides, she's been so busy with all this International Style Show that's coming off next Wednesday. And all the entertaining for all the celebrities who are flying in for it."

"Style shows seem to be bustin' out all over," Beany said. "We're having the Easter Parade at Harkness tomorrow evening. Dulcie saved me from a fate worse than death—being in it, I mean—but poor old Dulcie is so afraid she won't be clapped for."

Johnny said, "Which reminds me, Beany; Carlton asked me today if you needed him to take you to the Bunny Ball afterward."

Hank Willison broke in, "Who is this guy that wants to know if Beany needs him to take her to the Bunny Ball? Beany's my girl. I decided that the night she washed my shirt for me."

Beany laughed. "Carlton's the boy next door. He pinch-hits for me whenever—"

"You don't need any pinch-hitter when old Hank's available. Why can't I take you to the Bunny Ball?"

"Why can't I take Miggs and the four of us go?" Johnny asked. "We'll give Dulcie a thundering hand. You'd go with me, wouldn't you, Miggs?"

Miggs said, "Don't you have a girl?"

"Not now. She's moved to Utah."

"He's a lousy dancer," Mary Fred said from her bed. "Beany and I taught him, and he's no credit to us."

170

"Sure, I'll go," Miggs said. "I'm a good clapper, too."

Beany sat and listened to their plans. Hank said they could all go in his car, and what time should he come? . . . I'm so happy, I could purr, she thought. Miggs going with Johnny. That seemed so right. . . .

Johnny was not as girl-crazy as most college freshmen. It wasn't that he didn't like girls, but his mind was always so full of some colorful event or character in history. And, having no conceit, he felt he was no treat for a girl. (If he only knew how many girls had cultivated Beany because of her brother.) After Kay left, Mary Fred had said, "Get another girl, Johnny. You can't be a hermit." Johnny had only grinned. "Supposing I got one that wanted me to cut my hair every week?"

So happy she could purr. Something told Beany that Hank Willison, like Andy, would be a joy to dance with. It was the tense ones, like Norbett, who danced jerkily. Or the absent-minded ones, like Johnny, who meandered aimlessly about the floor and were constantly bumped into.

Praise be, Beany Malone wouldn't be one of the unattached at the fashion show or Bunny Ball. She'd be with a School of Mines senior. She thought then of Dulcie. Poor Dulcie, dateless—and filled with fear.

Hank was saying, with his eyes on Mary Fred's wan face, "We'd better get out of here. The hothouse flower looks a little wilted."

Mary Fred smiled wearily. "It's disgusting, that's what it is."

They carried their trays back to the kitchen. Beany was just grumbling, "That Johnny can mess up a kitchen worse than any six people," when Mike's barking almost drowned out the ringing of the doorbell.

Beany answered it. Norbett Rhodes stood there. He said with a defensive toss of his head, "I thought maybe

Cathy Carmody was here. I called her, and her Cousin Helena said she was with you."

Oh-oh! He was giving Beany to understand that he had not come to see her. "Yes, she's out in the kitchen. Come on out."

Johnny greeted him heartily. He insisted on Norbett's sampling his Italian Eggs. He poured him a cup of coffee. He said, "Say, we're all cooking up a deal to go to the festivities at Harkness tomorrow night. Beany's going with Hank, and my first love, Miggs, with me. How about your scrabbling up a date and going along with us?"

That blundering Johnny! Beany wondered, as she often had, how he could go through life and be loved by everyone. Didn't he know that Norbett had been picked by Helena Stearns to beau Miggs about? Didn't he realize that even though Norbett wasn't beauing Beany Malone about, he was still resentful of her other dates? But no, Johnny was so devoid of resentments and malice himself, he never expected it in others.

Norbett swallowed a mouthful of Johnny's egg and mushroom mixture, and grunted, "I don't have a girl. I must be the repulsive type. Every girl I get turns around and dates someone else."

H'mm, that was a jab at both Miggs and her. Again Beany thought of the dateless Dulcie. Maybe if she subtly steered the talk to the fashion show—and built up Dulcie as the crowning triumph—maybe she could find out if Norbett would go with her.

She said, "We have to go early because of the Easter Parade. You remember that deliciously wicked formal Dulcie made? Hilb is keeping her for the very last, because if it came on first all the others would be anticlimax."

Johnny, the unsubtle, broke in, "How about taking Dulcie, Norbett? Beany said she didn't have a date. Go ahead and ask her, and we can make a sixsome out of it. That way we could all swap dances. That way no gal is stuck with having to dance too often with me."

"I don't even know how to get hold of her," Norbett demurred. "She's never home."

"She's working at the Ragged Robin this evening," Beany said.

Johnny had an answer for that too. "Why don't we all drive up there and order a Coke and fix it up with her? Come on."

"You folks go ahead," Hank said. "Beany has to type her dad's article, and then I have to rush it down to the *Call*. Nine o'clock is the deadline. We'll just about make it."

In the suddenly quiet house, with the sound of Johnny's car leaving the driveway, Beany sat down at her father's typewriter. She rolled paper in it. She looked up at Hank to say, "I was sure that when you met Mary Fred, you'd prefer her to her younger sister."

"Let not your heart be troubled," he assured her and patted her shoulder. "I like 'em young. I like Beany, because she's dumb and stubborn. . . . Here now, type your dad's copy, and then I've got some more to add to it. I didn't get here until shortly before he left. I was held up at the assayer's."

Beany typed the title in caps, INVESTORS BEWARE! Her eyes followed the copy, her fingers the keys, automatically. But her mind was on the exciting sixsome Johnny had worked out for tomorrow evening—the bleak evening Beany had looked ahead to.

She wondered if she could find a formal on sale for—

let's see, she had twelve dollars, and she'd get five more tomorrow from Eve Baxter. She had worn her apple green to so many events. Of course, she could wear Mary Fred's pink—the pallid pink, Mary Fred called it. But it was pretty "blah," and the bodice wasn't snug enough.

Yes, she'd hurry downtown after her stint at Eve Baxter's and hunt for a formal. What a lark it would be to show up with Hank Willison, and have girls say, "Beany, you've been holding out on us. We didn't know you had a new love."

Suddenly, as she typed, the words took on meaning to her. This column of her father's was not only a warning to investors, but a blast at certain companies being formed to sell uranium stocks—penny stocks. He named them: Everyman's, Foursquare— With relief she typed the period. No mention of the one Miggs's father was in.

Beside her, Hank was saying, "Now for my addition, which is pure dynamite." He read to her, "And the Mid-Century is the shakiest of all. According to reports by geologist W. A. Naismith and his assistant, Hank Willison, their land holdings in Utah and Arizona are wild and woolly wasteland which looks promiseful on folders, but shows no trace of uranium. The small investor would—"

"No—oh no," Beany broke out. "You can't add that. The Mid-Century company is the one Miggs's father is in."

"It's Helena Stearns's. So be sure and get the name Hank Willison in. I want friend Helena to read that. I'd give a back filling to see her face when she reads that, and knows I had a hand in pulling the wall-to-wall carpeting out from under her feet."

Beany looked up into his pleased face. "Is that all you care about? Just gloating over Helena Stearns because she called you a dumb Okie years ago?"

174

"That's right," he agreed on a chuckle. "I lose sleep for gloating."

"But it's pulling the rug out from Katie and Miggs and Perry Carmody, too. I don't see how you can gloat over that."

"I'm shedding no tears over Katie and Miggs and Perry Carmody."

"You wouldn't!" she flung out, her voice shaky with anger. "All you care about is evening up your old grudge against Helena. I never thought you would be so callous —so mean. You said yourself Katie tried to fill you up. You told about Miggs's giving you the money she had for ballets when you bashed in the fender on her dad's car. I should think you'd feel a little loyalty."

"Get on with the typing," he ordered. "We haven't much time."

"I won't," she defied him. "I won't put that in. Dad wouldn't want it in his column. They're *his* friends—he wouldn't hurt them. He said himself it was like old times, seeing Miggs with me."

He didn't answer.

Her voice rose higher with anger and accusation. "Dad appreciates what Katie did for me. Not that it means anything to you that Katie saved my life when I was a baby—" Her very wrath choked her. "This is just something you cooked up to add on—just to feed your old grudge—just to see your name in print. If you think I'll type it—"

"You're durn tootin' you'll type it. My hunt-and-peck system would take too long. Get on with it."

"I won't," she repeated.

She started to get up from the chair. His strong hands shoved her back. There was iron under his drawled-out words, "Type it, and don't waste time, calling me names."

175

There was iron in his hands that held her in the chair.

She looked up into his set face and sensed a will stronger than hers.

In helpless fury, her fingers fumbled out the words on the keys, even to the last line, "The small investor would be taking far less risk in feeding his money into a slot machine."

She pulled the paper out and thrust it viciously at him. "Dad wouldn't have put that in. You're taking advantage of him because he's gone—because he trusted you. Trust, hah! You're small—and hateful. I'll never speak to you again. I hope I never lay eyes on you again."

He took the copy and opened the front door. He turned back to say, "You might manage not speaking to me. But not laying eyes on me is going to be hard, when I'm taking you to the dance tomorrow night."

She hurled out, "I won't go with you."

But the door had already closed behind him.

Before the evening was over, Beany knew that she would have to go to the Bunny Ball with Hank after all. That nothing short of being stricken with a virus or breaking a leg would save her.

For Miggs came back to the house with Johnny, to report that Dulcie had said yes, with pleasure, to Norbett.

Miggs had all her plans made. "Johnny promised to take me out to the farm early in the morning. I'll tuck in the clothes I'll need for the dance, and then dress here with you. That way I can put in a longer day out there. When I told you I knew someone who'd take care of the farm, I meant me. I can hardly wait to clean up the house after those tenants, and move the furniture around the way it was when we lived there. And if Orville doesn't

176

move all his claptrap out of the barn, I'm going to—with help."

"I can't help tomorrow," Beany said.

"Don't worry about tomorrow or Sunday," Miggs said. "But Monday, when school vacation starts, we'll work together. Bring out jeans to work in."

. . . But by Monday, Miggs Carmody wouldn't want any of the Malones working with her. By Monday, she would think of Martie Malone as the sheep-killing dog Helena said he was. . . .

Miggs had more to say to Beany when Johnny went outside to call to Mike; they could hear his barking as he chased a car down Barberry Street. "Beany, it seems that all your girl friends fall for Johnny. He was telling me about Kay, who moved away." Her laugh was shaky. "But then I've been crazy about him since I was four."

. . . All that would be different, too, after Sunday's paper came out. Just because Hank wanted to gloat over Helena Stearns. Just because he didn't care about ruined friendships or budding romances. . . .

Beany changed the subject. "I'm glad Dulcie's going with Norbett."

"So am I. By the way, Norbett tells me he's an old flame of yours."

"He was my first beau," Beany said absently. "Mary Fred always said, 'When bigger and better fights are had, Beany and Norbett will have them.'"

. . . But Mary Fred was wrong. Beany had just had a bigger and better fight—if a fight it would be called, for a School of Mines senior to hold her like a vise in a chair and say, "Type that, and don't waste time calling me names." . . .

"You're not the right kind of girl for Norbett," Miggs mused. "I don't know why—"

"I know. I bruise too easily. I took him too seriously."

"I'm not right for him, either," Miggs said. "Even if Helena hadn't thrown us at each other, we still—"

The back door opened on Johnny with the uncontrite Mike under his arm. "I'm about to give up on this blockhead," he said. "The perennial pup. Here he is, going on two years old, and no signs of growing up."

"It is kind of painful," Miggs said and bent down to pet the bundle of black, tan, and white dog. He looked up at her with doleful eyes, as though all the world misunderstood him.

Miggs said again as she was leaving, "Beany, this is the way I dreamed it would be when I heard we were moving back. That you and I would be dressing together and going places together."

No, Beany couldn't spoil it all by saying, "I'm not going to the Bunny Ball. I had a fight with Hank Willison because he tacked on a paragraph to Dad's column. Just so he could gloat. I can understand his gloating over Helena, but not over you and Katie."

No, let Miggs and Johnny have their date, unshadowed by what was to come. It would be their first—and their last.

18

WELL, this was certainly a new experience for a girl—this looking ahead to an evening with an escort she was furious with. And one she wouldn't speak to. Oh, she'd try and not make it conspicuous, Beany resolved, as she dressed on Saturday morning to go to Eve Baxter's. But she certainly wasn't going to carry on any sweet chitchat with him.

Eve Baxter had an appointment with her eye doctor and hurried through her dictating without taking time for either coffee or visiting. All the while Beany made pothooks and dashes in her shorthand notebook, all the while she drove to the *Call* office and typed the letters and answers, her resentful anger against Hank built up.

The top of his list, indeed! A lot he cared that he had shattered relations between Malones and Carmodys. How could a fellow with such a heart-warming smile be so heartless?

Beany didn't go downtown to look at formals. Mary Fred's pallid pink was plenty good enough for a date with Hank Willison. She wouldn't even take the trouble of pressing it, or giving herself a manicure. She would make cookies to send to Andy Kern instead. Andy was loyal to *his* friends.

She returned home in the middle of the afternoon and promptly reached for the cookbook. She doubled the cooky recipe. She had more than she could pack in the fancy box she selected. She filled a cooky jar and set it on the sideboard. She might even break her vow of not speaking to Hank long enough to say, "I worked all afternoon making cookies for Andy Kern."

The cooky-making took longer than she thought. She plunged hurriedly into fixing dinner. Meat balls, because if time was short, they could be eaten on the fly. The fashion show was to start at seven-thirty. Mrs. Hilb wanted the models there by seven.

Oh dear, there was the hall clock striking six. She was thankful when Adair, just returning from the art gallery, came out to help her.

Beany said, "I suppose Johnny's gone out to get Miggs. She'll eat supper with us too. And maybe Dulcie."

"And Hank?" Adair asked, reaching for the plates.

"I didn't ask him," Beany said shortly.

The side door was opened by Dulcie. She was still in her carhop togs—the tight-fitting red jacket, flared skirt, and white boots—and was carrying her formal in a suit box. The blackening of her eyebrows and lashes looked smudgy around her frightened eyes.

"I'm glad you came here to dress," Beany said. "I wish Miggs and Johnny would come."

Dulcie only stared blankly at Beany and Adair. "It's

180

going to be worse than I thought. Mom and Dad are going to be there. I tried my best to talk them out of it."

"Why no, Dulcie," Adair chided. "I'm glad they're going."

"I didn't want them to know that nobody likes me at school. Everybody will clap for everybody else, but none of the kids will clap for me," Dulcie said.

"We're going to clap like crazy for you," Beany told her.

"That won't help. Everybody will think I put you up to it. Just one little bunch of clappers."

"You've just got stage fright, honey," Adair comforted. "Have you had supper?"

"No, I guess I haven't," Dulcie said in an uncaring voice.

Beany was fixing a tray for Mary Fred. She dished up a plate for Dulcie, and Adair said, "Eat something, and then I'll help you into your formal."

The roar of Johnny's car announced his arrival with Miggs. Miggs's nose was bright pink, her hair mussed and wind-blown from a day outdoors. Her copper taffeta dress, with its built-in petticoat of gold silk, was over her shoulder and a hatbox dangled from one hand.

"And here," Johnny said, tossing her a black evening wrap lined with gold velvet, "is your bullfighter's cape."

"You're late, Johnny," Beany said. "We have to have Dulcie there at seven—or fairly close to."

"Battery trouble," Johnny muttered. "Here," he said again, handing Miggs a slice of bread on which he had mashed a meatball. "You take a bath first, and don't use all the hot water."

"I can dress fast," Miggs promised.

The hubbub started. The running of bath water. Johnny's yelling, "Beany, where's the black shoe polish?" Miggs and Beany crowding each other in Beany's small room while Beany zippered herself into the pink formal, and Miggs shook out the rustly skirts of her copper taffeta.

Miggs was telling, "The two little Kern kids have been out at the farm all day. They pulled enough clover to fill a hay mow. Stork's Stopover is right. I thought yesterday the mama rabbit looked a bit auspicious, and today she's been pulling fur out of her hide to make a nest. Beany, will you call the Kern family and tell them we couldn't pry the boys out of the lean-to?"

The hurried dressing overflowed from Beany's room into Mary Fred's. She was sitting up in bed, saying, "Come here, Dulcie, and let me straighten your lipstick." And to Miggs, "Look in the bathroom for a Band-Aid and I'll glue it over your skinned elbow." And there was Johnny calling out as he started up the stairs, "Man in the dorm!" And Mary Fred scolding, "Beany, why didn't you have me do your nails?"

"They're good enough." . . . Plenty good enough for Beany's beau of the evening. . . .

Dulcie said in a leaden voice, "Well, I'm dressed. I'll go on down."

Beany followed her down the stairs. "Dulcie, I'll get you a cup of coffee. Drink it, and you'll feel better."

Dulcie drank it, standing at the foot of the stairs because sitting would muss her clouds of white tulle skirt. She was standing there, with her look of doom, when Norbett came in. Her only answer to his awed, "Hello, Miss America," was a wan, "I wish I could drop dead."

"Good grief! Why?" he asked. He pressed up close to her to make room for Johnny, who was racing down the stairs, his bow tie untied, and carrying one black sock.

182

Beany muttered, "Maybe you can find the mate on the line in the basement."

And then came Hank Willison.

Beany was thankful for Johnny's covering up her lack of greeting with his, "You're just the guy I need. I can't tie a bow tie for sour apples."

Hank tied it for him in front of the dining-room mirror.

"Look at our Hank," Johnny said. "Flower in his buttonhole, and a pleased smirk. Looks like the groom at a wedding," and went in search of a mate for his black sock.

Hank did look very well turned out and very pleased with himself, and somehow that made Beany all the angrier. Her anger grew when he reached for one of her cookies on the sideboard and ate it with relish. It grew more when he turned and said with a teasing glint in his eyes, "Do I look like the groom at a wedding to you?"

Of all the gall! "No," she said icily. "You look like Frankenstein's monster to me."

Then came the hurried loading into Hank's car. Beany climbed into the back seat with Dulcie and Norbett. Let Miggs and Johnny have the honor of sharing the front seat with the driver. Beany didn't crave it.

Johnny said on a great heave as they drove off, "My socks aren't mates, but they're both black." And Dulcie said, "Norbett, hold my hand—hold both of them so I won't jump out of the car."

Mrs. Hilb was waiting in the hall at Harkness. A very dressed-up Mrs. Hilb, who greeted the people moving in groups toward the auditorium, while her nervous eyes watched for the arrival of her models. She hurried toward Dulcie. "Go in the stage entrance of the auditorium, before everyone sees your costume."

Without a word, Dulcie obeyed. At the stage door, she

turned and looked back at them—like a lamb going to slaughter.

The five who were left moved toward the open auditorium. Beany hoped they wouldn't be able to find five seats together.

"Here we are," Johnny said and stepped back so that Beany and Hank could file past him and sit side by side.

Beany said, "I'd better sit on the aisle. Claude might need me out at the table to sell *Hark Ye*'s."

It didn't work. Johnny merely shifted the seating so that Hank should occupy the seat next to Beany's aisle seat.

Beany left to confer with Claude Metz. He was in the hall, sitting behind the table on which were stacked issues of *Hark Ye*, and the placard announcing, "Programs and Pictures of the Easter Parade. Get Your Copy Here. Ten Cents."

"I came out to help you, Claude."

"I'm keeping it under control. They've gone like hot cakes. We had to dash up to Journalism and get more copies. My date's modeling her toreador pants in the show. So you go on back and sit with Lover Boy."

Lover Boy, indeed!

Beany returned to her aisle seat. She kept her eyes straight ahead on the stage curtain, which bulged and billowed from the activity behind it; and on the Negro piano player, his long fingers playing music that was all but drowned out by the noise of seats being thumped down, of friends calling to other friends, "Over here! We're saving seats," and the rustle of paper as people turned the pages of *Hark Ye*'s they had bought.

Beany didn't need to turn to the program. "Around the Clock" was the theme idea of this fashion show. It would start out with school clothes, and work through play togs—

Oh there, the curtain was parting. In the framework of a store window, girls, wearing the blouses and skirts and jackets they had made, sat or stood in the rigid poses of mannequins. They held their poses, with barely a flick of eyelash, while the girl narrator gave a short description. Mrs. Hilb had asked that applause be held until the narrator finished.

The stage clock struck eight times. The mannequins became human. They picked up schoolbooks or lunch boxes and strolled off to the music of "School Days," and much clapping.

Somewhere behind the scenes, Dulcie would hear that clapping, would be thinking, "They like those girls." When the lights went on briefly, Beany glanced around to see if she could find Dulcie's parents. Yes, there they were across the aisle; the stout, ruddy-faced Mr. Lungaarde and Mrs. Lungaarde with her tired eyes. And both looking pleased and anticipatory, as though they were thinking, "Just wait till you see our Dulcie."

The show moved on. Two numbers brought a special gust of applause. A girl in a red suit with a black caracul capelet had a black poodle in the act with her. The dog held his wooden pose until his mistress came to life. Then he fell into step and walked sedately off with her.

Johnny leaned across to say to Beany, "Bet he gets a haircut oftener than I do."

The other number was a little sister, big sister one. A Negro girl had fashioned full skirts and square-necked blouses out of red bandana handkerchiefs. The little sister looked so shyly important that they were clapped back for a bow.

Poor Dulcie, Beany kept on thinking, I can't stand it if

185

she's slighted. The clock was moving on toward prom time and the showing of formals. Here was the first group of girls in their pink, blue, and yellow ones. Beany gave an extra clap to the stout girl in her sewing class who had made the yellow one and laboriously worked a bead design on the bodice.

Norbett whispered to the group, "Dulcie's next."

The curtains parted. Mrs. Hilb, with an eye for the dramatic, had set the stage to resemble a garden with a profusion of white flowers. The spotlight was lavender, like moonlight. And in it posed a slender girl with burnt-sugar hair and creamy white skin, in a breath-taking froth of black lace and diaphanous white tulle.

A gasp went up from the audience. Both girl and dress were so lovely. Dulcie held her pose, one hand stiffly outstretched with a rose in it. Only no mannequin ever wore such a sick and panicky stare. The narrator's voice went through her piece, "Yes, folks, she really made it—"

Finished, the narrator stepped back. It was the signal for the model to come to life. But she still stood as though frozen—

You could hear a pin drop while the audience waited for her to take her first step. You could hear someone in the wings—probably Mrs. Hilb—say, "Go on!" The piano player, who had been playing softly, broke into "A Pretty Girl Is Like a Melody."

But this pretty girl stood like a scared and woebegone child.

Someone behind Beany said, "Gosh, she's scared stiff."

Beany found herself breathing out, "Oh, don't, Dulcie —don't cry—"

Perhaps the audience knew that same rush of sympathy, for a thunder of applause broke out.

A look of unbelieving wonder came over Dulcie's pale face. Like one in a dream, she walked to the music. But without her usual hippy swing, without one flip of burnt-sugar pony tail. Her smile, as she bowed herself off, was shaky and grateful.

The clapping and wolf calls went on until the curtain fell.

There flashed through Beany's mind what the girl had said in the *Hark Ye* staff room, "If just once I saw that girl acting as though she didn't own the world, I could take her to my bosom." . . .

At last, Harkness had seen the shy, insecure Dulcie under her bold front. They had taken her to their bosom.

Beany forgot for the moment that she was ignoring her partner. She clutched his arm and choked out, "They clapped louder for her than for anybody." And he said, "Wipe the tears off your face."

The Easter Parade was over.

Beany got limply to her feet. She heard the grumbles from students that it had lasted so long, the Bunny Ball would be cut short.

Well, that was all right with Beany Malone.

19

THE music for the Bunny Ball in the gym down the hall
started even before the auditorium was cleared. Norbett
said, "You folks go on and dance. I'll wait here for Dulcie."

Beany told herself she dreaded this part of the evening
—this having to dance with Hank Willison. But it wasn't
true; she felt an odd shiver of excitement. And with it,
a vicious longing to puncture his happy smugness. He
had no right to be having such a good time.

Inside the gym door, he held out his arms to her and she
fell into step with him. She said nothing. Neither did he.
Just as she had guessed, he was an expert, effortless dancer.
And she took unexplained pleasure in showing him that
no matter what tricky steps he took, she could follow without fumbling—thanks to her having danced so often with
Andy Kern.

Maybe now he would say, "I'm sorry about that column.

I didn't want to hurt the Carmodys. I didn't want to make trouble between you and Miggs."

But he didn't say it. He only danced with an amused half-smile on his face. They danced two dances, and then Johnny came up with Miggs and said, "Show her what a good dancer is like, Hank. Let Beany suffer along with me."

Beany tried to match her step to Johnny's. He was certainly no treat as a dancing partner. He always seemed more interested in something else than in keeping time to the music. "This is a rumba, Johnny," she reminded him.

He took a dawdling step or two and then came to a complete stop to ask, "We've got a diggin' shovel around someplace, haven't we?"

"Yes, in the garage. If you're going to dance, dance, so everyone won't be bumping into us. What do you want a diggin' shovel for?"

Johnny danced on, keeping a slack hold on her while he explained, "Tomorrow after Mass, Miggs and I are going out and reset a clothes post because she wants to air a lot of blankets, clothes, and whatnots they left in trunks there when they left. She's anxious to get out as soon as she can, because she thinks some baby rabbits are due."

"Yes, she told me."

"Hey, did you call up the Kerns and tell them we tried to bring the kids home, but they wouldn't budge?"

"Um-hmm. And Rosellen said she'd have Sidney go out with her this evening and get them."

At the side of the dance floor, Beany stopped, realizing that Johnny was too interested in clothes posts and shovels and possible little rabbits to come even close to a rumba.

She listened absently as he talked, noting that Hank,

dancing with Miggs, was also holding a lively conversation. Only Hank wasn't missing a beat of the music. Something Miggs said brought forth Hank's hearty laugh. The hypocrite—the low-lived hypocrite. Pretending to be a friend of Miggs's.

Change partners. Johnny claimed Miggs again—and Hank, Beany. He said amiably, "I was telling Miggs that Mrs. Naismith where I live wants some strawberry plants for her garden. Miggs says they have a plot of ever-bearing ones on their place. Only, she says, it's an art to nip off a runner at just the right psychological joint. Otherwise, it won't put down roots. She says I'm welcome to all I want."

Vow of silence or not, Beany had to burst out, "I should think you'd feel like a snake in the grass, asking for strawberry plants from the Carmodys."

She wanted to make him mad. She wanted him to defend himself. Instead he chuckled. "A very satisfied snake in the grass."

Beany froze into disdainful silence again. The dance ended and they drifted over to the table where punch was being served—but *not* in tin cups.

Norbett and Dulcie were there. Dulcie said, "I haven't danced with Hank. I've been robbed."

"The very next dance, you're going to be unrobbed," Hank said.

Beany's punch was untasted in her hand when the next dance started, and Dulcie's billowy white skirt swayed off in rhythm to Hank's step. Norbett said, "Let's sit down over here and drink our punch. I never could do a mambo."

Beany said brightly as they sipped their punch, "Aren't you glad now you came? Aren't you proud to be with the hit of the Easter Parade?"

190

He nodded. "And Dulcie's happy as a lark."

Beany tried to think of something else bright and chatty to say. "Good crowd. Maybe our staff will make up the deficit."

She needn't have worried about Norbett's noticing that her gaiety was all on the surface. For Norbett was thinking his own thoughts. "Beany, you were right when you said we could go on—and be friends. I blew my stack when you first suggested it, but I can see now that it's better for us both if we don't go steady."

Well, well, I asked for it, she thought. Yet, somehow, it was a mite jolting to have Norbett coincide so wholeheartedly with her idea.

"You weren't good for me, Beany."

"Oh, Norbett, do you have to be so deflating?"

He reached out and touched her arm. "I don't mean to be," he said earnestly. "I just mean that I leaned on you so much. Remember how I was always running to you with my tale of woe about being unwanted? So you'd build me up. Remember how I had to have you to strut and brag to?"

"I cared so about whether you were happy or not," Beany admitted.

"And I needed you to care. It did a lot for me. And then I needed to be pushed off, so I could stand on my own feet."

Eve Baxter had said something like that—something about pity being the worst thing for someone like Norbett. Beany couldn't quite remember, because her eyes kept following Hank and Dulcie. What fun they were having! How Hank was laughing!

"You didn't need me," Norbett went on, "and maybe the reason I had such mean spells with you was because I was jealous of—"

"Jealous? Golly, Norbett, when I was going with you I never looked at—"

"I don't mean of other fellows. I mean of your solid niche in life—of Johnny's brilliance and popularity, and your dad's being Martie Malone. I guess I always felt I had so much to live up to. Maybe this doesn't make sense to you, but I've changed."

"Yes, it makes sense. As Mary Fred says, 'You are a different you as you go along.' When we met, the you you were, and the you I was then, couldn't help being crazy about each other. I guess we needed each other then."

"That's right, Beany. But now we need somebody different."

The dance ended; another started. Hank and Dulcie were dancing it, too. Well, let them.

Norbett was saying, "Dulcie was so scared for fear no one would clap for her. I knew just how she felt. Because I always wanted people to like me. Dulcie's sort of a maverick like me. She's been kind of kicked around, too. We understand each other."

"You mean that Dulcie is more right for you than I am?" Beany had never thought of Dulcie and Norbett being right for each other.

"I feel more like being me around her. When I'm with her, I'm not fishing for sympathy, or trying to impress her."

Beany giggled. "No, you wouldn't get very far, putting on an act for Dulcie."

What queer quirks life had. Who'd ever think she'd be sitting out dances in the Harkness gym with Norbett Rhodes, listening to his telling her that another girl was *righter* for him than Beany Malone? Who'd ever think she could listen to it without a heavy heart?

Another dance ended. This time Johnny claimed Dulcie, and Hank danced with Miggs. Beany's lips thinned.

More talk about those strawberry plants Miggs had promised him, no doubt. Didn't the man have any feeling, any shame?

She noticed that Johnny and Dulcie danced only halfway around the floor, when they stopped to talk to Johnny's favorite teacher, Miss Hewlitt. Even from her distance, Beany saw Miss Hewlitt's lined face light up. She had always doted on Johnny, always predicted a brilliant literary career for him.

Norbett was saying, "I've sure made a jackass out of myself lately. Trying to be big stuff because I wanted to get in good with the penthouse folks."

"I wanted to, too," Beany said on a sigh. And then, because it was uppermost in her mind and heart, she confided, "Norbett, don't say anything to anybody tonight, but this is the last time Miggs will be friendly with us. Tomorrow morning, when the paper comes out, she'll hate us. And so will Katie. Just as soon as they read Dad's column, blasting that new uranium company Mr. Carmody and Helena are in."

"Holy Toledo!" Norbett said. "Helena's been afraid of that."

Before he could say more, Johnny came hurrying over to them, calling out, "Norbett, Miss Hewlitt was asking about you. Come on and say hello to her before the shindig breaks up."

The two boys went off, leaving Dulcie and Beany. They walked back to the table while Beany put down her punch cup. Already the table was being dismantled.

"Just one more dance after this," Dulcie said, humming in time to the dance music and tapping her foot. "What a ball it's been, huh, Beany? I feel so different about Harkness now."

"I'm glad, Dulcie." Beany added, on a sudden thought,

"Do you wish now Carlton had come with me tonight so as to see what a hit you made? You did look like Miss America up there on the stage."

Dulcie's musing smile broke into a laugh. "Carlton? Beany, I haven't thought of him this whole evening. Whatta you know, I guess my broken heart is mending. . . . Darnedest thing, here Norbett asked me because he was desperate for a date, and I came with him for ditto reasons—and the desperate date turns out just dandy."

She flushed a little and added, "I always said Norbett was all right, if someone could whittle him down to size. . . . Hey, why aren't you sticking closer to Hank? Here he comes for the last dance with you. He's something. You ought to appreciate him more."

"I appreciated him before I knew him so well," Beany said.

Beany wasn't sure whether it was Dulcie's flirtatious instinct, or whether the contrary side of her was aroused by Beany's belittling of him. But as Hank joined them, Dulcie said, "Ah, the man with the enigmatic smile. Beany, the guy has unplumbed depths."

"I know," Beany said coldly. "Slimy ones."

The anger in Hank's eyes was like a lightning flash. Beany felt a heady exultation. At last she had jabbed under his smiling smugness.

The last dance at Harkness was always a moonlight waltz. The lights shifted to silver, to lavender, to no lights at all for a turn or so. Oh, very romantic! But not for Beany and her partner.

She could feel his held-back anger under his drawl as he said, "Beany, I want to warn you. All these easygoing Willison relatives I told you about—they're not easygoing when it comes to taking back-talk from their women."

"But I'm not your woman," she said pertly.

"I'm warning you," he repeated.

That must be what is known as a deadly smile, Beany thought to herself. She held herself stiff and silent.

On the ride home, they stopped first at the Park Gate to let out Norbett and Miggs. But Johnny said, "Miggs is anxious about the rabbit obstetric ward. So we're going on to Barberry Street, and I'll take her out in my car for a quick reading tonight."

There were all the good-bys as Norbett got out. He was starting up the steps when Dulcie leaned far out of the car window, and in the feeling voice and gestures of a stage diva sang out loudly,

"Oh-h-h, thank you for a lovely eve-en-ing,
You are so mar-har-vel-ous, you are so—whatever—it—is—"

It was Hank who yanked her back, said on a laugh, "Hush, you—or the whole Park Gate will think you're serenading them!" Even Beany forgot that this was a tarnished evening for her and chortled. For Norbett, at the top of the steps, looked both embarrassed and pleased.

Dulcie was let out next on South Wyman.

And then, in front of the Malone house, Johnny and Miggs were out of Hank's car almost before it stopped. "We're off to the rabbitry," Johnny said.

Miggs only took time to say, "Hank, you were swell to take us." And to reach in and squeeze Beany's arm and say, "Now you've got Mary Fred to carry trays to and look after. Don't worry about Miss Goldie tomorrow. But be sure and come out Monday morning."

Maybe if Hank hadn't said, "I'll be out for said strawberry plants," Beany's anger wouldn't have come seething back. As though nothing were changed. As though Miggs would welcome Beany Malone when, or if, she went to the farm Monday.

Even as Hank walked Beany to the door, Johnny's car went sputtering out between the wide gateposts of their driveway. Mike ran after it barking, entreating to be taken in. Beany heard the car stop and Johnny say, "O.K., get in before you get athlete's heart, chasing after us."

Hank opened the door for Beany. He stepped inside with her.

Maybe he was lingering to say, "I'm sorry about the article, Beany." If he said only that, her heart would soften toward him.

Instead he asked with a quizzical smile, "Aren't *you* going to say, 'Thank you for a lovely evening'?"

No answer from Beany.

"All right," he sighed. "Then old Hank can mark off the price of the tickets, the haircut, the bow tie, to profit and loss."

Fury, like steam, heated through her. "Wait a minute," she snapped.

She ran out to the telephone stand in the hall where she had left her billfold. With shaky fingers she flattened it, took out the five-dollar bill Eve Baxter had paid her that day. She came back and thrust it at him.

"There! There! I won't have you grieving about the money you—"

The sentence wasn't finished. Before she knew what was happening, strong fingers grabbed her bare shoulders, and she was shaken so thoroughly and roughly that her teeth clacked together, and one braid shook loose.

He was saying, "That's for calling me Frankenstein's monster—and a snake in the grass—and slimy—"

His hands dropped. He turned, without a word, and went out the door.

Beany's knees were so weak under her, she had to back against the newel post. Her breath hurt. She heard his car drive off just as she was looking down at the red finger marks on her shoulders.

20

THE next day, Sunday, was the first of April. Turn the calendar. And, as though the weatherman knew a page was being turned, the day was almost hot. A bright sun slanted through the yellow checked curtains of Beany's room as she dressed.

. . . Ouch! She felt a sore twinge of shoulders when she lifted the comb to her hair. Even her neck felt stiff. She thought wryly, I was "shook"—but good, last night. . . .

What high spirits Johnny was in this morning. He had got up and gone to an early Mass. Beany could smell his coffee. She could hear his lusty singing as he carried breakfast to Mary Fred.

Johnny's singing was as off-key as his dancing was off-step.

Beany had to see the morning paper. Someone had already brought it in and left it on the couch in the living room. Hastily she thumbed through the pages, hoping somehow for a miracle—hoping that Stan Lowell, the financial editor, had deleted that part about the Mid-Century—

No, no miracle. There it was, every damning word, under her father's name and picture.

Adair was already in the kitchen, where Johnny was frying ham and baking waffles. A plate was already stacked high with them. But when Beany sat down at the table and reached for one, Johnny said, "Nuh-uh! Keep your cotton-pickin' hands off. I'm taking those out to the farm for Miggs and the hungry Kern kids. I'm baking them pale, so she can warm them up in the oven."

"Miggs and the Kern kids? On the farm?" Beany asked.

He was spooning batter into the black smoking waffle iron, which the Malones preferred to an electric one. He put the top down, recited his timing chant,

"One, two, three, four, five, six, seven,
All good children go to heaven—"

and flipped the iron over, before he answered her.

"Miggs stayed out there all night. Gosh, she had to. The little rabbits were born after we left for supper. Yeh, while we were at the Bunny Ball, Mrs. Bunny gave birth. Rosellen and Sidney went out to bring the boys home. They were still there when we got out after the dance—and poor Rosellen was in a tizzy because she couldn't pry the little fellows away from the new rabbits. So Miggs decided to stay with them. I left Mike with her."

"He'd be a lot of protection," Beany said in sarcasm.

"Believe it or not, I believe he would. . . . Find a Mason jar for me to put syrup in, Beany. . . . Funniest thing

199

about the fool dog," he went on to Adair and Beany, "he kind of took over that little farm. He spread himself on the step outside the house as though he'd suddenly grown up and was ready for responsibility."

"But, Johnny, what about Miggs's folks," Adair asked. "Won't they be worried about her not coming home last night?"

"I phoned them when I came back. They weren't home —evidently out social-gathering—but I left a message at the desk for them. Miggs couldn't do anything else. The Kern kids claimed some neighbor's dog was trying to get into the rabbits' lean-to, and they had to stand watch. And, believe it or not, Mike chased the dog away."

Adair laughed. "What Mary Fred's psychological mind will do with that. She'll probably say that poor little Mike was over-shadowed by our well-behaved Red here."

"I know," Beany said with mock gravity. "Mike only chewed up everything on the clothesline, and leaped all over us with muddy paws, and chased every car on Barberry Street to satisfy his trampled ego. . . . How many little rabbits are there, Johnny?"

"Five, we think. Don't expect too much when you go out tomorrow. I thought Mrs. Bunny had made a mistake and was nurturing a nest of mice. But Miggs said, give them a week and they'll look like the ones on Easter cards."

He wrapped the stack of waffles and ham in oiled paper, stuck a jar of instant coffee, a hammer and nails in his pocket, and said from the doorway, "I fed the patient in number twenty-three, but you spoiled females are going to have to bake your own waffles. Miggs and I have a big day of house cleaning and post setting ahead."

Beany watched him out the door, thinking, You and Miggs can have one more day together—one more day of grace—because she spent the night at the farm. Because the Sunday *Call* is not delivered out there. She wondered if the penthouse folks had read Martie Malone's column yet.

Already the telephone was ringing. Mary Fred's school friends, her riding pupils, were calling to inquire about her. Two more plants arrived for her. Adair said, "Beany, you'd better go to the next Mass, and I'll go later. Someone should be here to answer the phone and look after Mary Fred."

At St. Mary's, Beany slid into the pew on the aisle where the Malones always sat. This spot held so many memories for Beany. She and Miggs had come here together when they were so small they had to stand on the kneeling rail to see over the back of the pew.

It was that very young Beany who had asked her father once, "Do you say prayers, too?"

"You bet I do. I grab onto God's coattails and pray hard."

"You do? What do you pray for?" For it seemed to the child that a man who had no one to boss him, who had money in his pocket to spend as he saw fit, had little to ask for.

He had answered on a tired chuckle, "Mostly for strength to keep on sticking my neck out. And for strength to take what comes of sticking my neck out."

That memory was a little startling. And so was the more recent one of her father's kissing her good-by Friday and saying, "Maybe after tonight you'll wish you had a carpenter or a haberdasher for a father." Was he really saying, "I know it'll be hard for you when my column comes out Sunday"?

The vague, half-formed doubt she had kept pushing

aside began to take more solid shape. That last paragraph about the Mid-Century Company was not Hank Willison's. He was only completing the column for her father. Oh dear!

She thought of Carlton Buell last fall when he was only a pledge, and one of his fraternity brothers had come up before Carlton's father, Judge Buell, for a serious traffic violation. "The convictions of the father are visited on the children," Carlton had said. "Gosh, Beany, they almost depledged me when Dad took the driver's license away from the guy."

The convictions of Martie Malone might be visited on more than his children in this case. On Adair? Helena might well meet her at the penthouse door tomorrow morning with the unfinished portrait of Mrs. Carmody and say, "Go, and never darken our Sunset Room again."

And on Miss Goldie? Miggs might well tell Beany tomorrow that the Malones could make other provision for the sorrel mare.

If only Beany could talk it over with someone. Not Johnny, who was even now grubbing in happy innocence at the farm with Miggs. Not the convalescing Mary Fred, who could read Martie Malone's column and never dream that it remotely affected Miss Goldie. Adair?

Oh dear, again. Did other people have trouble keeping their minds on prayers instead of their own problems? "Give us this day our daily bread—" In memory she heard her mother's voice saying, "It means spiritual bread —strength."

It looked as though Beany Malone should pray for strength so as to face whatever came from her father's sticking his neck out.

A sobered Beany walked out of the church.

Yet as she walked homeward she was murmuring wrathfully to herself, "But Hank didn't need to gloat. He didn't need to say he was shedding no tears over Katie and Miggs. He didn't need to shake me the way Mike shakes an old shoe." She wouldn't even listen to the small inner voice that reminded her, You didn't need to take so many mean cracks at him, either.

Mary Fred's friend Lila had come to see her. She was sitting in Mary Fred's room, turning the pages of the society section of Sunday's paper when Beany went in to return Mary Fred's pink formal.

Mary Fred said from her bed, "Beany, Johnny tells me Dulcie got a big hand last evening."

"She brought down the house," Beany answered from the closet.

"How'd you get on with Hank? I wish I'd seen him first. Was it an evening you will long remember?"

"Indeed it was." That was the truth. Every move she made for a while, she would remember that evening. She wondered how long it took bruises to heal.

Lila said, "Beany, did you see your friend's picture in the paper? Mrs. Perry Carmody. She's to be one of the society-matron models at the Style Show."

Lila read excerpts aloud to them: " 'Society's next soiree—the International Fashion Show—is already causing quite a stir. It is earmarked as *the* social gathering next on the list.' "

"They always hold it in the gardens of that rich senator. You know that house that has twenty-one chimneys?" Mary Fred put in.

Lila read on: " 'About a hundred debs will give out programs. They will be garbed in pastel formals with ribbon corsages composed of the colors of the various nations participating in the show. The Symphony Orchestra will be playing at the rear of the gardens. The cocktail bar will be located at one side of the runway.' "

Lila dropped the paper and added, "The show lasts two hours, and then a buffet supper is served. It ought to be good. It costs twenty-five dollars per head—for the whole doings, that is."

"Twenty-five bucks! You'd have to drink a lot and eat a lot and see a lot and be seen a lot to get your money's worth," Mary Fred said.

A day of visitors coming, going, staying at the Malones'. Carlton Buell came over with a bouquet of his mother's daffodils. Mrs. Buell always had early flowers, late flowers. But then, she didn't have two dogs, as the Malones did.

Wally Thomas, Mary Fred's most devoted escort, called with a box of candy. An artist friend of Adair's from Santa Fe, wearing a fiesta dress of turquoise velvet, came to see her. The artist friend, Lila, and Wally Thomas stayed for dinner.

Beany had no chance to talk to her stepmother about the dynamite in Martie Malone's column.

21

MONDAY morning came.

Beany dressed in jeans and an old plaid shirt of Johnny's. Miggs had told her to wear working clothes and come to the farm. But that was before she knew about the column. Even though the day was a sunny replica of yesterday, Beany felt shivery inside.

She heard faltering steps in the room next to hers. She went to the door. "Mary Fred, you're up!"

Mary Fred's red robe hung on her like a sack. Her eyes looked big in her thin face, and she steadied herself with a hand on the bedstead. "Today is my day to be perpendicular. The next step is to browbeat Dr. Hunter into letting me go out and see Miss Goldie. But you're going out to see her this morning, aren't you?"

"Yes—yes, I'm going." She couldn't tell anyone as tottery as Mary Fred that she didn't know the outcome for her—or for Miss Goldie.

In the kitchen, Adair paced back and forth as she drank a cup of coffee. Johnny and Carlton were there, too—both with grimy hands. "Had to take the battery up for a recharge," Johnny said. "Thought I wasn't going to get Miggs back to the penthouse last night."

"But I was going to drive your car out to—to the farm," Beany said.

"I can take you," Adair said. "I have to go to the penthouse because I left my easel and paints there. But I don't expect to be there long."

Beany turned from the toaster and the slice of bread she was dropping into it. Adair's eyes were as full of panic as Dulcie's had been Saturday night before the Easter Parade. Then Adair knew about Martie Malone's article, knew what to expect.

Adair even added on a pleading note, "Yes, come with me, Beany."

Beany's shivery qualms rose to her throat. The toast she buttered and swallowed went down in lumps.

Carlton Buell was saying, "Then I won't have to take Mom over to the Park Gate. I can help Johnny with his battery." He went to the side door and yelled loudly, "Hey, Mom, you can go with Adair. She's going— How soon are you going, Mrs. Malone?"

"Right away," Adair said with a look that added, I might as well get it over with. And to Beany, "You'd better not wear jeans to the Park Gate."

Beany ran upstairs and changed to a skirt and slipover. . . . It would be a little more dignified to be shown the penthouse door in a proper garb. . . .

Mrs. Buell was in the front hall when Beany came down. Mrs. Buell was invited to a brunch at the Park Gate, but she wanted to go early and have a manicure in the shop

206

there. "I've been working in the yard until my hands are a disgrace."

She did most of the talking as the three rode to the Park Gate in Adair's convertible. They walked into the lobby together, and Mrs. Buell left them to go to the beauty shop. Adair hurried to the elevator, Beany following.

Sidney Peale was running the elevator. He waited until his last passenger alighted on tenth, and then turned to them to say, "The whole place is buzzing about the Martie Malone column in the paper yesterday. That's all the men have been talking about in the elevator."

"What do they say?" Adair asked tensely.

"Most of them say it's a good thing to have it come out. Rosellen called me yesterday morning and I told her about it. If it hadn't been for that—the write-up, I mean—she would have invested Andy's money in it, and I would have mine."

They were at the top floor now, and he slid the doors open for them.

Some ten steps till they reached the penthouse door. Adair said, "Beany, I'm scared," and pressed the bell.

"So am I," Beany murmured. They listened to the musical sound of the chimes inside. Adair fidgeted with her gloves, and Beany wished she had something to fidget with.

The door was opened by Helena Stearns. Their dazed eyes saw her greeting smile. Their dazed ears heard her warm and welcoming, "Oh, do come in."

They followed her through the hallway and into that overwhelmingly large and bright-hued room and took the chairs she motioned them to. She pointed out Adair's easel in a corner of the big room. "Nothing's been touched. Just as I told you Friday, Mrs. Malone, our weekend was so filled with engagements, we'd only be home to sleep, and you needn't go to the trouble of taking it home with you."

Beany stole a glance at the unfinished canvas on the easel. Heavens, she didn't know much about art, but she had never known Adair to paint a human being looking so stiff and wooden. The best thing about it was the sapphire bracelet on the wrist.

Adair sat gingerly on her low lavender chair. "Is Mrs. Carmody here?" she asked.

Helena laughed her silvery trill. "She had to run down to the beauty shop to have her hair done. After our luncheon today, the models are all to practice, and she wanted her hair done for it."

Beany asked if Miggs—Cathy—was home, and that too brought a silvery ripple from Helena. "She's still sound asleep. So sunburned from yesterday. And the poor child's simply exhausted. She's been working so hard out there on the little farm, looking after the Malone horse—"

Not horse, *mare,* a corner of Beany's mind corrected her.

"—but then," Helena added, "we all feel so responsible for the horse—even Catherine and Perry. We were all so happy to help you folks out."

Beany and her stepmother exchanged puzzled glances. They had been braced against her enmity. Could it be that Helena, what with her very social weekend, hadn't read Martie Malone's column?

"Oh, the detail—the detail," she was saying, "to make this International Style Show an outstanding affair. Our luncheon today is to discuss the costumes of the debs." She smiled at Beany. "Oh, my dear, why didn't I think to have you as one of the ushers along with Cathy? When you two are such inseparables."

"That's all right, Mrs. Stearns—I'm pretty busy," Beany

said. Again she thought, She *can* make you think she's wonderful.

And now Helena turned her smile on Adair. "What all this is leading up to, is to invite you and your husband and Beany here to be my guests Wednesday evening at the style show."

Again Beany's eyes met the equally startled ones of her stepmother. Three guests at twenty-five dollars apiece. Adair could only stammer, "Why, thank you—that's certainly nice of you—but Martie is out of town."

Momentary silence fell. Beany had an odd feeling that it was the lull before the storm.

Helena was still smiling as she said, "By the way, I happened to notice the well-read Martie Malone's column yesterday. I know it wasn't his fault but, somehow, he was misinformed on the resources of the Mid-Century Company—"

Adair straightened in her lavender chair. Beany stirred uneasily in her pale yellow one.

Adair said, "Martie was very unhappy about having to write what he did about your Mid-Century Company. But Professor Naismith, the geologist, and Hank Willison went all over the Mid-Century holdings quite thoroughly and—"

"Thoroughly!" Helena's scoffing laugh was harsh. "Your husband doesn't know lazy Okies the way we do. This Hank Wilson, or whatever his name is, doesn't know the meaning of the word 'thorough.'"

Oh yes, he does, Beany thought. He's thorough when he shakes you.

"And then, of course," Helena's deriding voice went on, "your husband didn't allow for this Hank's malice toward us, because I had to fire him for incompetency. So, Mrs.

Malone, I'm sure you won't feel it's too much of a favor to ask you to have Mr. Malone print a retraction."

Adair stood up and moved over to the easel and lifted the portrait off it. She said, "Martie even hoped there *was* some mistake when he got the first report from Professor Naismith and Hank. He bore the expense of sending them back a second time, just to corroborate their first findings. He had them bring back samples of ore and take them to the assayer's. Hank brought the assayer's report—and it wasn't good—shortly before Martie flew to Washington."

So that was why her father hadn't finished the column himself. Why he had left the ending for Hank to finish.

Beany got up and walked over to where Adair was folding the easel into its compact foot-long lengths.

Adair's hands were shaking. "I'm sorry, Mrs. Stearns," she said, "but under the circumstances, I wouldn't think of asking Martie to retract a word of what he wrote."

Helena was standing, too. She was flipping on and off a cigarette lighter she had picked off a low table. Her words had the same clicking metal sound:

"We've all tried to be friends to you Malones because of your old-time friendship with the Carmodys. I commissioned you to paint Catherine's portrait because it was very evident from your shabby home that you needed the money. I knew, before Catherine had two sittings, that you were no portrait painter, but I thought it only generous to carry on."

Beany had to swallow down defensive anger.

Helena Stearns went on, "And look at all little Cathy has done, in taking that horse off your hands."

"That's true, and we appreciate it all," Adair said. Her hands were shaking even worse. Beany took the tubes of paint from her to fit in the paint-smeared wooden box.

She wanted to get out as quickly as they could. Maybe Adair could hold on to her temper, but Beany wasn't sure she could.

"It's true, too," Adair went on, "that I've made a botch of Katie's portrait. . . . Is Mr. Carmody here? I'd like to see him."

"He's out of town on business."

"I'd like to explain to him and Katie that Martie didn't write his column out of malice, as you choose to think. I'd hate for them to think he did."

"I haven't mentioned it to Catherine or Cathy. I hoped for their sakes, and for this so-called friendship, that Martie Malone would forget his malicious attitude toward any new companies—"

"He didn't write it out of malice," Adair repeated. "Can't you understand that he wanted to protect investors?"

Helena hurled her words back at her. "Yes, I can understand. Perfectly. He's a little unsuccessful man, and so he has to attack the successful." She turned accusing eyes on Beany. "I suppose this was his way of retaliating for some imagined slight."

Anger goaded Beany into answering back, "No. I didn't tell him that you called me a pushy little person in a feather hat at the party. And a clutcher. But even if I had, it wouldn't have made any difference, because he—"

Adair nudged her to keep still.

The three were standing in a corner of the large, many-windowed room. Silence fell, except for the small noise of Beany's trying to fit the tubes of paint in the wooden box. And then—although there was no sound—she felt another presence in the room. She turned her head.

"Why, Miggs," she breathed.

Miggs was standing in the doorway that opened from the hall into the Sunset Room. In her rumpled jeans and faded blue shirt, she looked incongruous in the studied elegance of the big room. She seemed to huddle there in the doorway, looking small and lost. Even under her two-day sunburn, her face had a wan and jolted look.

Helena turned her head toward the girl. With an effort she smoothed the anger out of her voice and said, "Cathy dear, I didn't know you were awake. You should have slept until time to dress for the luncheon. You were so worn out."

Miggs's eyes rested on her Cousin Helena, as though she were staring at a stranger. She said, "I have to go out to the farm."

"No, child, you're not to worry about that messy place again," Helena told her. "The Malones are making other arrangements for their horse. You go ahead and bathe and get ready for the luncheon."

Miggs only repeated in her toneless voice, "I have to go out. Beany and I are going to spread the straw over the barn floor."

Helena Stearns's voice sharpened. "Not today, Cathy. I'm using my car."

Beany offered swiftly, "You can come with us, Miggs. Adair has her car."

Beany and Adair were moving toward the door, Adair carrying the easel and the painting, which she kept turned toward her as though she were ashamed of it. Beany carried the paintbox, which wouldn't close over the long brushes. One of them dropped, and Miggs stepped over to pick it up. "I'll go with you," she said.

But Helena stepped in front of her. "I said you were not to go, Cathy. We've humored you long enough in all this running back and forth—even in your staying out there overnight. There's no earthly reason for it now."

"Except that I like it there," Miggs said, "and I hate it here." Her eyes rested long on Helena and she said wonderingly, "I always thought you were kind. I thought you cared about *us*, because you always said we were the only family you had. I wish I never had to see you again. I wish I never had to come back here."

Helena followed them to the door. Her laugh was not pleasant to hear. "Maybe you're enjoying your dramatics, Cathy. But you're forgetting a good many things. Your mother wouldn't have all she has—or your father, either —if I hadn't helped them. They're happy here. They wouldn't find that ramshackle farm as enchanting as you seem to think it is. They won't go near it."

Miggs only answered wearily, "I know. But we want to fix up the barn for Miss Goldie. Then, I suppose, I'll have to come back."

22

On the ride out to the farm, the three sat in the front seat of Adair's convertible in constrained silence, as though each were absorbed in her own thoughts.

Beany's kept turning to Hank Willison. She owed him an apology—well, half an apology. He still needn't have been so pleased with his part in procuring the dynamite for the column. . . . No, by darn, *she* had bruises on her shoulders. Why should the bruis*ee* even think of apologizing to the bruis*er?* . . .

Once, as they drove, Adair said, "She was right about one thing: this is the poorest portrait I ever put on canvas." Once Miggs said in her flat voice, "I didn't know she called you a pusher and a clutcher at the party, Beany."

There was no question as to whom the *she* referred to.

Adair laughed. "And I didn't know you wore my feather hat."

"I did the hat no credit," Beany admitted.

They were nearing the little farm, and Beany said, "Slow down for the turn, Adair. It's the yellow house ahead."

Adair drove more slowly up the rutted road than was necessary, her eyes resting on the budding willow tree nearby. "Oh, Miggs, can I paint your willow? The lovely laciness of it—the sort of a hush because the tight leaves are just waiting to be born. It would ungravel my soul. I'll use this canvas and paint out what isn't a likeness to your mother."

"Sure, you can paint it," Miggs said.

"I wish you'd look!" Beany exclaimed as they drove into the yard. "The watchdog."

There was Mike, the problem pup, lying halfway between house and barn. Even when they got out, there was no onslaught of greeting. Only a certain preening on Mike's part, that said, "I'll let you folks come, but it isn't everyone I would."

The two girls helped Adair carry the easel, canvas, and paints over to a spot near the willow tree. As Adair set up the easel, Miggs asked, "If you get in any of the house in the background, could you do it a soft green the way it used to be?"

Adair nodded. "I certainly don't want that gruesome yellow in a picture of spring. Is this the strawberry patch the kids talk so much about?"

"*Was.* There're more weeds than strawberries now," Miggs said.

Adair couldn't wait to unscrew the caps from her paints, to start mixing shades on her palette. As they walked away, they could hear her humming. Beany said, "She always hums when she's happy at her painting. It bothered her because she couldn't do better on Katie's portrait. She said she couldn't get the feel of it—that Katie didn't come through."

All this was skirting the question that Beany, the forth-right, had to ask, "Miggs, will Dad's column turn you against all of us?"

Miggs leaned against the clothes post, which Beany noted was now set solidly. The bright morning sun seemed to emphasize the drawn unhappiness in her wind-burned face.

She said slowly, "I'm so confused—so unsure—about everything. It started that day when Rosellen and Sidney talked about putting money in the Mid-Century Com-pany—and I thought of Rosellen's brother ushering nights in a movie house to make it. And I thought of Sid-ney saving what he made running the elevator at the Park Gate. I guess it was then I began to doubt Helena. But not Dad—"

Her voice broke. She swallowed, said, "And of course Miss Goldie can stay here, unless," she added on a dubi-ous thought, "Helena persuades Mom and Dad we can't keep her."

There was so little Beany could say. Her eyes lighted on the blankets hanging on the clothesline. Miggs had said she wanted to air things that had been in the trunk. Beany said practically, "We better take the blankets in. The sun will fade the blue one."

They went through the back door and across the nar-row screened porch into the kitchen. Beany said, "I re-member this big kitchen. And the couch. We kids always lined up on it and watched Katie cook."

They dropped the folded blankets on it.

Miggs said, "The Kern kids took turns sleeping on it Saturday night, while the other one watched over the rab-

216

bits. They'd have been out here the first thing this morning, except they had to go to the dentist's."

The dining room was not as large as the kitchen and, out of it, stairs led to the bedrooms on the second floor.

"When Mom and I first left here we used to plan how we'd come back and make this house over," Miggs mused. "We found a picture of an outdoor patio with a fireplace. See, Beany, we could cut down the west window in the kitchen and put in a French door. And this one in the dining room to open outside. We planned how we'd have outdoor suppers there."

"The Sunset Room," Beany said, glancing out the window toward the mountains. Nearer by, she could see Adair painting with swift, absorbed strokes.

"I loathe that Sunset Room in the penthouse," Miggs burst out. "It's a stage setting. But I can understand how Mom likes it. It's like a playhouse to a little girl that never had one." She broke off to say, "Miss Goldie must be hungry for her breakfast, and here I stand, mooning about this and that."

But Miss Goldie didn't seem hungry. She was out in the pasture, the sun glinting on her pale sorrel coat. She didn't come when Beany stood in the back door of the barn and shook the measure of oats and called to her. Beany walked out, intending to take her mane and bring her in. But the mare, as though sensing her intentions, gave a defiant toss of head and moved restlessly on.

"I don't blame her for preferring the sunshine to this messy barn," Miggs said. "Johnny and I didn't get to it yesterday. We were fixing up rabbit cages. Papa has to be kept separate from Mama, now that she has her family."

"I'll help you move some of Orville's car parts out," Beany said.

"There's a pair of extra jeans in the house and a not very glamorous shirt," Miggs told her.

Beany hurried in and changed, thankful that there was no one to witness her peeling off her slipover and ask, "Where did you get those black-and-blue marks on your shoulders?"

While Adair painted in the strawberry patch, Beany and Miggs worked in the barn. They carried out the lighter pieces of machinery. They huffed and puffed as they pushed the heavier pieces far back. They swept all the debris off the rough floor. They pounded down nails that had worked halfway, and pounded in new ones where floor boards were loose. Beany pounded her thumb into the bargain, and Miggs tore the knee of her jeans on a bent nail.

Time flew.

And finally Miggs panted out, "Let's let the dust settle, and take a breather before we start covering the floor with straw. Let's go down and see what Adair's done with the willow tree."

They walked down to the weed-grown patch and Adair and her easel. She was just wiping her brushes and capping her paints. "I had no idea it was noon already," she said. "I'll have to leave and see what I can do for Mary Fred before I go down to the gallery. I'll have Johnny come out and get you two later on."

Beany and Miggs looked at the wet canvas on the easel. Beany couldn't believe her eyes. Adair had painted more than the willow tree. In fact, the tree was only a suggestion, as was a corner of the house, done in soft weathered green.

The picture was of Katie—the old Katie. Somehow, with hurrying strokes Adair had transformed the woman in the silver lamé to a woman in a mussed blouse and skirt—why, even a streak of loam clung to the skirt. Beany moved closer. The sapphire bracelet had been changed. It was a clinging tendril of strawberry plant that lay across her wrist.

Adair said, "Miggs, you'll think I'm crazy. But I've heard Beany and Johnny talk so much about Katie, that I guess I had that picture of her in mind. I guess that's why I couldn't paint her against the black and silver draperies."

Miggs didn't answer, but stared on in wonder at the canvas.

Adair apologized, "It isn't a finished picture. I mean, it's what we call a mood picture. I know it sounds silly, but it was what I felt, and my fingers just ran away with it."

A mood picture. And the mood was happiness. Beany could feel it in the flushed half-smile on the face of the woman Adair had painted—the woman standing in the sunlight with the mountains in the distance and the willow tree casting lacy shadow. She was looking down at the strawberry runner in her hand as though she were thinking, I'll plant it, and it will grow and bear fruit to feed the ones I love.

Miggs asked, "What are you going to do with the picture?"

Adair shrugged. "Nothing. I've had my fun just in painting it. Toss it out if you like."

"Oh no!" Miggs said. "I want it—to keep."

Adair handed it to her, showing her how to carry it with her finger tips under the frame so as not to smudge it.

As they walked to the car with Adair, Miggs said,

"Maybe Mary Fred would feel easier about Miss Goldie if Johnny brought a vet out to look at her and tell us when to expect the colt. Maybe he could bring him out when he comes later today."

Mike. Taut and quivering and wistful, the small dog looked at the yellow car he loved and claimed as his own. But he let the car drive off. He didn't even chase it down the lane.

Miggs carried the picture into the house and set it on the sideboard in the dining room. She turned at the kitchen door to look back at it. Beany, standing beside her, murmured, "It does look like her—like she used to. You can almost see the side comb sliding out of her hair."

"I know. Oh, Beany, it's so silly and childish—yes, and selfish—but I do miss her the way she used to be. Sometimes I feel so lost—and alone—"

She was crying softly, and Beany's arm slipped around her. She said almost to herself, "It's like the dream I had about you—the one Mary Fred said was thought communication."

"Maybe it was." . . . Miggs wiped her tears on her shirt sleeve. "After all, everyone has to live her own life. Dad is so proud of Mom. He just beams when people mention his beautiful wife. He loves buying her clothes and jewelry. Well, let's get back to carpeting Miss Goldie's quarters."

In the barn, they unfastened the wires that held together two of the seven bales of straw Helena Stearns had sent out. They spread it thickly on the floor. Ah, now the barn had the nice musty fragrance a barn should have.

Often, as they worked, Beany glanced out at Miss Goldie. She was in the farthest corner of the pasture. Beany could see the blond tail switching, switching. She walked out to see if she had eaten the oats Beany had left for her. She hadn't.

A car was stopping in the yard. "I'll bet that's someone bringing out the Kern boys," Miggs said.

The two girls stepped to the barn door. It was the Kern two who tumbled out of the car and headed for the lean-to, carrying carrots and something in a paper sack.

One look at the car, and Beany's heart started a hard, uneven beating. It was Hank Willison's car.

23

Hank Willison climbed out of the car. He said to Miggs as she walked to meet him, "Look what I brought out with me."

He opened the car door for Katie Carmody, helped her out.

Miggs said in amazement, "Mom! This is the first time you've come out to the farm."

"I kidnaped her the minute she stepped out from under the dryer at the beauty parlor," Hank said. "I told her Mrs. Naismith had her heart set on strawberry plants, and I had the furrows ready and waiting. But that I needed an expert like her to nip them off, or show me how."

Katie said on a nervous laugh, "He put up such a plea that I begged off from my luncheon."

"But I stopped and bought her a hamburger," Hank defended himself.

"We picked up the little boys on our way out," Katie

said. "And it's a good thing we did. I don't think I'd have known the place. It looks like a Halloween pumpkin sitting out here."

Beany couldn't stand apart from the group like a sulky child. It was too noticeable. She walked over to them, without a look at Hank, and for want of something better to say, said, "You look awfully pretty, Katie. Is that what you're going to wear when you practice for the fashion show this afternoon?"

"That" was a coral-colored knit dress with a matching cardigan which Katie wore over her shoulders.

"Oh no," Katie said on another nervous laugh. "I'm to practice in what I'll model Wednesday night—a cocktail sheath of cocoa-colored *peau de soie.*"

Nor was Hank addressing any remarks to Beany Malone. It was to Miggs he said, "Lead the way to the strawberry patch." It was Miggs's arm he took.

And what could Beany do but trail along? And feel like the little girl who wasn't there?

Katie picked her way in her teetery pumps. "I don't know whether I still remember how to nip off the runners," she demurred.

"It'll come back to you," Hank assured her. "Like praying or milking—you never forget."

Katie stopped at the edge of the patch. "Heavens, the weeds." She leaned over gingerly and poked at the ground. "And it's dry as a bone. We'll only break off roots, taking plants now."

"Couldn't we soak it good with a hose?" Hank wanted to know.

Wasn't he the persistent one? Dragging Katie out here, in spite of her luncheon date, just because the woman he boarded with wanted strawberry plants?

223

"It'd take a while to soak it," Katie said. "And we'd need a sharp-pointed hoe."

Hank was undaunted. "Couldn't we turn on the hose and let it run? And I'll drive down to this little hatchery —I noticed when we passed that they had tools—and bring back a hoe?"

"If you don't take too long," Katie agreed. "I don't dare be late for the practice. This is the dress rehearsal with the orchestra, and I have to figure what size steps to take in my—"

"Go through that routine again," Hank urged. "The kind of dress you'll be wearing that sounds like a pot of soy beans."

Katie laughed. *"Peau de soie*. I'd hate to have to spell it."

"I will return, as the general said," Hank promised, "with a sharp-pointed hoe."

The three stood in uneasy constraint, watching Hank's car bumping down the rutted lane. Miggs said, "It wouldn't take but a few loads of pea gravel to smooth up that stretch of road."

Katie didn't answer. She looked at the jeweled watch on her wrist. "I hope nothing holds him up. Helena didn't like it any too well because I skipped the luncheon—but it was just to be a lot of discussion of which deb should wear which pastel shade."

How out of place Katie Carmody looked here in her old habitat, wearing a coral-colored costume, and with her dark hair molded in a beauty shop. But this was Mrs. Perry Carmody of the Park Gate penthouse. . . . The old Katie was just a picture on the sideboard, just a memory. . . .

The Kern boys were calling from the lean-to, "Looks

like the rabbits have grown a little teeny bit. Come on in and look."

"We've already looked," Miggs called back. "And Beany and I are starved. We're going in the house and open a can of beans I brought out Saturday."

Donnie Kern said, "Here, take our hamburgers. He bought them. But Pete already had lunch, and the dentist told me not to chew on my filled tooth for a while."

"Thanks, thanks," Miggs and Beany said in chorus. And Miggs said, "While you're waiting, Mom, come on in and have a cup of tea. Johnny brought out tea bags with him."

They went into the kitchen together.

Beany was suddenly very tired, very hungry. While Miggs opened the can of beans, she put the teakettle on the gas stove.

"Beany, that left back burner always used to heat faster," Katie remembered.

While the kettle heated, Beany took off her loafers and shook out the dirt and straw. Wisps of scratchy grass stuck to her anklets, and she took them off too, wiggled her toes in relief. What a hot day it was for the second of April.

Katie didn't sit down, but moved restlessly about—as though the spirit of the past Katie and the present Katie were at odds. Starting into the dining room, she stopped short at sight of the picture Adair had so recently done.

"Shades of the past!" she said on a forced laugh.

The girls explained that Adair had visualized the old Katie from hearing so much about her and her strawberry patch. Katie added, "Dirty trick of Adair's to put those extra pounds on me after I suffered to starve them off."

Katie gulped down the tea Beany poured. She talked about the International Style Show—about the Italian designer who wanted to design her a dress of silver-blue satin. Yet her eyes kept roving about the place and she would say in one breath, "Imagine tenants pounding a spike in the plaster," and in the next, "Helena will never forgive me if I'm late for the rehearsal."

Hungrily, Beany ate the canned beans, and the hamburger sandwich that was not hers by right, inasmuch as it had been bought by a person who would not even glance her way. . . . Maybe when that person returned for Katie, Beany Malone could say, "I hope you don't mind my eating the hamburger you bought for one of the Kerns." Oh, but supposing that person turned on her a cold, level look and said, "I do mind." . . .

She put down her cup of tea, suddenly conscious of a not-rightness, of alarm. How dark and chill the air was! But the sun had been bright and hot when they came in. She heard the first sharp ping on the roof. She stepped to the door to see a few white marbles bouncing on the ground as they fell. She saw Mike scurrying to shelter under the house's wide eaves.

And with that, a loud rat-a-tat of hailstones sounded on the porch roof.

Beany ran back for her loafers, shoved her bare feet into them. "I've got to get Miss Goldie in out of the hailstorm," she said.

The hail was a solid roar as Beany ran across the yard toward the barn. If only—oh, if only Miss Goldie had come into the barn herself—

The barn was empty. Beany ran through it and into the pasture, the hail pelting on her bare head and shoulders, blinding her, as she made for that part of the pas-

226

ture where she had last seen the mare. Through the pounding polka-dot curtain of white, she dimly saw the dark outline of Miss Goldie.

She kept calling to her, hoping the mare would run to meet her. Why did she stand there, her head to the ground? Why was she nuzzling, nudging something on the ground? It was something dark and flat—it looked like a gunny sack—

And then, even before she saw what the mare was standing over and poking with her nose, Beany sensed the slim, gaunt body of Miss Goldie— Oh, heavens!—the colt was born.

24

BEANY dropped on one knee beside it in the sloshy white grass.

This—this lifeless little thing of long legs and dark reddish hide on which hailstones were bouncing—this, Miss Goldie's colt? She grabbed it up in her arms and started toward the barn. If only it would squirm a little— but it lay a wet and dead weight. If only those long knobby legs didn't dangle so limply—

A dozen pictures flitted in and out of her mind. . . . Old Tom McDevitt leaving the mare in her care. . . . Mary Fred at home, trusting Beany to look after her. . . . Why hadn't she brought Miss Goldie into the barn? . . . Why, oh why had she, Beany, wasted time in the kitchen, drinking tea, and thinking of what Hank Willison would say or wouldn't say? . . .

It didn't help to say to herself, But we never dreamed the colt would come so soon.

She couldn't run. Her feet kept slithering on the hail-stones. And the anxious mare made it even harder by darting in circles about her, whinnying, trying to nose the burden Beany carried.

Miggs and her mother were waiting in the barn door. It was to Katie that Beany sobbed out, "It's her colt—and I don't know—it hasn't moved—"

It was into Katie's arms Beany thrust her burden.

For only a brief second the woman stood, holding it. Then she dropped down on the barn floor, cradling it in her lap. "It's far gone—but there *is* a heartbeat. Miggs, those blankets on the couch. Warm one quick and bring it out. Beany, get something so I can rub him dry."

An anxious voice said, "Here, take my shirt."

The Kern boys. Donnie was stripping off his T shirt. Katie took it, began rubbing the long legs, the ribs that showed under the damp plush covering. She called after the girls, "Oh, hurry with a warm blanket before the chill hits his heart."

They hurried. They lit the gas oven full blast and shoved blankets in. Beany snatched a coat off a hook on the back porch and covered her warm blanket to keep it dry.

By now the hail had changed to a lashing rain. She raced through it with the warm blanket.

In the dim barn with the rain pounding on the roof, Katie held the colt close as though she hoped the warmth of her own body would reach through. She took the blanket from Beany and laid the foal on it, wrapping him snugly.

Those limp, limp legs, that lifeless small head lying flat, the glazed eyes that stared without sight. But still Katie rubbed the legs, the chest, the throat, soothing,

"There, there, little boy colt—there, there, little frozen thing—"

Miss Goldie hovered close, trembling, whinnying in mother-anguish. Katie said, "Tie her to the manger while we work with the colt. Soon as you bring another warm blanket, you'd better rub her dry, too."

All Beany could ever remember about that frantic, prayerful afternoon was Miggs and her racing through rain between barn and house for warm blankets. They scorched the yellow one—but that didn't matter. Beany was conscious of a hurting lump on her forehead; she didn't know whether an extra-large hailstone had hit her, or whether, in her haste, she had bumped into a clothes post. But it didn't matter. Once she fell as she ran and bruised her knee. That didn't matter, either, because she didn't drop the blanket she was carrying.

It did matter—matter greatly—when she reached the barn, for Katie to say, "Look—no, you'll have to kneel down close—see, his little ribs moving."

Beany relayed that news to Miss Goldie, who was whirling in her stall, knocking against the sides, against the manger. Her eyes rolled in a torture of anxiety, she gave out low heartbreaking neighs that were like moans of distress. "Your little fellow is breathing, Miss Goldie. He's going to be all right."

They formed a rapt semicircle around it—Miggs, Beany, Katie, and the two small boys—and watched the almost imperceptible lift of ribs in that flat colt body. They all whispered, as though even a voice might affect the faint breaths.

And at last, just as Beany was thinking it, hoping it, one of the little boys cried out, "Hey, its eye blinked—it blinked."

They waited on. And then came the most heartening sight and sound of all—a weak scrabbling movement of hoofs in the straw. As though some instinct urged the foal to get to his feet.

"As soon as he's a little stronger, we'll hold him up to his mother. Just a tug or two of warm milk in his cold little belly will do wonders for him," Katie said.

Now they could turn their attention to the markings of white on the newborn. Beany said, "I wonder if he'll look like his father, Sir Amber."

Katie laughed. "He's a little Sir Echo of his mother, if I ever saw one."

It grew darker in the barn. When Miggs brought out another warm blanket, she brought a candle. She stuck it in a bottle and set it on one of the two-by-fours that ran around the side of the barn like a shelf. She reported that the rain was almost over, but that their lane to the highway was a rushing torrent.

A whinny that was wild entreaty came from Miss Goldie. Katie said, "Look, girls, that's pure mother instinct—her standing with her leg back so as to make it easier for her baby to nurse. O.K., you blessed, we'll bring him to you."

There was tenseness in the dim barn as Katie lifted the colt, a swaddling of blanket dragging in the straw.

Miss Goldie stood trembling. Katie held the limp head, guiding it toward its nourishment. Beany edged in, waiting for the instant to push the teat between the foal's groping lips. Miggs was in the act, too, holding Miss Goldie tight against the stall partition. The little boys pressed close, anxious—

"There now!" It was a chorus, as the colt's mouth fastened on his mother. There now!—they watched the movement of his lips, the muscles moving in the soft neck—

And then, as though even that small effort was too wearying, the head of the foal sagged in weakness and milk trickled from his mouth. Katie carried him back and bundled the blanket around him, murmuring, "That should get the little fellow over the hump."

They all drew long, grateful breaths. Katie said, "Miggs, and you, Beany, are soaked. Have you anything to change to?"

Yes, Miggs had a change of clothes. Beany had the pullover and skirt she had worn out to the farm. In the house, they changed into them. Beany had no dry shoes. Miggs said, "Take them off and they can dry here on the oven door."

They gravitated back to the barn. The two boys were working over a squat, rusty stove, and Katie was adjusting the elbow in the pipe to reach out a window. "It's the stove out of my old brooder," she said. "A little fire will take the chill off out here. We'll practically have a steam-heated apartment. No, Pete—or Donnie—don't put too much wood in."

They all lingered on in the flickering candlelight, in the new warmth.

Mike set up a barking outside. But the threat in his bark changed to one of welcome. "Somebody must be coming," Donnie Kern said.

"I don't know how anyone could get here. The lane is still a river," Miggs said.

Beany opened the barn door. She stared at a tall male figure that was splashing through the wet yard, carrying a lantern to light his way and the way of someone behind him.

"Why, Johnny Malone!" Beany said.

"I thought maybe it was Hank," Katie said. "He promised to return with a hoe."

Johnny, his Levis rolled up to his knees, his shoes under his arm, said, "The man with the hoe phoned me this afternoon to tell me he was stalled. He got water in his generator during the rainstorm. Said to tell you he'd be here soon as he could. I didn't know whether I was going to make it out with the vet or not."

Beany recognized the big, slow-moving man who followed him in as Dr. Sackman, the one Mary Fred had called when her black horse was alive. He, too, had his pants legs rolled up and carried his shoes in one hand, his grip in the other.

He looked about the barn at the uneasy mare, the colt poking its head out from the blue blanket. "The old stork can beat the vet the same as it can the M.D.," he said on a throaty chuckle.

"I almost didn't bring Dr. Sackman out," Johnny said. "Because Mary Fred got word from old Tom McDevitt today. He's already had one eye operation, but he has another one to go through. And he told her the colt wasn't due till April tenth."

"Storks don't bother to read calendars, either," the man said. "Johnny, hold the lantern and I'll check the mare."

He deftly tilted up Miss Goldie's head and administered a draught of brown medicine. "That'll calm her down." He motioned to Beany. "Untie her halter rope so she can lie down when she feels like it."

"Now look at Sir Echo," prodded one of the little boys. "He was almost dead when Beany brought him in—and Katie had to rub him with my shirt—"

Katie nudged him to silence.

Dr. Sackman dropped down beside the foal and felt over it with gentle hands; he tested its heart with a stethoscope, said as he folded it and put it back in his worn grip, "The heart's even. A little weakness, but one more nursing should take care of that. Keep the two of them quiet for a day or two, and Nature will do the rest."

He walked over to the pile of baled straw and said, "Move over, boys, while I put my shoes on. I'm not the barefoot type."

A small and plaintive voice sounded, "I'm kind of hungry."

Katie said instantly, "Why, of course you are. We forgot all about supper. I'll fix something—" and then in a stricken voice, "my goodness, Miggs, there isn't a thing in the house."

Johnny said, "I brought up a sack of groceries and put it on the back porch. I'll wade back and get the other one in the car we had to leave beside the highway. Hank told me, when he phoned, that you were out here, Katie. I wasn't sure what you put in your potato pancakes, but I got spuds and flour and eggs—"

"Milk?" Katie asked.

"Milk, sure. And butter and honey and sausages."

And, knowing Johnny, Beany knew that he had bought enough of everything for a crew of threshers.

Katie threw back her head and laughed. This was no studied trill but the hearty laugh the Malones had remembered through the years. "What're we waiting for?" she said. "Come on." She motioned to the two little boys. She went out the door, one arm around them, one around Johnny.

The veterinarian said, "I hope there's coffee. I'll be in, soon as I get my shoes on."

"There's coffee," Johnny turned back to say.

25

OVER an hour later Beany softly entered the barn, lighted by the lantern Dr. Sackman had left for them.

The supper of Katie's potato pancakes was over. They had all taken turns in helping to grate potatoes and beat eggs, and in running between the noisy hubbub of the kitchen and the barn to report on Miss Goldie and her leggy colt. To little Pete Kern had fallen the exciting honor of announcing, "Guess what? The colt is up and sucking away all by hisself."

Everyone had to flock out, tiptoe in, and watch that sight, until Katie said, "Come on back, before the pancakes get cold."

And now, fully as gratifying was the sight that met Beany's eyes. Miss Goldie was lying down in the soft straw with her newborn snugged up close beside her. If Mary Fred could only see them!

Beany walked over and put out the candle, which was guttering low. She picked up the blue blanket that had wrapped the colt. Little Sir Echo didn't need it now.

She carried it with her over to the bales of straw. She sat on one of them and leaned against another. It was drafty here in the corner, and she pulled the blanket around her shoulders.

Johnny, having gorged himself on potato pancakes and sausages, had left. He had taken the Kern boys, whose folks must be uneasy about them, and Dr. Sackman, who had another call to make. He had said, "Hank will be out later to take the rest of you home."

But would he take Beany Malone home?

Yet she couldn't very well tell Johnny that Hank was paying her back in her own coin, and wasn't speaking to her or even looking her way. She tried to reach for her old resentment toward him, but somehow there was none to reach for. It had been crowded out by the events of the day—and perhaps by all the supper she, too, had so hungrily put away. She knew only a drowsy content as she slouched on the bale of straw, wrapped in the blanket.

Her loafers were still drying on the oven door. She pulled her cold bare feet up under her. She was achingly tired from all her morning's work here in the barn, from all the running back and forth from house to barn.

With an effort she opened her eyes wide and focused them on the foal. Mary Fred would want to know every detail as to markings. She could see the white on his hind legs running almost to the knees. She couldn't see the front legs, for they were doubled under. Cute, the way he lay with legs folded under him in grown-up fashion like his mother. Cute, that short little stub of tail. Who'd think that one day it would be thick and curly and blond like

236

his mother's? Or that the little brush of mane would one day be—would be—

In a drowsy haze she heard someone enter. It was Katie, and Beany murmured, "I'm just waiting till little Sir Echo stands up—so I can see—"

"Yes, wait there and rest. I'm just checking the fire in the little stove. And I want to look at the rabbits—I haven't had time to see them yet." Katie's laugh was the last thing Beany heard.

She fell into a sound sleep.

She only half roused when a man came into the barn and said in relief, "Katie, you're here! I was worried when Helena said you'd gone off, but she didn't know where."

"Perry! I didn't think you'd be back for days. Oh goodness, we mustn't talk so loud—Beany's sound asleep there on the straw. The poor kid's just bushed."

The mention of her own name roused Beany further. But sleep was still too heavy upon her to let her move a muscle or say a word.

The man's voice said, "What in the world are you doing out here?"

"I've been having the most wonderful day I've had in years. We had to work like fiends to keep a new colt from dying—the poor little thing was so wet and frozen."

"You look bushed yourself, Katie," he said with concern. Beany sensed more than saw that he had put out an arm and pulled her close.

Heavens, this would be no time for an eavesdropper to sit up and announce, "I'm awake."

Katie's words came in a tumbled rush, "If only I didn't have to leave here. Tomorrow I could pull weeds out of the strawberry patch. They come up so easy when the ground is soaked. I belong out here—not in a penthouse.

It seemed so *right* to hear a little boy say, 'I'm hungry.' I'd forgotten how I loved feeding people."

"You mean you'd like to live in the country again?"

"Yes. Oh, Perry, I tried so hard to be the right kind of a wife for you. Helena said that a successful man would be unhappy with a wife who didn't keep up with him— that he was ashamed of. She kept telling me about broken marriages because of it—and so I tried. I know I was over-weight and dowdy. I know you think Helena is wonderful—"

"There was a time when I thought she was," he admitted.

Beany in her blanket longed to hear him say, "But I loved you the way you were." Instead he said, "And you didn't like the suites in hotels where the meals were brought up to you? I kept thinking of all the times you cooked on that stove in there with only one burner hot enough for frying. I wanted to make up to you for all the hard years."

"They were happy ones. I'm a worker—I'm not the decorative type. I tried to like the penthouse, but it seemed such a playhouse life. I don't want to live in a hotel. I'm sorry to disappoint you, Perry."

His wry chuckle interrupted. "No, Katie darlin', I'm relieved. Because the penthouse is out, anyway. I had a set-to with Helena before I came out—"

"You did! What about?"

Beany felt a shiver of excitement. Yes, what about?

He didn't answer the spoken or unspoken question, but asked, "Did you see the vicious slap Martie Malone took at the Mid-Century in his column yesterday? No. Well, I got the Sunday paper in the hotel lobby late Saturday night. I was furious at Malone when I read it. And
238

then the darnedest thing happened. That young Rhodes kid that's been bobbing up at the penthouse—I can't remember his first name—"

It was all the eavesdropper could do to keep from prompting him, "It's Norbett." The guilt she had felt in listening to their conversation was nothing now, compared to her curiosity. What about Norbett?

"—he came over to me, and I never heard such an earnest plea as he made for Martie Malone. Made him sound like a St. Francis. The Rhodes kid told me Helena had been afraid of Malone all along, and that's why she urged him, the kid, to write that special story in the *Tribune* on folks who'd made money buying uranium stock."

Katie's husband paused, and every nerve in Beany's body was urging, Go on! Did you believe Norbett?

Katie said, "In the note you left at the desk, you said you were taking a late plane out on business."

"That was the business. I wanted to see for myself if Malone was right. I saw—or, at least, I saw enough. I got off the plane in Utah and hired a car and a couple of experts with Geiger counters, and we went all over that country. I was a fool not to have investigated more fully in the first place. Of course, today when I had the split-up with Helena, she told me they're acquiring new holdings to make the company solid. But I want no part of it. I'm pulling out. I'm sticking to peddling oil equipment and maybe taking a flyer in an oil well now and then—but with my own money, not Helena's. So you can be a hayseed—and if you turn your head, I'll brush the straw out of your hair."

"Perry, I'll bet you're hungry."

"I'm starved."

Katie's warm laugh sounded. "Johnny Malone said he

239

hoped I hadn't lost my fryin' arm—and I haven't. Look, Perry, the old brooder. And today Hank drove me past a hatchery where they sell day-old chicks—"

Beany felt the draft of chill night air as they opened the door and went out.

She stretched her cramped body and lay there, turning over in her mind all she had heard. Her mind flicked back to that Sunday when she came back from church, grieving that she would never be able to make up to Katie Carmody for the favor she had done her. She had been thinking that the very moment her eyes rested on the sorrel coat of Miss Goldie.

And yet it was Miss Goldie's foal that had helped Catherine Carmody change back to Katie. . . .

Norbett had even had a part in it. He had told Beany at the Bunny Ball that he wanted to be a friend. He had been, when he defended her father; for he had sown the first doubt in Perry Carmody's mind about Helena Stearns and the Mid-Century Company.

Someone was fumbling at the latch on the door. More company for Miss Goldie and her colt. Beany heard Miggs's low laugh as she came in with—with Hank Willison.

Miggs said, "Sh-h, Mom said Beany was sound asleep out here on the straw."

Beany had had enough of playing 'possum and listening in. She sat up and announced, "I'm not asleep now."

"I was dead to the world, too, on the couch in the kitchen," Miggs answered her, "till Hank came and wakened me. I wanted him to see Mary Fred's colt that kept us on the run all afternoon. I'm like Mom—I don't know whether this place is Aching Acres or Stork's Stopover."

No word from Hank for the girl sitting on the straw,

clutching the blue blanket to her. Not even a hello. He and Miggs stood looking at the mare and colt, talking in low tones so as not to disturb them. Even when Beany said, "I'm waiting till the colt stands up, so I can see the white markings on his legs," Hank didn't even look in her direction.

Miggs said, and laughed again, "Mom and Dad are staying out here tonight. But we're short on bedding. Short on everything until, as Mom says, we make a trip to Montgomery Ward's tomorrow. So I thought I'd spend the night with you, Beany, if that's all right? I wanted to, anyway, so I could help tell Mary Fred about things. You'll take us in, won't you, Hank?"

He answered promptly, "I'll take you any place you want to go. But not Beany. We parted company Saturday night."

Miggs gave an amazed gasp. "You did? Why?"

"Because she got all wrathy about my part in her dad's column. Because she called me Frankenstein's monster and a snake in the grass and slimy—"

"But *you* just did what Martie Malone and Professor Naismith told you to do," Miggs said. "She oughtn't to be mad at *you*."

Well, this was a new experience, too—this hearing herself discussed as though she weren't there.

She spoke up defensively to Miggs—as though Hank Willison weren't there. "I wasn't mad about his investigating. I was mad because he gloated so. I could understand his gloating over Helena because she called him a dumb Okie, but he said he was shedding no tears over Katie or Miggs or Perry Carmody."

"I wasn't," Hank said to Miggs, *not* to Beany. "Because I hoped it would jolt your dad enough so he'd look into

241

it himself. I figured the wool had been pulled over his eyes. I thought maybe a sizable jolt would break the hold of your sweet-talking Helena."

He went on to Miggs, definitely not to Beany, "I couldn't bear to see Katie without her old laugh. I tried my durnedest to get her out from under Helena and all that *pot of soy* clothes business. I even exposed her to new baby chicks at the hatchery. But it wasn't enough. It took a half-frozen colt to shake her loose."

Beany had to get into the conversation. "Katie's going to get some day-old chicks for her brooder."

No comment from Hank. A troubled Miggs looked at the two. She said, "Beany, I'll get your shoes. They're dry now."

She left them alone in the barn. Silence, except for a long contented heave from the mare. The lantern was sputtering and Hank stepped over to it and adjusted the wick until it burned evenly. He took a step toward the door as though he were going into the house. As though he would say to Miggs, "Come on," and leave Beany to spend the night in the barn.

She flung out in desperation, "Why didn't you tell me what you told Miggs? I mean, about hoping the column would help them."

"Because you were a conclusion-jumper. You didn't give me a chance. You instantly accused me of being callous and hateful and heartless."

"You shook me," she accused him. "I've still got bruises and a stiff neck."

"You're lucky I didn't paddle you into the bargain," he grunted.

Miggs reappeared with Beany's loafers and anklets. Again she looked at the two, and the expression on her face seemed to say, This is your private fight. She said, "Here!" and thrust the shoes into Beany's hands and scurried out again.

Beany sat on the baled straw and pulled on an anklet. She shoved hard to put her foot in the shoe. It felt so tight and stiff, she bent over to see if it was on the right foot. It was. She stood up and wriggled her toes to the end.

She faltered out, "Hank, the reason I was so mad when you—when I thought you were acting mean and hateful —was because I—I liked you—and I didn't want to think—"

"And the reason I was so stubborn about not telling you, was because I liked you—and I couldn't understand why you'd think the worst of me."

"The editor of *Hark Ye* said that was one of my vices," Beany admitted humbly. "But I'll never be—anyway, I'll try not to be—a conclusion-jumper again if you'll stop being mad at me, Hank."

"I ought to stay mad," he said, "and maybe I would, if you weren't standing there in one bare foot, with a lump on your forehead and your braids sticking out in pigtails—"

Her hands reached guiltily to her short stubby braids. "I lost all the hairpins," she murmured.

Hank picked up her other shoe, worked it in his hands to limber it up. Beany sat down, pulled on her other sock. He helped her on with the shoe, asked, "That better?"

"Um-hmm, lots."

The scrabbling sound of hoofs caused them to look toward Miss Goldie and her colt. They were both unfolding legs and standing up.

Beany cried out, "Look, Hank, Sir Echo's front legs both have white on them. And look, that splash of white on his face. Doesn't it look something like the map of Ireland?"

"Not as much as your freckled face does. Haven't you got a sweater or something to wear home? You're not going home with your best boy friend, wrapped in a blanket like a squaw, are you?"

Beany murmured, "Maybe Miggs has an extra sweater." She added, "This is the way I thought it would be on my birthday. I thought maybe Katie would fix supper for us. I planned on Miggs coming home with me to stay all night. Isn't it funny about days? I looked forward to that party with Miggs—and it turned out so sour. And today, I dreaded—I dreaded to see Miggs again. And you, Hank, because I did feel bad about all the names I called you. And today has turned out so wonderful. So special. Today seems more like a birthday than the seventeenth of March did."

Hank Willison reached out and cupped her face and kissed her on one cheek. "Today *has* been kind of special, so that's for dissolving our Hatin'-Helena partnership. You know, I ought to send her roses. If she hadn't banged the door on me so hard, I'd still be back in the sand hills. I wouldn't have gone to the School of Mines. I wouldn't have met Beany Malone."

He kissed her gently on the other cheek.

"And what's that for?" she asked.

"Oh that," he said in his easy drawl, "that's to say, 'Happy Birthday, Dear Beany,' on your belated birthday."

About the Author

LENORA MATTINGLY WEBER is one of this country's most beloved writers of family stories. Her home is in Denver, Colorado, and it is here that she has lived and worked most of her life.

She was born in Dawn, Missouri, but her family left there when she was twelve to homestead on the Colorado plains.

"I came up to Denver to attend high school," she says. "In my senior year I was captain of our basketball team and Al Weber, the young coach, always had to come home with me to carry the extra balls, score books, etc. So instead of going on to higher education, I married, and now have children and grandchildren—I have to stop and count to know how many.

"I have been writing for many years and, next to writing and riding, I'm happy to say, I like cooking—and there is always plenty of that to do in a family of our size."

Mrs. Weber has written many novels for girls, the best-known of which are the stories about Beany Malone. She has also written short stories for America's leading magazines: *Saturday Evening Post, Ladies Home Journal, McCall's Magazine,* and *Good Housekeeping.*